CANOEDLING IN CLEVELAND

A NOVEL

Richard Morris

To Dan,
Enjoy! —
Richard Morris

SQUARE DEAL BOOKS,
HYATTSVILLE, MD

First Edition

Printed in the United States of America

Cover design and story illustration by Audrey Engdahl

Map sketch by Richard Morris

ISBN-13: 9780692217191
ISBN-10: 0692217193

Library of Congress Control Number: 2014943370

Square Deal Books, Hyattsville, MD

For
Barbara,
Jennifer, Alex, and Audrey,
Rick, Aisha, and Dave
Brandon, Ben, Robin, Joe, Elvy, and Paul

and

Dave, Tom, Duane, Chay, Don, Bob, and all other canoeists

and

The heroes who brought back fish, ducks, and eagles
to the Cuyahoga River
and people to the beaches of Lake Erie
and who created Cuyahoga Valley National Park

Chapter 1—Bombs Away!

Junior year is over. It's the summer of 1960. I've got nothing to do but mow lawns, babysit my two brothers, tell them canoe stories, sleep, and listen to the Cleveland Indians on the radio. I'm as bored as a caged monkey. Two and a half months with nothing to do. What kind of a summer will that be? Last summer, I took a two-hundred-mile YMCA canoe trip on a lake in Ontario halfway to the Hudson Bay. What a blast. But my family can't afford that again. I can't go anywhere, really. I'm locked in a prison, and I've gotta get free. Another year and I'm out of here and off to college, thank heavens. But not now. What do I do now?

I want to canoe! That's what I want. I have to canoe! It's imperative. I think about it for a really long time (for me)—at least five minutes—and come to a decision. Here's my goal for this summer: I will canoe every lake and stream around here that's canoeable. It's a great plan, a noble objective. Now all I need is a canoe (my family doesn't own one), a car to carry it on with a licensed driver, and someone to canoe with—someone I can con into sharing my adventure.

I tell Brett about it. He's my jockstrap big brother. He was our star quarterback in high school and is going into his senior year at Ohio State studying, what else, phys ed. He has a steady girlfriend named Annie, a car he won't let me drive, and a summer job at the supermarket. And he's dad's favorite. They're always playing golf together. Me? I always find an excuse not to go. *What, you want me to go hit a little ball with a stick and see if I can get it in a little hole? Why?*

Brett sneers, "Where are you going to go canoeing around here?"

I tell him: "Hinckley Lake, Vermilion River, upper Cuyahoga, lower Cuyahoga, Lake Erie, and Shale River, if it gets high enough."

"Ha. And you don't have a canoe or a car to carry it on. Good luck."

"So?"

"So you better get a new goal, dumbo."

"Nope. That's my goal."

He tilts back his head and gets that snotty little grin of his and says, "Okay. How 'bout a little wager? I'll bet you a hundred dollars you don't do it."

I feel my upper lip rising. "Oh yeah? You're on."

"You've got till Labor Day, Jeffrey. And a bet's a bet. Remember."

Late Thursday afternoon, I walk over to Randy Clark's house. The sun is still strong, and the air sultry. I don't know if he'll be around or not. I didn't want to call him. I hardly ever see him or talk to him, and I can't stand him because he's so stuck-up. It's because he wins all those swim races. And he looks really strange—goggle eyes, pointy chin, gangly arms, and enormous hands that droop when he bends his forearms up. I think he looks like a praying mantis. I don't know why girls think he's cute. No, I'm not jealous.

Now don't get me wrong. I really like Randy. Why? Because he has a canoe and a car with a rooftop carrier, which our car doesn't have, and he lives near me, he drives, and he's pretty good with a paddle. He and I got stuck in the same canoe on that trip last summer and fought all the way: "You're not paddling!" "Pull harder." "You splashed me, you rat!" I'd start singing, and he'd yell, "Shut up!"

The house is a light-blue ranch with an attached double garage. The doors are up, and it's empty. I don't see the canoe; it must be behind the house. I ring the bell. He comes to the door and says, "We already paid."

"Okay, wise guy. I haven't delivered your paper in two years." I carried the *Cleveland Plain Dealer*, under the morning stars, in rain and snow, for four years.

"Oh. Yeah. Well, whaddyou want?"

"I need to talk to you."

He steps outside, in front of the garage, under the overhang. "Now, what's on your mind, Klossen?" That's my last name.

"Well, I keep thinking about our canoe trip last year. Man, that was fun, wasn't it?"

"The best."

We are examining the driveway at our feet.

"I wish I could go again, but we can't afford it."

"Same here. I gotta caddie every chance I get and stash the money for college."

"But you'll probably get a swimming scholarship."

"That won't be near enough money. So, I gotta stick around here all summer, you know, and be up at the club at 6:00 a.m. every crummy morning to get in line. And if I miss too many days, I get dropped down on the list, and then I don't get to go out as much and don't get the good golfers and the double-bag jobs."

I look out at the street. "Yeah. I've got eleven lawns to keep in shape. That keeps me busy part of the time. I do them in the morning when it's cool." I look back at him. "But listen, you could get away once in a while in the afternoon to go canoeing, couldn't you?"

He looks up. "Canoeing? Where? There's nowhere good around here."

I can see I have some persuading to do—but that's nothing for me. I'm an expert at canoodling. I squint my eyes and say, "There are lots of places. I admit they're not quite like the north woods." I reel off the list I gave to Brett.

"They're no good. The Cuyahoga is polluted and catches on fire, and you can't even swim in Lake Erie, the bacteria's so high."

"Yeah, I know. The beaches are closed. But we'll be *on* the water, not *in* it."

"Shale River is just a shale bottom everywhere with a trickle of water down the middle."

"Yeah, but we'll get at least one big storm this summer that'll raise it up. We'll just have to keep on top of the weather and be ready to go."

He slowly shakes his head, unconvinced. "What about those damned concrete fords? The canoe won't go under them, and every time the road crosses the river, we'd have to get out and portage around them."

"Ah, but if the water's high enough, we could just float right over them and go diving down the little waterfall on the other side."

We walk behind his house, back by the swamp. The air smells wet and earthy and feels cooler under the trees.

We look at his canoe with reverence; this is the vehicle that will take us away, out of our boredom, into a world of excitement. It's lying bottom up, and I reach down and pat the hull.

"Looks pretty good," I say. "A few dents, but not bad."

"Garth put those in. He's a wild man. But it doesn't leak." Garth, his brother, is going into his senior year at University of Colorado.

"Is he coming back this summer?"

"Nah. He's staying out there. He's leading white-water rafting trips."

We start walking back to the front yard. Randy stops. "So, Klossen, tell me this. Suppose we do go down a river. How do we get the canoe back to the car?"

I had to think. "I don't know. I guess we'll have to take someone with us to drive and meet us."

"'Who?' is the question. What sucker would give up his time just to ride along with us and drive the car?"

I glance down the concrete street lined with new homes and newly planted trees and shrubs and focus on someone walking a small black dog on a leash. I stare for a while.

"What are you looking at?" Randy asks.

"I don't know. Someone's coming. I think it's . . . uh, Lori Matthews."

He looks up the street too. "Oh, jeez. Can't you find someone better to look at?"

At this stage of her life, Lori's short—not much over five feet tall—slender, with slim hips and an almost flat chest. She's wearing plaid Bermuda shorts. Her stringy, light-brown hair is cut well above her shoulders, and she wears braces. She's shy, quiet, and studious—one of the brains in our class. But she's kind of nice.

"Get rid of the braces and give her a perm, and she wouldn't look too bad," I say.

"What? You think you could go out with her?"

"If you put a bag over her head."

He smirks, looks at me, and asks, "What would Jean say?" Jean Phelps was my girlfriend from last year. She's really pretty, and we were in lots of things together—drama club and the *Whitecaps*. That's the newspaper.

"If I started going out with Lori?"

"Yeah."

"Oh, she wouldn't mind," I say, "as long as I kept her happy too."

He laughs. "Sure, big talker."

"What about Connie?" I ask. "What would she say?" Randy and Connie have been dating for almost a year. Her parents are members of the country club. She's real snooty. She was made for Randy. All she cares about is money and clothes and her hair and the country club.

"Connie? She'd get really pissed. She wouldn't believe I could stoop so low." He grabs a two iron out of a bag in the corner of the garage, sights an imaginary ball on the driveway, draws back, swings, and then looks off in the distance.

"Listen, Randy. I know this is crazy, but what would you think about asking her to drive?"

"Lori? Well, at least we wouldn't be bothered with a lot of chatter. She hardly ever says a word. But I don't know how much fun she'd be. Does she have a license?"

"I've seen her driving that old '52 Nash they've got."

He leans both hands on the club with his left leg straight, his right leg crossing it, and his toes pointing to the ground, and asks, "She doesn't date, does she?"

"I don't think so. She didn't go to the junior prom."

"I didn't see her at the senior prom either." He's bragging. A senior girl invited him to the prom, and it was at the country club, and he wants people to know it. "What senior boy would invite her? He'd have to be a real loser."

I try to imagine what she'd be like on a canoe trip. "I don't know how she feels about thrills. But we could test her—try her out on something and see how she does."

"On what?"

I give him an evil grin. "I know. We could take her on a bombing run in the valley, have her help us sink a convertible with water balloons."

"What?" He bursts out laughing and tosses the club on the lawn. After he recovers, he says, "You think she'd go along with that?"

"We can ask."

We're quiet while Lori approaches, and our silence must have made her suspicious. She is probably thinking, "What are those boys talking about?" and "Why did they stop? Are they talking about me?" She stares straight ahead as she comes to the driveway, not acknowledging our existence.

"Hey, Lori," I say. "How're you doing?"

She turns her head in total shock, blushing. "Fine."

"Say, can we talk to you for a minute?"

She blinks. "Me? What about?"

I walk closer, and her dog, a Scottish terrier, starts wagging its tail and sniffing my shoes. I squat and pet him. "What's his name?"

"Scottie." *Now that's original.*

"How can he see with all this hair over his eyes?"

"X-ray vision."

We laugh, and I stand up and look down into her eyes. "Say, Lori, we've been a little bored lately, and we were thinking about doing something kind of wild, and we were wondering if you might want to go along with us."

"Me? Do something wild? What?"

"Well. You know how all those rich, snooty couples like to drive down through the valley in their big convertibles, you know, to show off?"

"I guess."

I tell her what we're planning.

"What? You're kidding," she says.

"No," I say. "We're serious, Lori. It's time we poor upper-middle-class people stand up for ourselves and teach those rich show-offs a lesson. Don't you think so?"

She smiles broadly but shakes her head no. "You're crazy."

"We're very serious about this," Randy puts in. His voice is deep and smooth. She looks at him with something like awe. Inwardly, I laugh, but I still feel jealous of the insect.

"Why do you want *me* to go along? We hardly know each other."

"Well, Randy's gonna drive, and I'll ride shotgun and do the deed. But I need someone in the backseat to resupply me, especially if they start chasing us and I have to engage in a retrograde rearguard defensive operation."

Her eyes widen. "You mean they might chase us?"

"An unlikely scenario," I say. "They would have to turn around to chase us, and by that time, we'd be long gone."

"But why do you want me to help you? There are lots of other kids you could get."

"Listen, Lori," I say in a sincere voice. "You may not know it, but Randy and I have been observing you for many years, and we know you're a dependable and studious-type person who can keep quiet about something like this and not blab it all over and get us in trouble."

"That's right," Randy says.

"Ha! You two are crazy!"

"So, will you do it?"

Tuesday afternoon, Mom asks, "Where are you off to?" as I head for the door.

"Randy's. I'm not sure what we're doing."

I find him in the garage. The door's open, and their station wagon is in the driveway. His dad's white '59 Buick LeSabre is gone. Randy is standing beside the outdoor faucet.

"About time you showed up," he says.

"Where's your mom?" I ask.

"She's at a meeting. They picked her up."

"What about Lori?"

"She said she'd be right down."

"Are her parents home?"

"No. They're both at work."

She shows up and we start filling the balloons. Randy works the spigot, I hold the balloons, tie them off when they're full, and hand them to Lori, who puts them in the buckets.

"How can you do such an evil thing?" she asks me with a smirk. "Aren't you a church person?"

"Yes, past president of the youth group," I say proudly. "And sometimes I sing solos in the choir."

"So how could you concoct this dastardly plot against innocent people you don't even know? Don't you believe in the golden rule?"

I have to laugh. "Of course. And I understand that it's not 'do unto others before they do unto you.' Of course I believe in it; I believe in it, treasure it, and live by it—whenever I can."

"Well?" Randy asks, as he turns off the faucet and reaches for another balloon.

"Well," I say as I stretch the neck of the balloon and start to tie it, "this is more of a prank or joke than an evil deed, and everybody ought to be able to take a joke. Right?"

"For sure," he says.

I look at Lori as I hand her the balloon. "And really, these people are responsible for their own destruction; they're laying themselves wide open, you know, by driving a car with a gaping hole in the passenger area." She lets out a little shriek. "Why would anyone buy a car like that?" The corners of her mouth turn upward, and all her braces and teeth appear, and eyes to the sky, she shakes her head from side to side. "To put it another way," I continue, "they're asking for it. Begging for it. Hoping that someone will come along and start their adrenalin pumping . . . and relieve their summer boredom. We'll be doing them a favor."

We turn down the residential street, past the line of houses on the left, and creep down the steep hill to the river. It's me and Lori and Randy in his '55 Ford station wagon with a luggage rack on top—white on the hood and below the side windows and red on the roof and swooping down the sides from the front fenders to over the wheels.

The temperature's steaming already, and our T-shirts and shorts are sticking to us. We turn right at the road along Shale River. The water is less than a hundred feet wide and shallow enough to walk across in most places. It winds along the shale cliff, almost 150 feet high, on the west side, and the two-lane road snakes along beside it. Between the road and river are picnic areas, ball fields, trails, and woods.

We drive for over an hour, turn around, retrace our route, and reverse our direction again. Still don't see one. A few cars pass, but no convertibles. By now, it's getting close to three o'clock. The shadows from the trees and cliff are starting to blanket the valley, and the air is getting cooler.

"Where are they?" I ask. "What's wrong with these boys? Some of them must be down here—playing golf, riding horses with their girls, hiking . . . "

"Or parking," Lori says.

I'm shocked. "You don't do that, do you, Lori?"

"Not me, but I know girls who do."

Then, there it is, coming right around the corner—a cream-colored Cadillac with whitewalls and an evil toothy grin, heading straight for us, its great pointy fins rising like dorsals on a pair of sharks.

"Slow down!" I shout.

"Get it!" Randy yells back.

Out of the car goes my arm with the smooth and squishy sphere in hand. Up goes my catapult, and into the air goes the projectile, over the station wagon roof and down into the open convertible with a splash.

"You got him!" Randy roars.

"Drive!" Lori squeals, and off we go.

"Wait," I say. "Turn around."

"What? Why?"

"Let's get it again! They're sure to do a U-ee to chase us."

"Ha!" he whoops, and he does the U, going into a pothole on the shoulder with a jarring bump and back onto the road, then wheeling off in the other direction.

Sure enough, here it comes again.

"Slow down," I command. "Lori. Another one. Quick!" She hands it to me. My arm shoots out the window as the giant beast with the gaping hole on top comes toward us. Up goes the balloon, over the top, and down it comes—yes!—into the car again.

"Did I get it?" I yell.

"You creamed it," Randy replies, his head out the window.

"Yes!" Lori screams, looking behind us out the rear window. "It landed right between them in the front seat. I could see it splash all over." Then she starts giggling.

"Man. Two perfect shots. You can really throw those things," Randy says.

"Let's get out of here fast," I say, "before they come again." We race away down the road, up the steep drive out of the park, and into the afternoon traffic.

Now the momentous event is over, and Lori's a changed woman. There's mirth in her eyes. She's holding a secret inside her that's itching to get out, and Randy and I are the only people she can talk to about it, and it's drawn her to us. She starts calling us every day to see what we're doing.

"That girl called again," Dad says as I come in from outside. "Who is she?"

"Probably Lori Matthews. She lives over on Rose Arbor."

"That little girl you used to play with?"

"Yeah. Same one, just older now. She's always bugging me and Randy." *No need to give him too much information. The only freedom we teens have is in our own private worlds.*

And now, when Lori walks down the street toward Randy and me, she has a springier step. You can tell that she likes sharing that secret with us. And she wants to know what we're going to do next and wants to be part of it.

Everything couldn't have worked out better.

And that night, I stick my head in Brett's room. "Hey, Brett. I just wanted you to know that I have a canoe, a car, and a driver now."

"Doesn't matter, slimehead. You'll never do it." *Oh, yeah?*

Chapter 2—Racing Randy

The afternoon after the bombing raid, Randy and I meet in his driveway. "So what do you think?" I ask. "Did she pass the test?"

"Damn right. I think she got a kick out of it. Do you think she told anyone about it?"

"I don't know."

"She's pretty tight-lipped," he says.

"So what do you think? Should we ask her about going canoeing? She might come in handy."

"It's okay with me. Where do you want to go first?"

"Hinckley Lake."

"That mud puddle?" he says, shaking his head. "It's barely big enough to get the canoe in. And it's all flat water—no rapids at all."

"I know. I just thought it would be a good place to start out. It's close; it won't take long to get there. We can do it in an afternoon. And they'll let us use our own canoe."

"My canoe."

"Yeah. And it won't be crowded during the week. It's a good place to get Lori accustomed to what canoeing's all about. Then we can cross it off our list and move on to some better water."

"You can't even swim there except below the dam," he says.

"I know, but accidents happen, Clark, especially with you in the canoe."

This trip has a complication. Lori has to get permission to go, and Randy and I have to face the Grand Inquisitor to get it.

Lori ushers us into the living room. Mr. Matthews—judge, jury, and executioner—is sitting in a captain's chair reading. Randy and I—the defendants—perch on a sofa facing him across a coffee table stacked with books and magazines; Lori observes from a chair on the side, and her mom stands guard in a doorway.

Glaring at us through wire-rimmed glasses, he begins in a crisp monotone, "So—I understand you boys want to take Lori canoeing with you. Why?"

I leap in. *It's always better to start talking than let fear fill the void.* "I thought it might be fun for her, sir. And Randy and I need someone to help us carry stuff and pick us up with the car if we take the canoe out at a different place than where we put it in. It would really be helpful to have her along, and I think she would have a good time."

He stares, unsmiling. "Will Lori be going in the canoe?"

"Sometimes," I say, "if she wants to."

"Do you have life jackets?"

"Yes. Three. Right, Randy?" He nods affirmatively.

"Are you both good swimmers?"

"Yes, sir. I got my swimming and canoeing merit badges in the Boy Scouts, and Randy's on a swim team in Lakeshore. And we both went on a two-hundred-mile canoe trip in Canada last summer."

"During the school year, I practice most mornings," Randy adds. "This summer I can't because I'm caddying to make money for college."

"Well . . . I guess you can swim. Who will be driving?"

"I will, sir," Randy says.

"How long have you been driving?"

"Counting my learner's permit, a year and a half."

"Have you ever had an accident or received any tickets?"

"No."

He nods his head affirmatively, adjusts his glasses, and looks at each of us in turn.

"Ever been stopped by the police?"

"No, sir."

"Do you boys drink alcohol?"

"No, sir. I've never had any," I lie. "And my parents rarely drink." Mr. Matthews looks down over his glasses, squints, and looks at us sideways as if he doesn't believe a word I'm saying, but to my relief, he lets it pass.

Randy shakes his head no.

"Do you know how to get there?"

"Oh, yes, sir," I say. "We've been there several times. I know how to get there. And I have good maps too."

He tilts his head backward and asks, "Do you go to church?" That one's out of left field; Lori told us her family never went. Why should he care?

"Yes. Regularly," I say.

"Once in a while," Randy says.

Now Mr. Matthews looks at Lori's mother. "I think it's all right," she says. "They're both good students, and Jeff was a dependable paperboy, and I know his mother. She works at the library with me."

They nod to each other, and he looks back at us. "Okay. She has our permission. But I want to know when you are going and when we can expect you to have her back."

Whew. My first near-death experience.

We're rattling along down the two-lane highway, windows open, on our way to Hinckley Lake on a sunny June afternoon, just shooting the breeze. I'm riding shotgun, and Lori's in the back. The bow of the canoe on top extends over the hood. Taut ropes stretch from its point to the middle of the bumper, and others reach from the bow seat to the ends of the bumper. Others tie it to the rooftop carrier, and still others run from the point of the stern to the ends of the rear bumper.

We're all in swimsuits—mine are boxers and Randy's are tight racing trunks. Lori has on a one-piece black suit with a little dressie-like thing on the bottom and a top that goes all the way up and is tied to a strap around her neck for extra security, as if she needs it with those little boobs of hers. Her dad must've bought it. She does look cute, though, except for the braces and that limp hair. And here she is. She has dared to go canoeing with two boys. That's exceptional.

We drive past fields of knee-high corn and newly baled hay, pastures with cattle, barns, and woods. The air smells fresh and rich with the grass and hay.

We get close to the park, so I go over everything for them. I scoped out the objective a few days ago, and I know exactly what it's like. There's a boat-launch ramp near the parking area and a building on the left where they rent rowboats and canoes. The store in the building sells bait, fishing gear, hats, clothing, candy, and snack food—typical park stuff—and that's where you pay for rentals. Outside, they have maybe ten or fifteen rowboats and canoes pulled up on the beach and two pontoon boats with flat roofs tied to a dock that juts into the water. A guy in a ranger suit checks people out and hands out paddles, life jackets, and so on. A "No Swimming" sign stands guard at the boat-launch ramp, another one tells you to wear life jackets, and another describes the varieties of fish in the lake. The lake is only a few hundred yards wide and is in the midst of forest. The dam is at the other end, about a half a mile down. To the right, the water curves around a bend to an area that can't be seen from the boat rental area. Part of this cove is roped off with buoys because it's too shallow for boat motors. The lake looked deserted when I was there, like we would have it all to ourselves.

"So, it's easy," I tell them in the car. "We just pull up, unload the canoe, carry it to the ramp, and shove off."

And that's what we do. Randy and I unrope the canoe, take it off the car, and carry it to the ramp, and Lori brings the life jackets and paddles.

"I get the stern," Randy says. "It's my boat, and my car brought us here."

"Okay, Clark. Don't be so defensive. But remember, I get it half the time."

"The hell you do."

"How would you like me to turn it over in the middle of the lake?"

Randy and I stand on each side of the canoe and hand-over-hand it onto the water. I drop in my paddle and life jacket, climb in, and walk forward, bent over, holding onto the gunwales on each side, stepping over the stern seat, the thwarts in the stern, center, and bow, and the bow seat. I put the life jacket on the bottom in front of the seat and kneel on it to keep our center of gravity low. I glance over at the boat rental and see the man on the dock looking at us.

Lori follows me into the canoe and sits down in the center, rocking the boat just a little. She's wearing her life jacket.

"You're doing great, Lori," I say. "It's like you've done this before."

"I've been canoeing before."

Randy throws in his life jacket and the snack bag, puts his hands on the gunwales, pushes the canoe into the water, steps in, and kneels on the jacket.

"We're off," he says as we glide onto the smooth water.

It's exhilarating—fresh air, big sky, calm water with trees around the shore, paddle in my hands, reaching into the water and pulling it past the canoe, my arm and back muscles stretching and working.

"It takes me back to Temagami," I say.

"Sure does, Klossen, and don't think I've forgotten what happened on that rock."

"What, do you still think about that accident?"

"What accident?" Lori asks. I explain how I accidentally bumped Randy and knocked him into the frigid water.

"It was no accident," Randy says. "He pushed me on purpose."

"Give it up, Clark." I change the subject. "Say, I think we better stay away from the dam. It drops off about twenty or thirty feet. Let's go around the bend to the right. That ranger at the boat dock can't see us from there."

We paddle for a while and go gently around the bend up to the yellow line of buoys.

"Why don't you want him to see us?" Lori asks, her forehead wrinkling.

"In case we want to do something against the rules," I say.

"Like what?"

"I don't know. Like maybe we might want to go for a swim. I'd like that. How about you two?"

"Sounds good to me," Randy says.

"How 'bout you, Lori? He can't see us from there." *Don't worry. We'll keep our suits on.*

"Sure. I'll join you. It is hot today. But you two better keep your suits on. I'm not swimming skinny."

I guess she read my mind. Sure would be fun to go nude, though. I can just see it.

"We'll be good. Let's go," I say.

We glide up to the shore, I step out, tie the canoe to a branch, and lunge backward into the cool water. "Agh," I gasp. Then I right myself and stand up. The water comes halfway to my knees. "Terrific," I say. "It's not even up to my belly button."

"Maybe it gets deeper farther out," Lori says.

We wade out twenty yards and it's still below our knees.

"We sure don't need life jackets here," I say.

"I don't wear those things anyway," Randy reminds me. "They restrict my motion."

"Is that why you don't use them in swim meets? You'd all be safer if you did."

"You're a nut," Lori says.

"You said it," Randy says.

"I know, but speaking of competitions, how about a little race, Clark, just you and me."

"What? You and me? Swimming? Ha! I'll kill you. Where do you want to swim to?" He puts his arms behind his back and flexes for us.

"How 'bout to the other side of the main lake—there and back?" Randy blinks. That distance is about a quarter of a mile each way—much farther than he's ever swum in a meet. I knew he would be flailing away on his stomach all the way and having to rest in the middle of the lake while I did my slow float on my back, resting the whole time. I knew I'd win. Slow and steady wins the race.

"What if the ranger sees you?" Lori asks.

"It's just a risk we'll have to take," I say. Of course, Randy's risk is much greater than mine, because when I swim, only my face and toes show (plus my arms a little when I'm bringing them forward), and I don't make much of a splash. But his back and arms will be out of the water all the time as he crawls along, and he'll be splashing constantly with his feet, so he'll be much easier to see. He'll probably get caught and taken in to the dock, in which case I win by default. "So what do you say, Clark. Are we on?"

"What's the prize?"

"The winner gets the stern for the rest of the day, and can just sit back there and steer like you always do."

"Okay, big shot. You're on. Let's go." He dives in and starts paddling away like a machine, turning from side to side, straightening his arms, each in turn, and pulling them back through the water with stunning power.

I lunge backward with a splash and begin the slow sweep with my arms to my sides, both at the same time, and synchronized with my frog kick. I immediately space out, lying on the water, moving my limbs, looking far into the sky, my ears immersed in the silence of the deep, listening for the gurgle of aquatic creatures. With only my face and feet in the air, I know that from a distance I might be mistaken for a canoe, but never a swimmer.

My mind roams. I think about school and working on the spring play . . . and winning the debate on capital punishment . . . leading the youth service at church . . . family camping in Canada

. . . canoeing Lake Temagami . . . visiting the Hudson Bay trading post . . . browsing Indian blankets and whistles and postcards with bears on them . . . pushing Randy into the water . . . talking him into canoeing this summer . . . throwing water balloons into the car (two for two!) . . . watching Lori's excited face . . . peeling off her swimsuit at Hinckley Lake to see what's under there, and . . . oh, no—that won't happen.

Once in a while, I roll over and look to see where Randy is. The first time, he's way ahead, cutting through the water like a speedboat. The second time, he's even farther in the lead. *When'll he get tired?* After about half an hour, I turn over and find him standing on the opposite shore like an exclamation mark. I look back and see Lori, another tiny vertical bar, following the race. I'm in the middle of the lake. *Maybe I'll lose,* I think.

I go back to swimming and try to dream of all the girls I'd undressed and had my way with in my lifetime (zero, in the real world), and I get so hot I'm afraid I'll start looking more like a sailboat than a canoe. So I change my train of thought and start thinking of favorite songs and make the meter match my swimming stroke. I wish I could sing out loud, but I don't want to attract any attention, and sound carries across water. After another quarter hour or so, I touch shore, turn around, and look. Randy is in the middle of the lake. Now I know I'm going to lose. I start swimming back, gazing at the trees on the land I'm leaving behind. Then I hear a strange little vibration in the water that gets louder and then dies. I turn over. Uh-oh. A motorboat has accosted Randy. It must be that ranger from the dock. As I gaze at the boat, I see a question mark bending down toward the water. Then a dot of yellow appears for a second, and after a few minutes, the boat leaves and heads back to the dock. I wonder what happened and why Randy didn't have to get in the boat?

I keep swimming, but now when I turn over, I seem to be gaining on him. Could I possibly catch up, just like that tortoise caught the hare? I know he must be getting tired. But my progress seems too fast.

As I near the inlet, I'm only twenty yards behind him, and now I can see why he's been going so slow—he's wearing a life jacket. Ha! He should've practiced some underwater evasion to get away from that ranger, but he didn't. He didn't have the cajones to. He's too straight arrow, and it just might have cost him the race.

I pick up my pace, and before we reach the canoe, I pass him up, and run aground in front of Lori. I look up at her. *Darned if she doesn't look cute.*

"You won!" she says in amazement.

"You bet. Now you know who the real man is. Ha!"

I stand with her there in the water and watch the poor boy come in. "The winner is . . . Jeff!" she announces. "The slower swimmer!"

Randy staggers up to us. He couldn't even swim the last thirty yards; his hands kept hitting bottom. He's angry. "The only reason you won was because I had to wear this life jacket. It's like having to drag another body along with you."

"Too bad, Randy. You should never have let yourself get caught. You should have dived under the boat and escaped underwater."

"You scumbag. I could never have outrun a motorboat. And he would've gotten mad as hell and had us all arrested or something. How would you have liked that, asshole?"

"Watch your language, Clark. There's a lady present. Anyway, he wouldn't have caught me. I was disguised as a canoe, and I kept a low profile."

"Yeah? Well, take this, you rat!" He swings his paddle and splashes me and Lori with a long sheet of water.

"Hey. Lori didn't do anything. Don't splash her." I seize my paddle and splash him back, and Lori joins in with hers. Then I splash her because she splashed me, and the three of us battle it out with each other until we're tired. Finally I say to Randy, "Okay, okay. You win."

"The swimming contest?"

"The splashing contest, stupid. But listen. I'm going to give you another chance to prove yourself."

"What do you mean?"

"I propose another contest. This one's to see who's the most powerful paddler. But if you're too tired, you can just forfeit now before we begin." This is all for Lori's benefit.

"Forfeit? I could beat you at paddling no matter how tired I am."

"Oh, yeah?"

"Yeah. Now how do you intend to go about this with one canoe—have separate runs and have Lori time us?"

"Nope. It's simpler than that. We put the canoe in the center of this inlet, get in facing each other, and the one who reaches the opposite bank first is the winner and the most powerful canoeist."

"You don't stand a chance, Klossen."

"We'll see about that, Clark."

"You're both crazy," Lori says.

We go to the starting point, as best we can gauge it. The water there is knee deep. Grabbing the gunnels on both sides, we throw ourselves in and sit staring at each other. I'm pointed toward the shore where Lori stands.

"Okay, Lori."

"Ready . . . set . . . go!" she shouts. And with that, we start paddling furiously toward each other. What we learn after a minute, however, is that we aren't going toward either shore. We're going in a circle. We keep it up for a full revolution.

"This isn't working," he says.

"Nope."

We switch sides to stop turning. We can hear Lori cackling.

"She's laughing at us," he observes.

"I know."

"What's making us go in a circle?" he asks.

"It's because the paddler in the stern always overpowers the man up front, so if he paddles on the right, the canoe tends to go to the left, and if we're facing each other, it's like both of us are in the stern, and we both tend to go to the left, which means we go around and around."

"So what do you think we should do, both do J-strokes?" That's where you push the blade away from the canoe at the end of your forward stroke; this straightens your course.

"Nah. I've got a better idea. We both paddle on the same side. Here. I'll paddle on this side, and you paddle on this side too. That way we'll go straight."

I make sure I'm paddling on my strong side, of course, which means that he'll be paddling on his weak side, since he's right-handed too, and I'll be sure to win. You've gotta have brains and quick thinking to win life's battles.

Off we go, digging and splashing furiously, but we have to be careful; it's easier to tip the canoe when you're both paddling on the same side.

Sure enough, it's clear from the beginning that I'm going to win, which makes Randy paddle harder and harder and get madder and madder. But we're halfway to Lori before he catches on as to why.

"Switch sides," he says.

"Switch sides? Are you tired already?"

"A little. So?"

"I guess that proves you're the weaker canoeist, Clark. You lose."

"You mean you aren't a little tired yet?

"Heck no."

"Well. Anyway. I'm the captain, so you have to do what I say, and I say switch."

"How do you figure you're the captain?"

"Because I'm in the stern."

"The hell you are. I'm in the stern."

"Oh. You mean because we're facing each other."

"This boat has two sterns, Clark. We're both sitting in the back."

"Screw you, Klossen. I'll beat you anyway."

He begins an impressive surge of paddling and starts to move the craft backward (from my point of view). But I know he can't keep it up, paddling on his weak side. Before long, my steady strokes are driving us toward Lori again.

Then, wouldn't you know, he starts accusing me of rigging this contest by making him paddle on his weak side and not letting him switch sides.

"You're just a weak paddler, Clark. Face it."

That got him.

"But you haven't won until you reach the shore by Lori. Is that right?"

"That's right, Clark. But we're almost there."

With that the scoundrel leans to the side and rolls the canoe into the water. Up we come spurting and spouting.

"There," he says. "Contest over. You didn't reach the shore, and you didn't win, and you haven't proved you're the strongest."

"You did it on purpose."

"It was an accident, Klossen, just like when you bumped me into the lake in Canada."

We jump around, splashing each other vigorously, each seeking vengeance for the other's crimes.

"Okay, boys. I get to paddle now since neither of you won the race," Lori says.

We look at her in shock. *Lori?* Then we look at each other. "What do you think?" I ask Randy.

"We're already wet, so if we tip over, I guess it won't matter."

Randy and I lift the canoe out of the water to drain it, and put it back in right side up. Then we all get in and head for the loading ramp with Lori in the bow. I'm in command in the stern since I won the swimming race.

"The girl does all right with the paddle," I tell Randy, who's sitting in front of me. "Not strong, but pretty good."

"Of course I do," she says.

When we get near the ramp, I yell, "Rudder right," for her to guide us in, and she puts her paddle in and points it toward the ramp.

"Not bad," Randy says.

We walk to the car in our wet suits past the "No Swimming" sign, which makes me smirk.

In the car on the way back, my mind flies to the morning paper. "Hey," I ask, "did you guys hear that Elvis is getting out of the army? It was in the paper this morning."

"I don't have time to read the paper before I go to the club," Randy says.

"It's now or never . . . " I sing, parroting Elvis's hit.

"Ooooh," Lori groans.

"Shut up, Klossen."

"He got lonesome, I guess," I say, and I croon a line from "Are You Lonesome Tonight?"

"Stop," Lori says.

"And did you see what those Negro college kids did down south yesterday? That was in the paper too."

"What?" he asks.

"They had another one of those sit-ins at a lunch counter."

"Big deal. They've been doing that all year long all over the South."

"It was on the TV last night too," Lori says.

"They're nuts," Randy says. "It's a good way to get beaten up or arrested. Southerners don't like Negroes getting out of line."

"I think they have a lot of guts—more than most of us have," I say.

"I think they have a right to eat at any lunch counters and restaurants they want to," Lori says. "They do up here. Most places, anyway."

I nod. "Yeah. Why not down there?"

"You two must be Ne-gro-lovers," Randy says, drawing out the words.

"They're people too," Lori says.

"Yeah," I say.

He hits a pothole, the car shakes, and the canoe bounces and slides forward. But the ropes hold, and we go on.

"Whoa!" I shout. "What're you trying to do? Wreck the car . . . and the canoe?"

"Shut up, wise guy."

"Now, Randy," I say.

He flips me a bird below the seat where Lori can't see it. I ignore it.

A memory pops up: "One time my mom told me that when I was two or three, I was with them at a parade downtown, and we got separated, and they found me choking and sniffling and holding the hand of a Negro cop. He was really nice to me. Mom and Dad always told me that if I ever needed help, I should find a policeman."

"And that made you a Negro lover."

"I think there are good ones and bad ones, just like us."

"Absolutely," Lori says.

"Yeah. There are bad ones, all right," Randy says, turning his head and looking at me, "like the two that beat up my grandfather and robbed him and left him in the gutter."

"White people beat up Negroes too," Lori says.

"And cheat them and murder them," I add.

Randy turns his head back to the front, grimaces, and says, "I don't care. I don't want anything to do with them. I think they're stupid, ugly, and vicious."

"Randy!" Lori gasps.

I can't believe it. I take a deep breath of country air, look out at the farms, listen to the air buffeting the car and canoe, and feel it pressing against my face. "Stupid like Thurgood Marshall?"

"Who?" Randy asks.

I say it louder. "Thurgood Marshall. He's the Negro lawyer who convinced the Supreme Court to integrate public schools," I say.

Randy gets a satisfied look. "We don't have to worry about integrated schools in Orchard Park, 'cause there aren't any Negro kids living there, and they can't bus them in from Cleveland 'cause we're in a different school district."

"Even though we're less than a mile from the Cleveland border," I say.

"Yeah, but ten miles from where they live downtown."

We come to a major intersection with a four-way stop and turn left onto the other two-lane highway. We get behind a tractor trailer loaded with steel pipe, but Randy zooms around it.

"I wonder why Negroes don't live in Orchard Park," I say.

Randy replies, "My dad said that when people came to Cleveland, all the white Republicans went west, and all the Democrats, Jews, and Negroes went east."

"He was kidding, wasn't he?" I ask.

"I guess. But I think it's true . . . pretty much."

"And all the culture went east too," Lori says. "The orchestra, and art museum, Case Tech, Western Reserve . . . "

"You know, now I'm really curious," I say. "I'd really like to find out why they don't live in Orchard Park."

"Maybe I could help you," Lori says.

I turn to the backseat and look at her. "That would be great." *I'll get Lori, the brain, working on it . . . And who knows what else might develop.*

"Whatever turns you two on," Randy says. *He's reading my mind.*

We pull down their street, and I say, "Well! We've accomplished objective number one: Hinckley Lake."

"What's next?" Lori asks.

"One of the rivers – white water!"

"I'm up for that," Randy says.

"I gotta check some things first and do some reconnoitering."

"Let me know if you need any help," she says. *Oh, yes, I will.*

Chapter 3—Getting Gas with Lori

I'm late for dinner, which is not permitted—ever. I was out riding around on my bike and stopped in to see Lori (she wasn't home). I won't tell them that, of course.

"You're late, young man," Dad growls. "Where were you?"

"Sorry," I say. "I was taking a bike ride and went too far and couldn't get back in time."

"Oh? Where did you go?"

"Along the lake out to Avon Lake and back." I knew that would impress him. Exercise is a good thing.

"That's over twenty miles, round trip," Dad says.

"Yep." *And I never broke a sweat.*

We're in the dining room. Mom's at one end of the table with Billy and Jimmy, who are five and three, on either side. They're up on phone books so they can reach the table. Dad's at the opposite end of the table from Mom, and I'm to his right. The room is open to the living room, and behind Mom is a bay window facing a sea of grass. Our backyard connects with our neighbors', and no one builds fences or plants shrubs to break it up, so it's a big field we all can play in. Brett's working, as usual.

"Well, I hope you like cold food," he says. It's tuna fish casserole with bread cubes and green beans. And yes, it's better hot.

After a punishing silence, Dad asks, "How was Hinckley Lake?"

"Nice, but kind of boring."

"Everything's boring to you."

"No, really. It's all flat water. And it's tiny. You canoe around it once, and there's nowhere else to go."

Dad smiles. "You should have done another lap for exercise."

"Yeah." *Always agree with him.*

"How did Lori like it?" Mom asks.

I'm relieved that someone else is talking. "She had a great time. We even let her paddle for a while, and she did pretty well. But usually, we'll have her along so she can drive and pick us up in the canoe. I think she was hoping we could go swimming, but they don't allow it there, you know, except below the dam in that stream that goes up to your ankles. I don't know why they don't let people swim in the lake. I don't think it's polluted."

"Obviously, they don't want anyone to drown," Dad says.

"Oh, right. But you know, they ought to give people who can swim licenses like driver's licenses. We could take tests, and then they could just give tickets to swimmers who don't have a license." Dad ignores me. It's too much for him to think about over dinner. "But anyway, we did have fun. And we had some good conversations in the car. That Lori is really smart."

"What did you talk about?" Mom asks.

"Lots of things—like the Negro kids sitting in at lunch counters in the South, and segregation, and segregated schools."

"They've always had segregation down there, Jeff. That's how they keep peace between the races. But the kids doing those sit-ins are breaking the law, and they're bound to get in trouble. They need to learn to follow the rules."

Dad's a follow-the-rules type guy, and I think he's pretty much a segregationist. He might as well be living in the Deep South. I know he thinks white people are smarter than Negroes, and that Negroes should be kept in menial jobs.

"Irv. You know I support those kids," Mom says.

"Yes, I know. We're just lucky we don't have those racial problems here because all our Negroes live on the East Side."

* * *

"Get up!" Mom shouts. "It's seven o'clock, and Helen will be here at eight. Clean up this room. It's a mess. I will not have Helen put a foot in this room until it's cleaned up. Get up. Now! The lawn needs mowed and edged. And I want you to babysit this afternoon while I go to the store. Get up!"

What a way to wake up on my summer vacation, to the sound of Mom, my drill sergeant, shouting orders at me. I sit up in bed, rub my eyes, throw my feet over the side, and look around. Dirty clothes are everywhere: on the floor, on my desk, my desk chair, and bureau—socks, underwear, shirts, jeans, everything. So what. "You don't hang up dirty clothes. Why would you do that?" I grumble to myself. I know there must be some other articles of clothing under the bed, but finding those would require me to get on my knees, put my head on the floor, and look with a flashlight. Better let them be. They've been there since antiquity, and no one will know they're there.

It's big cleanup time. Mom always runs around cleaning the house before the cleaning lady comes. Now does that make sense? She doesn't want Helen to think badly of her. Mom's responsible for the cleanliness of our abode, and she doesn't want Helen to think we live like pigs. What would Helen say to her friends? "Oh, those white folks. They live like pigs."

I stand up and slowly move my bones over to the closet, swing open the door, retrieve the empty bag lying in a corner under a pile of clothes, and start picking up and stuffing.

Helen's been coming once a week for several years now. Mom started getting help when Billy was born, five years ago. Helen's dark brown and stout. She keeps her hair tied up in a bun, and in cold weather, wears a heavy wool coat and small black hat. She carries a big black purse on her arm and hides her lunch in it. She and the other cleaning ladies in the neighborhood arrive on the bus from Cleveland just before eight and walk down the hill to the houses. They usually clean two houses a day. Then at ten minutes before five, there's a parade of them going back up to catch the bus home.

I don't know much about Helen, except that she lives on the East Side. I guess she has a family; I don't really know. Mom knows more about her. She eats lunch with Helen whenever she comes, and they sit in the kitchen and talk. Helen's a certified teacher like Mom. I don't know why she isn't teaching. I really don't have any other contact with Negroes since they live on the other side of town.

"Get up! She's coming up the drive."

"I'm up," I say. Now I have to hustle.

Helen's nice, but she can be stern sometimes. I usually sit on my bed and listen for the approach of the vacuum cleaner through the living room and down my hall and gauge my time by it, you know, how much time I have left to pick up my things. But sometimes she arrives too soon, knocks, and booms, "Mr. Jeff, I'm ready to do this room now."

Oh! I have to get out of here and clear my head. When Mom's in one of her shouting moods, I find it's best to get out of the house. Sometimes I hide in the garage and sit by the lawn mower and read so if she opens the door and looks in, I can say I'm working on the motor. Today, I shout in the door at her, over the roar of the vacuum cleaner, "Can I have the keys? I'm going to get gas."

"You're always going to get gas."

"Well, how can I mow without gas?"

I put the can in the trunk of our light-blue '57 four-door Plymouth with the white top and back down the driveway.

I stop at Lori's, ring the bell, and ask her, "Want to go for a ride?"

"Where?"

"I want to go exploring—see what I can find out about why there aren't any Negroes here. I don't know where to start, but I thought something might hit me if I look around."

"Bonk," she says, and laughs. "How long are you going to be gone?"

"Not long. I told Mom I was going out to get some gas for the lawn mower."

"You're bad."

"Sometimes you have to be."

She disappears and returns wearing a white blouse tucked into her shorts. And I think she brushed her hair. It's still straight, but looks neater.

"Where are we going?" she asks.

"I thought we could see what we can learn in downtown Orchard Park."

We pass the high school, the big Catholic church, some other churches, and Orchard Park Diner, and park in front of the stores near the Westview Hotel. I love that hotel. It's a big, pink building, nine stories high with a Spanish tile roof, a hundred rooms, a ballroom, and restaurant. It sits on the edge of the valley, a hundred feet above the river, and right next to Shale River Bridge.

"Let's look at the bridge."

We walk to the center and look down on the river and yachts, through the canyon between cliffs made by water from receding glaciers, past the railroad bridge and yacht club toward the lake.

I tell Lori, "I feel like that guy who walked across the valley on a rope—900 feet across and 150 feet above the river. That's not much shorter and shallower than the Niagara River Gorge. And did you know that when the bridge was built in 1910, its concrete arch was the longest in the world?"

"You're full of facts today."

We go into the hotel. The two-story lobby has glass chandeliers hanging from a decorative ceiling. Walls at the mezzanine level contain murals, one with a sculpture of a naked man riding a dolphin. Overstuffed furniture sits in conversation areas in a one-story section near windows overlooking the valley. A scent of cigars and cigarettes is in the air.

"Oh, look!" she says. "That's Poseidon, the Greek god of the sea. Or it could be Neptune, the Roman god. And it looks like a high-relief sculpture, you know, where more than half of the depth is shown, but I expect it was cast on the ground and attached to the wall. See how the pattern on the wall goes under the sculpture?"

"Yes. Where did you learn all that?"

"From books."

"Brain."

"So you don't like me telling you things, Jeff?"

I feel myself blushing. "No, I do. That was a compliment." *I better be careful or she won't tell me anything.*

We go to the desk where a man stands looking at some papers. He has graying temples and is wearing a suit and tie.

"Yes?" he says, looking up.

"Beautiful hotel you have here. Can you tell me when it was built?"

He glances at our attire, and says abruptly, "It was started in 1923 and opened in 1925."

"Great. Do you have any other information on it, you know, historical stuff?"

"Just a postcard. It shows a trolley car crossing the bridge and passing by the hotel." He hands it to me.

"Oh. Where did the trolley go?"

"From Cleveland to Lorain. Anything else?"

"When did it stop running?" Lori asks.

"Sometime in the thirties, I think. Too many people were driving cars." He reaches for the card.

"Can I have this?" I ask.

He leans his head back and says, "It's twenty-five cents."

I pull out a quarter and give it to him. We thank him and leave.

"Well. He was snooty," I say.

"He was just busy."

"But we did learn something: if you lived here after the thirties and worked in Cleveland, you had to have a car."

"Unless there was a bus," Lori says.

We cross the street and go into the hardware store. A thin old man is taking cardboard boxes of nuts and bolts from a rolling metal table and putting them on the shelves. His face is wrinkled like a raisin, and his piercing eyes and pointy beak remind me of an owl.

I address him. "Hi. . . . Say, we're interested in that trolley that used to come through here. Do you know anything about it?"

"Trolley. Humph." He doesn't look at us. He leans his head back to look through the lower part of his glasses and places two boxes on the shelf. "What do you want to know about it?"

"I guess it went from Cleveland to Lorain. Right?"

"No. From Cleveland to Toledo. Interurban. The LSE—Lake Shore Electric Railway." His lips are pursed even when he speaks.

"And did people from Orchard Park commute on it to go to Cleveland?"

"Yes, yes. Until they started driving."

"Did most people commute?"

He still hasn't looked at us! His head keeps bobbing down and up like a momma bird feeding her young as he picks up boxes, looks at them, and deposits them on the shelves. Maybe he's watching us through his peripheral vision, I don't know. "There were no jobs here," he says. "People had to commute. We just had greenhouses and farms and orchards and vineyards and a few stores."

"Did you ever ride the trolley?"

"All the time. It stopped right behind the store here. Took less than half an hour to get downtown, even with the stops."

"Did any Negroes ride it?"

Now he looks up at me with those big eyes and pointy nose like he's getting ready to feed me to his nestlings. "Negroes? Why do you ask?"

I shrug. "Just curious."

"Well, there were some—just passing through—except for some servants and cleaning ladies who worked along the lake."

I can't think of any other questions, so we thank him and head for home.

"Whew. Talk about grumpy old men!" I say.

"Indubitably!"

"Ha. That's an SAT word. You must have learned that by studying the cards in the box."

She tosses me a metallic grin and says, "Indisputably!"

"Ha!" I shout. "Undoubtedly!"

On the way home, she asks, "So, did any ideas hit you on the head today, Sir Isaac? Or should I call you Mr. Holmes?"

"About why no Negroes live in Orchard Park? Sure. We had no jobs here and no place for them to live. They'd have to have a car to commute, and they couldn't afford that."

"Unless they took the trolley or a bus."

"Yeah, but that would cost money too, and they'd still have to have a house. We don't have any apartments here, except those expensive high-rises by the lake, and the houses are expensive."

"So you think that poor Negroes coming to Cleveland from the South couldn't afford a house and a car, so that's why they jammed into the East Side."

"That's my theory. I suppose some of them eventually got good jobs and could afford to live here, don't you think?"

"I would think so," Lori says. "Lots of houses they bought on the East Side are nice."

I drive up to her house and she gets out. "I think you're pretty nice, too." I watch her blush. "Say, are you going to be around this weekend? Maybe we could get together. We might get some other ideas, and we still have to reconnoiter the next canoe trip."

"I'm not sure."

"You know, I've been thinking."

"Not again. That's twice in one day. About what?

"Maybe we ought to do more than just try to find out why there are no Negroes here. Maybe we should do something to open this town up to Negroes."

"Integrate it. Like those kids were integrating that lunch counter."

"Yes."

"Whoa! You are an instigator."

"But we still have to find out why we're segregated so we'll know how to change things."

She cocks her head and looks up at me slyly. "Yes. And we should keep it secret, too, you know, what we're doing, because some people won't like it, including Randy."

"And my dad. Yeah, you're right." *Yes. I'd like to keep a secret with you, especially one from Randy.*

She starts toward the house, and then turns around and shouts, "Oh, wait, Jeff! You forgot to get gas!"

"I've got enough. And if I run out, I'll just have to go get some."

Chapter 4—Fourth of July Weekend

Fourth of July weekend is like solitary confinement. It turns out that Lori is visiting relatives, so we can't pursue our investigation (or anything else), and Randy has to caddie every day. I'm all alone, except for my jailers (Mom and Dad) and my ratty little brothers skittering through the house.

I catch up my lawns on Friday and Saturday morning. The weekend's saving grace is Saturday afternoon. Dad is golfing with some friends, and Mom lets me use the car to recon the next canoe trip.

I look at the map and trace the Cuyahoga River south from Cleveland. The water's supposed to be just as polluted down there as in Cleveland, but who cares—we'll be canoeing, not swimming. It shows that the old Ohio and Erie Canal and towpath and a railroad all follow the river through a park to Akron. We could put in at Peninsula and take out in Brecksville. It looks like about seven or eight miles on the map.

I drive to Hinckley, turn east for about ten miles, cross Riverview Road and the bridge over the canal, towpath, and river, and bump over the railroad tracks into Peninsula. There's grass growing through the ties. I turn into the parking lot of a tavern by the railroad. A few cars are outside. I walk in and wait for the hostess at a counter with a cash register. Behind it is a bar with a half dozen stools and shelves full of liquor bottles on the wall behind it. I glance around. Most of the place has square tables with four chairs each. Diners, including a few kids, sit at several of them. Some are eating late breakfasts of bacon and eggs and pancakes, but an older couple is munching hamburgers and fries. A middle-aged woman comes out of the kitchen and approaches me. She's wearing a short-sleeve blouse and pleated white skirt, cut above the knees, and a flowered apron. "Can I help you?"

"Yes. Can you tell me a little bit about the canal and railroad and river?"

"A little. The railroad—the Cuyahoga Valley Railway—it doesn't run anymore, and the canal boats have stopped. The river has flooded and washed out the canal in places. The aqueducts, where the canal goes over the river—they're deteriorating, the locks are all broke, and the towpath is grown over with bushes and saplings."

"But the river still works, right?"

She smiles. "Yes, it still moves."

"Say, a buddy and me want to go canoeing on it. Can you tell me a little about it?"

She glances over to see if anyone at the tables wants her, then looks back.

"Did you see that sign at the corner outside? "'No Boating—Fishing—Swimming in the River'?"

"I missed it."

"You're not supposed to canoe on it or swim in it. It's real polluted with all that industrial waste and sewage from Akron. They didn't even need to put in that 'No Fishing' part. There aren't any fish in the river. They all died. So you won't see any herons or kingfishers or mallard ducks here, either. It's a dead river."

"Really? That's bad. But we're just gonna go *on* it, not *in* it."

"Yeah. That's what they all say. Until you hit a rock and tip over. Then you'll have to swim in that gunk. And maybe you'll swallow some of it. And if it'll kill fish, it'll kill you too." She shakes her head and glances around the room again.

"Have you ever seen anyone canoe on it?"

She sighs and shakes her head. "Once in a while some crazy people do. You know there are rapids in there, don't you?"

"That's what I want to know. I want to know where they are and how bad they are. Do you know anyone who's canoed it?"

"Yes. There's a mechanic down at the gas station who's done it couple of times, but he almost always goes other places."

"Oh, yeah? What's his name?"

"Jim. He might be there right now if you want to talk to him. Tell him Dot sent you."

Jim's standing under the rack in the garage greasing a car. I tell him, "I want to canoe down the Cuyahoga. Dot down at the restaurant said you could tell me about it."

He looks up. "Yeah, I'll tell you about it. Wear your nose plugs, because it stinks. And you don't want to get water in your nose if you tip over. I'd go someplace else if I were you."

"Well, we've gotta go somewhere close because we can't spend much time driving."

"Where do you live?" he asks.

"Orchard Park."

"Rich kid, huh?"

"Nope. Most people who live there aren't rich. But say, are there any rapids on the river?"

He gazes out at the park across the street. "Oh, it's pretty calm. About class I and II. Not many boulders. And it doesn't drop as much after Boston, so it gets gentler. And if you go when the water is fairly low and stay away from fallen trees, you'll probably be all right. It gets a little choppy sometimes. But that's just fun."

"Great." That's good news—just what we need, especially if Lori insists on paddling.

"But if the water gets near flood stage," he warns, "stay out of it. It's a monster. The river's in control, not you. You go where it takes you and hope it doesn't wash you up against some strainers or boulders and flip you."

"What's a strainer?" I ask.

"Usually a tree. You get carried against it sideways to the current and the water flows through it, and you can't get off it. It'll grab you like eagle talons."

"Really?"

"You better believe it. Another thing. When you come to that island outside of Peninsula, take the left channel. The other one doesn't have enough water. You'll run aground and have to portage through it and stick your feet in that muck."

"You really know the river," I say. "How many times have you canoed it?"

"Dozens when I was your age. Not now. I know better, and you should too. Find somewhere else to canoe."

"Thanks for the advice," (which I promptly ignore). "Say. Do you have a map of the river?"

"Yeah. There's a topo map on the wall in the office, but it's the only one I got."

He walks over to a workbench, sets down his grease gun, wipes his hands on a rag, and leads me into the crowded office.

I see the map and ask if I can trace it. He gives me two sheets of paper and a pencil, and I draw the route from Peninsula through Boston to Brecksville Station and Independence. It seems that the hills come close to the river between Peninsula and Boston. But then, after going through a tight place, the river flows into a wider valley and seems to meander north.

"Where are the rapids?" I ask.

"Just north of Peninsula, and just north of Boston, and just before you get to the dam in Brecksville. Watch that you don't go over the dam."

"Okay. And someone with a car could drive up to Boston or Brecksville and get us out?"

"They can just go up Riverview Road. It's rough, but passable."

On Sunday, we go to church, and then Monday is the Fourth of July. Dad puts out the flag, and Mom makes pancakes and sausages for breakfast. Outside, the temperature shoots into the nineties. I play croquet with the boys, and in the afternoon, descend into the basement, where it's cool, and listen to the Indians and watch the boys play with their cars on the concrete floor. Then at about five, we gather up lawn chairs, blankets, and stuff and go to City Park on the lake for the fireworks. We pass that sign I hate, "No Swimming," find a place on the hillside, and Dad grills hot dogs while Mom and I babysit.

We eat and bathe ourselves in insect repellent, and then I take the boys to the playground until the lightning bugs start to appear. We're starting back when my girlfriend Jean approaches with two other girls. I've neglected her since school was out; I haven't even thought much about her, and now, here she is.

"Jean! Where have you been? I haven't seen you in eons."

She smiles. "Jeff. I thought I might see you here."

The other girls and I say hello, and I introduce Billy and Jimmy. I'm carrying Jimmy now, and he's starting to squirm.

"So what've you been doing," I ask her.

"Oh, you know. I'm still trying to get ready for my college trip—calling schools and scheduling tours and interviews. And getting all that stuff together to take, like transcripts and letters and pictures and so on. What about you?"

"Not much. I did go canoeing on Hinckley Lake with Randy Clark and Lori Matthews." I shock myself by mentioning Lori. But I might as well. I'm beginning to really like her, and I'm not feeling close to Jean at all.

"Lori Matthews?" Jean looks perplexed and kind of insulted.

"Yeah. We needed someone to pick us up in the car if we put the canoe in at one place and take it out at another. She lives right in our neighborhood and was free, so Randy suggested we take her along." I don't think that satisfied her curiosity.

She asks if I want to tag along, but I tell her I have to babysit, and that I'll call her soon.

On the way back, I'm thinking that Jean would never have gone balloon bombing in the park and wouldn't have been half as much fun as Lori was at Hinckley. Funny thing.

The community band starts playing patriotic songs in the band shell. The sun sets at around nine, and streaks of gold and orange spread across the western sky. An armada of sailboats and yachts wait for the rockets to spread showers of sparks in the dark blue above them. The fireworks begin—booom. Jimmy ducks his head under Mom's arm, and Billy puts his hands over his ears.

Farther to our front, another type of fireworks is starting; a lightning show is approaching fast from the west, competing with the manmade starbursts. The moon fades and disappears, and wind gusts start hitting our faces. I can smell the rain coming.

"We better run," Mom says. We get up. Dad picks up the blanket and chairs. Mom grabs Jimmy and I snag Billy, and we pick them up and carry them.

The fury pounces on us before the fireworks are over. Lightning cracks and lights up the park and the angry gray lake. People run out from under the trees, and we race to the car as the downpour begins. Brooms of rain sweep over us, drenching our summer clothes.

On Tuesday, I meet Randy and Lori, in his garage. "The river sounds great," I tell them, "but it might smell a little."

"From sewage?" Randy asks.

"Yeah. And industrial waste from Akron. But it has some little rapids to make it interesting, between Peninsula and Boston, and a lot of gentle water too, from there up to Brecksville." I show them my map and where these places are.

Lori looks at me peevishly. "Are you going to let me paddle this time?"

"I don't know, Lori. You've never paddled in white water on a river, have you?"

"No."

"I'm not sure it's a good idea. You might tip it over, and the water is pretty bad. What about your parents? What would they say?"

"They'll never know."

Randy and I look at each other and smile and nod—the famous parent-child divide, camouflaged with deception.

"Didn't you say the water north of Boston is gentler?" he says.

"After the rapids."

"Well maybe she could paddle the part of the river below the rapids."

"I'd like to try," Lori says.

"Then one of us would have to drive from Boston to Brecksville," I say.

"So—that's no problem. We can flip a coin to decide who drives."

"Okay. Do you have one?"

"Right here, buddy."

"You flip it and I'll call." Up in the air it goes. I call heads, and it lands on the concrete with a jingle.

"Tails. You lose, Klossen. You drive from Boston to Brecksville. Lori and I paddle. But I get the stern, Lori."

"Wonderful," she says, her eyes dancing.

I'm ticked. "I can't believe it. I do all the work to get the trip together, and then you do all the paddling. That's just great."

"Don't be a sore loser," he says.

"We'll see who the loser is, bug."

Chapter 5—Down the Poison River

We're on our way to Peninsula, bouncing along in Randy's station wagon, with the canoe on top, windows open, and speakers blasting. Lori and I are careful not to discuss our secret. We cross Riverview Road, the river and tracks, turn left, and pass that "No Boating—Fishing—Swimming" sign and the restaurant. This morning there's a police car parked there.

"We better be quick, before that cop tells us we can't go," I say.

We wind through the parking lots and down the street by the railroad, turn left, cross the tracks into a parking lot, and stop the car. I look at my watch. It's 9:45. Randy and I untie the ropes, take down the canoe, carry it to the river, and set it by the water. Lori carries the paddles, life jackets, and a coil of rope. I have the map I traced wrapped in plastic wrap in my pocket.

"Okay, Lori. So you just drive along Riverview Road and under the Turnpike and go one-point-three miles. The river bends close to the road there, and that's where we'll make the switch. Right before Columbia Road. If you go past it, you've gone too far."

"Got it. Okay. Bon voyage!"

"Bon voyage? We're getting ready to battle and conquer a dangerous river, Lori. This isn't some cruise we're taking."

"Oh, yes. I forgot how polluted it is."

I put on my life jacket. Randy sees me do it and says, "What are you doing? Afraid of a little white water?"

"Just being prudent. I don't know what we'll run into."

"You won't catch me in one of those things. You know how it slows me down in the water."

I laugh. "I sure do." Lori chuckles.

Randy and I put the canoe into a backwater. I throw my paddle in, and it thuds against the aluminum; I climb in, bend over, walk forward, kneel, and look back.

"Randy! There's the cop! He just pulled in next to your car."

"Let's go," Randy says. He steps in with his paddle, shoves the bank with his other foot, and kneels on his life jacket. We pole our way through shallow water, and then glide away into the current as the policeman walks toward us in his black short-sleeve shirt, black pants, and gun belt. He points at us and shouts, "Don't you know it's polluted?"

We cup a hand over an ear and pretend we can't hear.

"You can get cancer from that water!"

He looks at Lori and they chat, while we move around the bend and are gone.

Soon the water starts rushing downward and we hear the roar of rapids ahead.

"Here we go," I shout.

"Dig," Randy says. "We've gotta be going faster than the water if we want our rudders to work."

"I know."

Then we're in it—bouncing up and down on the choppy waves, the bow dipping down toward the water and then lurching upward.

"Hug the right bank, Randy," I say. "We're turning to the right."

He does, but not too close.

"Tree on the right," I say. "Strainer." He changes sides and digs furiously, and I rudder to the left. We get around it, but see a big rock straight ahead.

"Rudder left again," he says. I do it, and we glide around it and into the foamy water again. He switches sides and we both pull briskly on the left to keep from turning around.

An island comes into sight, with channels to the left and right.

"Go left!" I yell. He does a stern sweep on the right side to redirect the canoe, and then we strain to make it into the left channel. For a few minutes, it's peaceful. Then the river begins its downward race again with choppy waves and foam. We paddle vigorously and guide the craft into the splashing current and around white haystacks, me ruddering sometimes and doing drawstrokes elsewhere to pull the canoe away from rocks. The turbulence continues for half a mile until we go under a railroad bridge. Then gradually the water calms, and we are gliding into a curving lake of flat water.

"Hoo-wee!" Randy shouts. "What a ride!"

"You said it!"

"But did you notice the smell of sewage while we were going through it? Yuck!"

I think of the atomizer on Mom's bottle of cologne. "Yeah. I think when the water smashes against the rocks in the rapids, the rocks must spray it up into the air."

"I hope we didn't breathe too much of it."

"Just be careful you don't splash me with your paddle," I warn.

"Me splash you? That's funny. You always splash me."

"Truce! Let's not do it here."

The remainder of the trip is a breeze—just floating down the river, paddling whenever we feel like it or when I feel like tormenting him.

"When are you gonna paddle, Clark?"

"When are you, Klossen?"

"I asked you first."

"I asked you second."

I start paddling. He follows, and we seem to make a little more progress.

We follow a big curve to the left and then a sharp one to the right. Ahead way up in the air are the new Ohio Turnpike bridges—two of them, side by side—resting on concrete arches fifteen stories high. We keep looking up as we go under, and then look back from the other direction. It's a sight. They're half a mile long, spanning the Cuyahoga River Valley, the longest bridges on the turnpike.

Half a mile farther, we go under the low bridge of Boston Mills Road, past the hamlet of Boston Mills, where they used to make paper in the eighteen hundreds. Then we hear that rushing sound again. "White water!" I shout. This ride isn't as much fun as the one at Peninsula, but it's good enough. We still have to dodge rocks and worry that the bow might go under. What a kick. Then it's over, and a little more than half a mile farther and around a leftward bend we arrive at our takeout point. Wouldn't you know—it's right in the middle of some rapids, and we'd have to scale a cliff to get to the road! Glancing at the top, there's no sign of Lori.

We dash through the rapids, avoiding two boulders, and arrive at some flatter water.

"Nice takeout point, Klossen."

"Yeah, well, the map didn't show the rapids and the cliff."

"What do we do now?"

"Just keep on going until we can find a takeout point, then hike up to the road and see if we can find Lori. That's all I know to do. What do you think, Clark?"

He shrugs.

The current is fast, and soon we arrive at a large gravel bar on the left where a stream joins the river. "Let's get out here," I say. "Maybe we can follow the stream up to the road. At least we won't have to scale a cliff."

We pull the canoe onto the bar and start up the stream. This water seems pretty clean; it may be coming out of a woods. We climb up, stepping on rocks and holding onto branches, avoiding poison ivy and getting wet up to our calves.

"Whose idea was this?" Randy grouses.

"I thought you were tougher than this, Clark. I really did. But now I know you're just a wimp."

"Oh yeah?" he says as he bends down and throws a handful of water my way.

"Missed."

At the top, we find ourselves at the junction of Riverview and Columbia Roads, and decide to wait there. Pretty soon, we see the red-and-white station wagon coming toward us from the north.

"Where were you two?" Lori asks. "I stopped where you said to and I looked over the cliff down at the rapids and said, 'They're not stopping here.'" We laugh. "And after I watched you go through those rapids, I jumped in the car and went north to see if I could find where you might stop. I didn't find you after a couple of miles, so I turned around and came back."

"Good thinking," Randy says.

"Have you seen any sign of that cop?" I ask.

"No. I guess he had more important things to do than to follow us."

"So what did he say?"

"He just ranted about how polluted the river is and how he tries to keep people out of it to save them from getting cancer from the chemicals or sick from the sewage. He was really serious about warning people."

"Well, we didn't get any of it on us, except we may have breathed some of the mist in the rapids," Randy says. "We're wet from this stream, but we think it's pretty clean."

I follow it with my eyes into a wooded hillside.

"I got some of the river water on my hands when I was paddling, but I rinsed them in the stream," I say.

"And we'll wash our hands good when it's over."

I look at Lori. "Imagine yourself paddling down a river of deadly poisonous excrement."

"You're just trying to get me to let you paddle the rest of the way," she says. "Forget it, Klossen." I chuckle inside. "He also asked if we have our Ohio registration, because if we don't have that, he'll give us a ticket and make us take the canoe out of the water."

"What did you say?" Randy asks.

"I told him I was pretty sure we did. Do we?"

"Heck no," Randy says. "It's just a little old banged-up canoe. There's no reason it should have to be registered."

"It only costs ten bucks," I say.

"Yeah, but then you have to put those big ugly numbers on the canoe," he says.

"Yeah. Indians never did that," I add.

"What else did he say?" Randy asks.

Lori looks at us sternly. "He told me we have to stay out of that town Boston Mills, especially at night."

"Why?" I ask.

"There's been some vandalism," she says, "and they don't want strangers in there. And you know how teenagers are. And we're just the type who'll tear things up: young people who ignore advice and warnings from people of authority and go canoeing on polluted rivers anyway."

"Okay, Officer," I say, holding my hands up and smiling. "We'll stay out of Boston Mills. Now, Lori, you don't still want to paddle down this sewer, against the law and all advice, do you? We promised your parents we'd keep you safe, and you'd be risking cancer and all kinds of other cruel afflictions that would end your life while you're still a young girl."

"I want to paddle! And you're not going to fast-talk me out of it."

"Ha! Good girl," Randy says. "Let's go."

I give up. I tried. "Now remember, about two and a half miles downriver as the crow flies—which should take you about an hour or so in this current—you'll come to a stretch where the river comes close to the railroad and pretty close to Riverview Road. I'll park and get out there and wave. A few hundred yards after that—just before you come to Station Road Bridge—pull over to the left and see if you can find a place to debark."

"Debark? You mean like take the bark off a tree?" Randy asks.

"No, idiot. Debark like disembark. Get out of the canoe. But don't paddle too far. If you keep going under the bridge, you might go over the dam and get that poison sludge all over you. You sure you want to go, Lori?"

"Stop begging."

"Okay," Randy says. "So we just go to Station Road Bridge and try to find a place to get out."

"Right. And then we can find somewhere to wash our hands and eat. I'm hungry already."

Off they go. They cross the road and railroad, and I watch him take her hand and help her down the steep stream bank. *I wish it were me. Oh, well. Life is not fair.*

There's no reason for me to hang around. I get in the car and drive to my destination, where the river comes close to the railroad and Riverview Road. The problem is that Riverview Road has an excellent view of trees and bushes, but not the river, so I can't find where I'm supposed to go, park, and wave at them. I have to keep driving for several miles, all the way to Valley Road. Turning right, toward the river, I cross the tracks, bear left to the small train station—Brecksville Depot—and park. It's deserted, and there's grass growing between the tracks. The road crosses the river through an old steel truss bridge that's flat on top. I hang over the railing and look down at the swift river. Then I walk back up the road trying to find a good takeout place and a more camouflaged spot to wait in case the cop comes by. I take a path to the river and decide to stay there so I can call to them when they approach.

An hour goes by and nothing happens. I find a place to sit and wish I had a book. It's really monotonous. I think about everything. I think about the colleges we visited during spring vacation and decide which one I liked best. I think about the solo I sang in church: "Why Should the Nations So Furiously Rage Together" from Handel's *Messiah*. I sing the whole thing to myself. I ain't great, but those voice lessons helped.

I think about the great Cleveland Indians and recite every member of their 1954 pennant-winning team in my head. *Why, oh, why would they trade away Rocky Colavito and Roger Maris and Norm Cash—all those great homerun hitters.* I think about Frank Lane, the general manager, and spit on the ground. Then I think of the Browns' Jim Brown, the best running back ever. But it takes more than one running back to win.

I look at my watch again. It's been an hour and a half. Now I start to worry. *They ought to be here by now. What's wrong? I hope they're all right. What happened? Did they capsize in some rapids? Were they trapped by a fallen tree? What?*

I'm hungry. Now that's serious. I was hungry two hours ago. I start reviewing all my favorite foods and try to smell them and taste them and experience them. Hamburgers, steak, toasted cheese sandwiches, hot dogs with brown mustard, and on and on. I know it's a prosaic menu, but I'm just a proletarian guy who had to study his vocabulary cards to do well on his SATs.

Maybe they stopped off somewhere. I let my mind wander and watch them making love by the river just like Burt Lancaster and Deborah Kerr in *From Here To Eternity*: *Randy and Lori lying in the river, kissing, with the water rushing and swirling over them. Then she runs up the hill and falls on her back in the grass, spreads her arms, closes her eyes and waits. Randy looks down at her with his insect eyes, sinks to his knees, bends over, and passionately kisses her. "Nobody ever kissed me the way you do," Lori says. Randy asks, "Nobody?" and Lori says, "No. Nobody." What a kiss. Man, he really planted it on her. He never even saw her braces.*

Maybe they stopped at a backwater marsh and watched a dying heron fishing for a diseased fish or stopped to observe a forest of dead trees standing in the water like charred corpses.

I look at the sky and count clouds. Then I count the diagonal braces on the bridge. I imagine people arriving at the train station in 1890 in buggies and carriages, lining up, and boarding cars for Cleveland.

At last, they arrive, just before I expire.

"Randy! Lori!" I shout. They see me, and Randy steers the canoe to me. He overshoots the takeout point a little, so they have to paddle mightily upstream to get back.

"We did it!" Lori shrieks. *WHAT did you do?* my mind screams back. "Rapids, rocks, trees in the water, and we did it! And we didn't get wet."

"Congratulations. That's terrific. You are officially initiated into the Shale River White Water Canoeing Club. But I thought you'd never get here. What took so long?"

"It's a long way on this crooked river," Randy says.

"So how did she do, Clark? Really."

"Better than you do, Klossen. She pulled her own weight, and was good at ruddering when we had to avoid rocks and things. She has a smooth, powerful stroke. Yeah, you could take some lessons from her."

I grit my teeth and smoke starts curling out from behind my eyeballs. "Yeah, well, did she rock the boat or try to sit on her seat instead of kneeling?"

"Never."

Lori glowed.

"And how did he do, Lori? Did he just lay back and let you do all the work like he did with me in Canada?"

"No. He was pretty good. He kept doing that J-stroke, unless he had to pry or sweep or rudder to get us going the right way. And he kept us in the current most of the time and guided us through the rapids like an expert. I'd give him an A minus."

"Minus?" Randy says.

"You talk too much."

We stop for sandwiches in Brecksville—and to wash our hands. Lori and Randy dominate the conversation with excited tales of their trip (*yuck*), and she chastises him a few times for not guiding them around certain rocks and trees.

"That one branch nearly took my head off," she says.

He grins back. "You complain too much. And if you'd ruddered left when you saw it coming, you could've avoided it."

"I thought you were in command of the vessel."

"Not when you're about to get your block knocked off. Anyway, I told you to duck. It's not my fault that you didn't duck low enough."

On the way back, I start thinking about pollution. "You know, we ought to do something about all this stinking water around here. It really makes me mad what the A-people have done to the water in the rivers and the lake and to the fish and birds."

"The A-people?" Lori asks.

"The adults, you know, the ones who know everything and tell us what to do."

"And just what do you think you're going to do about it?" Randy asks.

"I don't know yet, but we've got to do something and do it soon, before the summer's over and we forget about it. They don't have any right to poison our water. We can't just accept the world they give us. We have to change it!"

"What are you, a revolutionary?" Randy asks.

I can't let that go by. It's time to play. "What, you mean like George Washington and his friends rising up against the king of England?" His jaw drops, and I shake my head. "Nah. I just want cleaner water, Randy." He's speechless, and my audience in the backseat is hiding a grin.

We get home at about five. I hit the shower and wash off the river.

"How was your trip?" Dad asks at dinner.

"Fun. We had a good time."

"And Lori paddled too?" Mom asks.

"Yes. On about half the trip."

"Good. Did she do all right?"

"Yeah," I say, nodding my head up and down.

That's it. I leave it at that. I don't tell them I was mad because I organized the trip and then had to spend half my time waiting for them on a bridge, and that I was jealous of Randy for being with Lori all that time. That would have gotten me lots of free advice. You don't want to tell parents too much about what's going on in your life because then they'll try to worm in and give you all kinds of opinions and suggestions and warnings and instructions and tell you exactly what to do. No, you sure don't want that. They'll try to control you if you let them. But I couldn't resist saying one thing.

"The river stinks, though," I add. "It's so polluted all the fish are dead. It's from sewage and industrial waste from factories in Akron."

"Factories make good things for us and provide jobs, Jeff," Dad says. "You know that. And factories have to get rid of their waste somewhere." Spoken by the great industrialist.

"I know. And that rotten smell in the Flats is the bread and butter for all Clevelanders." ("Our bread and butter" is what my grandparents in Pittsburgh called the smoke there.) "We're just lucky we don't have to smell it here because the wind blows it east."

After dinner, Mom and Dad go to another church meeting, so I have to put the boys to bed again: bath, pajamas, bed, and . . .

"Canoe story!" Billy stridently demands, and Jimmy chimes in.

"What? Not another one. I'm too tired."

"We want a canoe story!"

"Too tired."

"You'll be sorry if you don't," Billy says.

I scowl at him. "What? You're threatening me?"

"You heard me," he says.

I hear Mom in his voice, and I hastily capitulate. "Okay, okay."

I decide to tell them one about the stinky river: "One time I went on a canoe trip on the Cuyahoga River. I ran outside, picked up my canoe, and ran down a country road until I came to a little town called Peninsula. I crossed the old Erie and Ohio Canal and the towpath and the Cuyahoga River and then the railroad tracks of the Valley Railway. Do you kids know what a canal is?"

"No," Billy says, shaking his head, and Jimmy shakes his head too.

"It's like a stream. But canals were built by people. They made them straight and level so that boats could float on them and carry stuff like wood and coal and flour. Mules pulled ropes attached to the boat, and they walked on paths beside the canal called towpaths, and a mule driver guided the mules. A mule is like a horse, only stronger. And whenever the ground went up or down, the boats had to go through what they called locks with gates on them to hold back the water.

"So anyway, I stopped at a restaurant in the town, and this woman in a white apron ran up to me and said, 'You're late. Where have you been? We thought you'd never come.'

"I didn't know what she was talking about. 'Late for what?' I asked.

"'The race, of course.'

"'Race? Race between whom?' I asked with my very best grammar.

"'The race between the canal boat and the freight train and the canoe on the river. Don't you remember?'

"I did not remember, but I didn't want her to think I was forgetful, so I said, 'Of course, I remember. But what's the prize if I win?'

"'There's no prize if you win, but the loser has to eat dog food for lunch.'

"'Dog food!' I repeat. 'Oh, no!'"

"Eeew," Billy says and sticks out his tongue. Jimmy does the same. He does everything Billy does.

"I rushed outside and picked up my canoe and ran down to the river. There I found a little man with a long nose wearing black-and-white-striped pants, shirt, and hat. He was looking crossly at his watch. 'Where have you been?' he asked. I told him I was sorry I was late. I didn't want to argue with him because he had a gun. Yes! He had a pistol in his hand raised up in the air like he was going to shoot a cloud. I didn't think he was going to shoot me. I looked to the right and saw a big freight train with smoke belching out its smokestack. I looked to the left and saw a canal boat loaded with sacks of flour. Farther that way, I saw two giant mules. They must have been twenty feet tall, and they were snorting and pawing the ground like angry bulls. I put my canoe in the water, jumped in, and heard the little man shout, 'Ready . . . Set . . . Go!' And with that he fired his pistol into the air with a boom and a crack, and the two giant mules lurched, jerking the canal boat forward, and the train engine began chugging and chugging as its wheels slowly turned. I knew that its wheels would turn much faster after it got going.

"I began paddling as fast as I could. I sure did not want to have to eat dog food for lunch. I knew that the current of the river would help me go fast, so I was sure I would win. I was sure I could beat two mules pulling a heavy boat in water that had no current. And the train was going so slowly; it must have had a heavy load to pull. I was heading into some rapids and going pretty fast. The only problem for me was that the river curved back and forth like a snake, but the railroad and canal were straight, so I had to go twice as far as they did. The other problem was that the river smelled so bad I had to hold my breath. But that made me paddle even faster; I had to finish the race quickly so I could get out of the water and take a breath of clean air!

"As I came to a bridge, I looked up and saw a policeman standing by the railing looking down at me shaking his finger saying, "You can't canoe in there. It's polluted." I couldn't answer him because I was holding my breath. I just had to keep going.

"Down through rapids and around rocks and trees I raced, and things were going pretty well until I looked to the left and saw that the mules had caught up to me and were approaching one of the locks they use to lower the boats. The boat has to go in the upper side of the lock; then they close the gates, lower the water inside, open the gate on the low side, and the boat goes out. I was sure the lock would slow them down; it would certainly take some time. Boy, was I wrong! The giant mules were going so fast that they just pulled that boat right out of the water and through the air, and set it down on the lower part of the canal on the other side of the lock, and kept on going. The boat went over the lock instead of through it!

"Then I heard a train whistle shrieking at me. I looked to the right and saw fire coming right out of the freight train smokestack, and I watched it roar right past me. I knew I was in trouble now."

This is the appropriate moment, so I stop talking. I tuck Jimmy in and bend over to give him a kiss.

"So what happened?" Billy screams.

"What? What?" Jimmy asks, refusing to slide down under the covers.

"Oh. The race. Weeell . . . I lost the race. I just couldn't beat those giant mules and that great big freight train. We got to the end, and a little woman with a short nose wearing a black-and-white-striped dress said, 'I'm sorry, Mr. Klossen, but you lost the race.'"

"Ooh, no," Billy wails. "So you had to eat dog food?"

"That's right. But lucky for me, in Peninsula they feed their dogs chocolate chip cookies."

"They made you eat chocolate chip cookies for lunch?" Billy asks.

"That's right. And that is the end of my canoe story."

"You were lucky!" Billy says.

Later, I see Brett. "Two down, four to go."

"So what, dipstick?"

"I'm just telling you."

He makes me mad. I go into the kitchen and call Lori. "Hey, do you want to recon the Vermilion River with me tomorrow?"

Chapter 6—Reconnoitering the Vermilion

I pick Lori up at nine and we head west on Detroit Road. The morning air is cool, so we keep the windows most of the way up, and the sky is blue with a few wispy cirrus clouds. She and her mom have packed us lunch in a basket, and I'm looking forward to a nice picnic. I try not to look too long at her pillowed chest, slender arms, and delicate fingers.

"That was a great trip down the Cuyahoga, huh?" I say.

"I loved it. But you looked a little unhappy at the end."

"I guess I was. I only had half a trip."

She turns and faces me. "Well, me too!"

"But I planned the trip."

"But you and Randy flipped a coin. It was fair and square. And he got stuck with me."

"He said you did pretty well."

"I did! That surprised him. I think he was nervous when we went into the first rapids. After that, he relaxed."

"Anyway, that's why I looked the way I did. I was a little miffed."

She leans her head back and nods. "I thought so. But you shouldn't have been. I told my dad about it, and he said there's an easy solution."

"What?"

"Divide the trip into three legs instead of two, and each of us takes two legs. That way everybody gets to paddle two-thirds of the time. That would make it perfectly fair."

I had to think about that for a minute.

Lori explains: "Like on the first leg, it could be me and you. And on the second, me and Randy. And on the third, you and Randy."

"I get it. I guess that would be more equitable. We can try it out on Randy and see what he says."

"It's just a suggestion."

It seems like a good solution to me. But she might be trying to pull something. She's smart, all right. And her dad is too.

I find myself glancing at her too often. I can't stop myself. She is a girl, after all, even if she does have braces and stringy hair that falls like a mop. Someday she'll have nice straight teeth and go to a hairdresser.

"What does your dad think about the two of us going off alone to look at rivers?"

"He doesn't know about it."

I blink. *Surprise. Lori isn't always honest and open. Sometimes she can be sneaky. Then I see Lori and her mom making the lunch without her dad's knowledge, and I ask myself,* Is a conspiracy afoot, with me the hapless victim?

"So it's okay for the three of us to be together, but maybe not just the two of us?"

"I don't know."

I look at her, my eyes wide. *What he doesn't know can't hurt him.*

Changing the subject, I hand her the road map and describe our route. "We stay on this two-lane road and North Ridge Road all the way to the Black River Reservation south of Lorain. It's about twenty miles. Then go another ten to Vermilion."

We drive along, passing farms, old houses, vineyards, a winery, and an occasional store. Yes, a winery. The lake takes a long time to cool down from the summer heat, and that gives us a long growing season in the fall. But we get no spring at all. The lake melts and suddenly it's summer. Yes, I exaggerate a little.

We arrive at the Black River. I turn and drive down a steep road to take a look at the river. I'd heard it was narrow and too shallow to canoe, and that's what we find: large areas of exposed gravel and fallen trees that completely cross the river.

"No canoeing here," I say.

"The other end, at Lorain, has a big steel mill."

"Yeah. It's like Cleveland. Big lake freighters go in there. And there are also lots of power boats. Not a great place to canoe."

Now we're flying down North Ridge Road toward Vermilion, past more farms and occasional houses.

"You know that power boats are our mortal enemies, don't you?" I ask. "Their wake will swamp us. Turn us right over and dump us in the water."

"How do we defend ourselves?"

"First, we stay away from them. We have the right of way over powerboats and sailboats; they're supposed to get out of our way and stay away from us. But—"

"But they still must be allowed to pass us."

"Yes. And if we can do something to get out of their way, we have to do it. And if we have to cross a traffic lane, like in the river, we're supposed to try to do it at right angles to the lane. That's the shortest route across."

"So we have the right of way over those thousand-foot ore boats?"

"Ha. That'll be the day. They just worry about not hitting the sides of the river."

"So what if wake from a powerboat gets too close? What do we do?"

"Our second defense is that when we see a big wave coming toward us, we have to turn the canoe at right angles to it—face it—or at least turn at an angle."

"We must face adversity."

"Ha. Yeah. If we let it hit us sideways, it'll rock us and turn us over. We can't ever let that happen. Once we get inside the *V* of the wake, we're safe. We do the same thing with any wave, like waves in a lake. We have to turn into them, at least partway. Then we go up and down when we cross them, but they don't tip us over."

"But I don't want to turn into a wave."

I smile. "Very funny."

She's cute, all right, and I can't help looking at her.

We're getting near the Vermilion River when she asks, "Are you going to let me eat? I'm starved. Also, I need a bathroom."

Girls. If she were a boy, all we'd have to do is stop the car and find a bush. I look at my watch. I'm surprised to see it's after noon.

"Okay. There are supposed to be some restrooms in the park."

We follow signs toward the Mill Hollow/Bacon Woods, cross a bridge over the river, and go down a hill and around a bend to where the road levels out. There we can see shale cliffs curving around in front of us. On the right is an old house. Some picnic tables wait by the river, and beside the house is a barn. I keep driving, looking for restrooms, and spot a building with faded wood walls and roof shingles.

"That must be the privy," I say.

I park in front, and Lori hurries to the door marked "Women." I go through the door marked "Men." It's old and stinky. I use it, and then walk over to the house to see if they have any information. No one's there, but I do find a brochure in a box by the door. It tells about the house and has a map of the river and nearby roads.

We drive to the picnic area, jump out, and look at the water. "This looks a lot like Shale River," she says. "A shale cliff, but not as high, and a shallow river, but not as wide."

"Yes, but it looks deep enough to canoe."

"And the air smells fresh here too."

"Yeah," I say. "The water must be okay, and there must not be any big factories upstream."

"I like the sound—the quiet rushing and bubbling."

We find a table by the water, and Lori brings out the basket from the backseat and spreads a cloth on the table. She hands me a paper plate, cup, and fork, and a sandwich wrapped in waxed paper. "Ham and cheese okay? And potato salad? And iced tea?"

"Sure." I take a bite of the sandwich and say, "This is good. Did you make it?"

"Yes," she says sort of shyly, "and I helped Mom with the potato salad."

Now, I find myself looking into her pale blue eyes. When she looks back, I quickly drop my gaze, but I know she saw me looking.

"What does the brochure say?" she asks.

"It says we're in an oxbow."

"The river loops around us."

"Yes. And a farmer named Benjamin Bacon bought an interest in a saw and grist mill down here in 1835 and dug a millrace, like a canal, from one side of the bow to the other."

"Why?" she asks.

"To increase the water power at his mill. The river drops as it goes around the bow, but the millrace is almost level as it cuts across, and this gives the water more power when it goes over the waterwheel."

"Interesting."

"It also says we're in a hollow formed by the cliffs."

"Ergo, Mill Hollow," she says. "A mill in a hollow."

We finish eating, and Lori says, "Let's take a hike along the river. This is a neat place."

We start out, and she says, "Look," as she peers upward and slowly pirouettes with her arms and hands stretched out to the side. "You can see all those cliffs now. They go right around us." I find her dance more stunning and delightful than the cliffs.

The path along the river is full of brambles and poison ivy, so we walk down the paved road till we come to the millrace. There we find a path that's not overgrown, but it forces us to walk closer together. I go behind her and find myself wanting to put my hands on her hips, but I don't. Fear conquers desire. We look at the dry canal, side by side, and I accidentally bump into her. Accidents happen. She looks up at me quickly.

"Sorry," I say. "This is an interesting place, isn't it?"

"Yes, but I guess we better get going."

She turns and passes me on the narrow path, and I assist her by grasping her shoulders and gently pushing her forward. I release them quickly, and we go on.

We drive north above the cliffs toward the city and never see the river. After a few miles, we pass streets and houses and summer homes, and when the river comes into view again, it's wide, and the water is flat. All the way through town, we see hundreds of yachts resting in slips and lagoons. Cabin cruisers grind up and down, and sailboats drift quietly by. A low truss bridge crosses the river—not a drawbridge. That means that the stink boaters can pass under the bridge and go up the river, but the rag boaters have to stay on the lake side unless they take their masts down.

We cross the bridge, turn south, and find the South Street launch ramp. "This would be a great place to put in or take out."

"Look at the sign on the bridge abutment," Lori says. "5 MPH Or No Wake."

"Huh. So you can go faster than five miles an hour if you don't make a wake. That's good. As long as there are no scofflaws cruising around."

Lori laughs. "Scofflaws. Lawbreakers. Another SAT word."

I smile. "Yeah."

"There's a police boat. Maybe they enforce the law."

We wander into a small shack near the ramp and watch a young man filleting fish. His speed and skill are amazing. I ask him what kinds of fish they are.

"Walleye," he says. "And those in the bucket are perch."

"Good eating?"

"You bet."

"The water's not polluted here?"

"Nope."

We cross back over the river and follow it south in search of wilder water. We pull into Birmingham City Park and find a young couple lifting a canoe off their car. I see an Oberlin sticker on the rear window. We watch them set it on the ground, and I ask where they're going.

"Up to Mill Hollow," the guy says. He's tall, slender, and strong. She's shorter, but sturdy, and has a long brown ponytail.

"What's the river like?" I ask.

"It's a nice ride, a few little rapids, but nothing difficult. The hardest part of the trip is right here. The portage to the river is steep and long. If there was snow or grass on it, you could sit in your canoe and ski to the river."

"Do you know any place to take out between here and Mill Hollow?" Lori asks. I know what she's after—three legs for the trip.

"The bridge at Gore Orphanage Road. That's about half-way."

"Didn't we pass that road on the way here?" I ask.

"Yeah," he says. "But that piece won't take you all the way to the bridge. You have to go around and take the road down from the north."

"How far is it by canoe to Mill Hollow?" I ask.

"About eight miles."

"How long does it take to canoe it?"

"At the race in March, the winner did it in about an hour and fifteen minutes." He looks at his companion and smiles. "We do it in about two hours."

"And how long to get from there to the city boat ramp in Vermilion?"

"About the same. It's not as far, but the last couple of miles are flat, so they go slower."

They open the car doors, retrieve their life jackets, paddles, and a small canvas bag, put on the jackets, and lay the paddles on the ground.

"Anything to look out for?"

"Just fallen trees. You might run into one of them once in a while, especially down at this end."

"Is the water pretty clean?"

"Oh yeah. There are no factories around here. It's mostly farmland."

"Great. Hey, thanks."

We take off for the bridge. It's one lane wide and has two curved steel trusses on each side to carry the road to an abutment in the middle of the river and then on to the other side. There are steep banks down to the river on both sides, one of which has a path I'm sure we can scramble down to get to the canoe. The river looks about forty feet wide here and is navigable, although I see the bottom showing through in one place on the north side.

"Look," Lori says. Downstream beside the river we see a great blue heron standing in an eddy.

"There must be fish in the water."

We look down the sides of the abutment, and she says, "We could switch here."

"So that's your plan. Divide the river into three legs, so you get to ride two-thirds of it."

"Well, why not?"

"We'll see what Randy thinks."

Back in Orchard Park, we stop at a market downtown to pick up some stuff, and when we step outside, I stop. "Look. Across the street." A Negro family is walking along looking in the store windows. The man is wearing a suit and gray fedora, the woman, a tight cream-colored suit. Her hair's up in a beehive. A teenage boy has on a short-sleeve, plaid shirt, and a younger girl, a flowered dress.

"Don't stare," Lori says.

"I can't help it. It's—it's a shock."

"Stop it," Lori says. "They'll think you're not friendly."

"It's weird. I don't think I'm prejudiced, but I can't stop looking at them. Not in an unfriendly way. I just wonder what they're doing here. I feel like they're not supposed to be here, like they're out of place." I look at Lori. "Maybe we should cross the street and ask them why they're here, you know, use the friendly approach."

"It might really embarrass them."

A few other shoppers are walking here and there, and I notice that we're not the only ones staring.

"I hope no one says anything ugly."

"Come on, Jeff. Let's go."

On the ride back she says, "You know, Jeff, I'm curious about why you're so interested in integration."

"I don't know. Mom grew up in a town near Pittsburgh, and her dad worked with Negroes in the steel mill and liked to sing with them at lunch. Mom went all through school with them, and after college, she taught Negro kids in high school. She says there was never any problem with the different races. So I guess I've been influenced by her. What about you?"

"Same sort of thing. Before we lived here, we lived near Washington while Dad was in school. We shopped in the same stores with Negroes. I saw them in the library. Everyone was polite. Mom taught me that. I was a little girl then."

"Were they in your school?"

"No. And they didn't live near us."

"Huh. Sometimes don't you feel like we live in a prison, and they won't let us get out and make friends with people on the outside?"

"They?"

"You know. The A-people. Our jailers. The segregationists. The ones who know everything and tell us what to do."

"Go on."

"You know, we're all of one blood with Negroes. The segregationists say that if you have one drop of Negro blood in you, you're a Negro. But when you get a blood transfusion, you don't know what race the donor was, and it doesn't matter."

As we pull up in front of her house, she asks, "So who are we going to talk to next about it?"

"I don't know."

"Maybe one reason they don't move here is that the banks won't lend them money. Maybe we should talk to a banker."

Whew. That makes my stomach jump. "Good idea," I say. "But first, we have another river to conquer!"

When I drop her off, she asks, "When are we going to talk to Randy about the two-thirds split?"

"Ha. You won't let me forget that, will you?" She shakes her head no. "I'll call him."

Chapter 7—The Puerile Madman

"So let me get this straight—each person gets to paddle two-thirds of the time?" Randy asks. The three of us are standing in his driveway.

"That's right," I say.

He shakes his head and laughs. "How did this happen, Klossen? You know, I like Lori a lot, but she was just supposed to go along to drive the car. Then we let her paddle a little, and now she wants to be an equal partner so we all only get to go two-thirds of the way."

"That's right, Clark. It's only fair," I say. Lori stands by, patient and silent, but firm.

"Fair?" he grouses. "I'll tell you what's fair. It's my canoe and my car, and I should get to go on the whole trip with you guys splitting up the rest any way you want to. That would be fair."

Darned if Lori doesn't speak up. "But, Randy. We're all working together," she says. "We're a team now, and we all should share evenly. That's fair."

"Fair?" he says. "What do you bring us besides your good looks? At least Jeff plans the trips."

"I helped plan this trip too. I went with Jeff. And I drive on the trips."

"Hmph," he snorts.

"Listen," she says. "I'll tell you what. I'll bring all the food and drinks. Will that make it fair?"

"No. I want to paddle the whole way," he says with finality.

"Then count me out; I'm not going," she says.

"Me neither," I say.

"Phooey!" he says, turning his back.

"Come on, Randy," she says. "That's a fair deal."

After a long silence, he grumbles, "Oh, all right."

"So, this trip has three legs," I say.

"You were sure you would win, huh?"

I ignore him. "The first is Birmingham to the bridge on Gore Orphanage Road; the second is the bridge to Mill Hollow Park; and the third is Mill Hollow Park to downtown Vermilion." I describe each stretch.

"How do we decide who gets which legs?" he asks.

"Just throw out our fingers, one or two. The two people that have the same number go together on that leg."

"That's stupid," he says. "You say the first two legs are wilder and the last one has a lot of flat water."

"Yeah," I say, not knowing where he's headed.

"Then I want the first two legs. You two can flip a coin to see who's going with me. Then you two take the last leg."

Darn. All I can think about is flat water and powerboats. But at least I'll be with Lori.

I sigh. "That's okay with me. How about you, Lori?"

"I suppose. It's not democratic, but if Randy's going to be that way, I guess we'll have to go along so he isn't crabbing all day."

She and I flip a coin. I get the first leg with Randy, and she gets the second.

I'm the one who should be crabbing. Originally, Lori was supposed to drive all the way, drop Randy and me off at the beginning of the trip, and pick us up at the end. Now, I get one good leg and one rotten one, and Randy gets two good ones. Hell. I'll only get a good ride for about half an hour. Women and their schemes! And my mom is not innocent in this matter either with all her harping: "Did you let Lori paddle?" "Oh, don't you think you should let Lori paddle? . . . " on and on and on.

"I suppose you've gotta have the stern too," I say. I'm in a dark mood.

"What do you think, Klossen?"

"Don't think I won't get back, Clark."

We arrive at the Birmingham City Park and unload. Randy and I carry the canoe down the steep slope with me up front. Lori carries the life jackets and paddles. I slide on some gravel once and almost fall.

"Slow down," I yell. "Don't push."

"What's the matter, Klossen. Can't hold up your end?"

We feed the canoe into the river, climb aboard, kneel on our life jackets, and wave good-bye. The sun is bright, the breeze warm and fresh (there's no pollution here), and the water is glistening. I perk up. You never know what excitement lies around the bend.

The river's about thirty yards wide with a high shale cliff on the right and trees on the left with fields beyond. My paddle immediately hits bottom, and I prod Randy to get us out into the current where the water's deeper. Soon we're zipping along. It feels good to work my arms and shoulders again and smell the clean air.

A rushing sound creeps in from ahead. I shout, "White water!" and our muscles stiffen in anticipation. But when we get around the bend, there is only a stretch of moderate waves with no big rocks or haystacks.

"Dig," Randy bellows, and we race through it.

"A pleasant run," I say as we reach the end.

That is the most excitement we have! For the next forty minutes it is easy water and no thrills. It is so easy that I just stop paddling for a while, lay my paddle across the gunwales, and take a break. I just gaze up at the sky and the cliff and the trees.

"Come on, Klossen. Paddle."

"I'm watching the birds. I thought I saw a hawk. Or maybe it was a crow."

"We're canoeing, not bird watching."

"What's the matter, Clark? You can't control this thing by yourself?"

"I just don't want to do all the work."

"You don't do any of the work. All you do is sit back there and rudder. I do all the work."

At one place, the river widens and gets really shallow. Our paddles hit bottom, and then the bottom of the aluminum canoe scrapes. We have to climb out and let the canoe float up without our weight and then drag it for about a hundred yards in ankle-deep water.

The rest of the way, it's just a nice float. Before I know it, we're at the bridge, and there's Lori, standing on the bank, waiting to evict me and get in with Randy.

He guides us to shore, I throw Lori the rope, and she pulls us in. I step onto the rocky bottom in ankle-deep water and climb up the bank. Then Randy steps out and he and I pull the canoe up on the bank.

She smiles and asks, "How was it?"

"Too easy," I say, "but not bad."

"I couldn't get him to paddle," Randy says, walking forward to get out and stretch. "He kept looking at birds."

I sing, "Down a lazy river by the old mill run."

"It's not the river that's lazy," he says.

He yawns and stretches his swimmer's physique (dammit)—his impressive shoulders and back, skinny hips and legs—then puts his floppy hands behind his head and flexes his biceps. I can't stand it. I know Lori is looking. To me, he looks insectile, but maybe not to her.

I get the keys from her, and they turn the canoe around. As usual, she's wearing her orange life jacket. She climbs to the front, kneels, and Randy shoves off.

"See you at Mill Hollow," I say, and they're gone.

I hop in the car, drive to the house in the oxbow, and park near the picnic area. It only takes ten minutes. I sit on a picnic table and wait. I remember the path to the canal where Lori and I walked. We were here all alone, together. Why didn't I make a move—do something? And now she's out there with Randy again. Phooey.

Now I wait. And I wait.

At last, in they come, chattering excitedly. *What do they talk about?* She gives me a smile as they glide to the bank by the tables. The aluminum bottom scrapes, and they get out.

"How're you doing, Klossen?" she asks, grinning.

What has he been telling her about me?

I pull the canoe onto the grass and tell Randy, "Now it'll be your turn to wait."

"That's okay with me. I'll just find a place to take a nap."

Lori gets the basket out of the car, and we have our picnic. Then Randy and I turn the canoe around and put it in the water. Lori climbs in and walks to the bow, and I push off. I marvel at how Lori is now taking her second ride of the day. *How did she wangle that?*

"We're off," I yell at Randy. "See you in a couple of hours, at about two thirty if that guy in Birmingham was right."

This ride is really easy. It's all class I with no rapids at all—only decisions. Should we go this way or that? We come to a marshy island. Should we go to the right or take the shortcut straight ahead? Which way will have more water? Which will be fastest?

"Let's go to the right," Lori says. "Follow the cliff."

We do, and the current swings us around the big horseshoe to the end of the island with no difficulty. It might have been quicker the other way, but we'll never know.

"So what did you two talk about?" I ask as we paddle along.

"I'll never tell."

"Oh, come on. You were talking about me, weren't you?"

She stops paddling and turns to face me. "You're so paranoid and self-centered. What makes you think we'd talk about you?"

"Because I know Randy, and I'm sure he would tell you every little embarrassing thing he could think of about me, especially from our Canadian trip."

"Like what? I know, you tell me all the embarrassing things, and I'll tell you whether he told me about them."

"You're trying to trick me."

"Noooo."

She turns forward and starts paddling again.

"He probably told you that I pushed him into the cold water, on purpose, when it was really just an accident."

"He already told us that," she tosses over her shoulder. "You already argued about it, remember?"

"Oh, yeah. So what did he tell you?"

She stops again and turns around. "All about himself, of course. That's what boys do. All about winning swimming races, and carrying bags of golf clubs, and funny people on the golf course, and mean people who like to order you around. And how he helps people find their balls in the rough if he likes them, but suddenly goes blind when he's with people he doesn't like, and stuff like that. There. How's that? Satisfied?" She faces the front again and resumes paddling.

Gradually, the river gets wider and flatter, and the current slower.

"Switch sides," Lori says. *Uh-oh. She's getting tired.*

After five more minutes, she says, "Switch sides," again.

Then after another five, she says, "I'm tired. I have to take a break." She places her paddle across the gunwales and scrunches up her shoulders and moves them forward and backward, one at a time.

"Okay." What else could I say? I glance at my watch. It's already two o'clock. I start to wonder if we'll get to the wharf in time to meet Randy.

We start zigzagging along with me doing an exaggerated J-stroke to try to keep us going straight. And after about fifteen minutes of paddling solo, I start to tire. "I have to take a break too," I say, and I resort to an occasional pry stroke or drawstroke to keep us going in the direction of the current as we float down the river. *We're never going to get there. I may fall asleep first.*

"There sure are a lot of cottages," I say, looking at the both sides of the river.

"They must be expensive."

"Yes—right on the water."

Finally, I say, "You know, we're never going to get there if we don't paddle."

"Okay. I'll try again." She starts paddling again, but with weaker strokes than before.

Yachts and sailboats begin to appear along the western shore—moored to docks held against the current by steel cables anchored to trees. Then we pass inlets with multiple docks and boats.

"I need to stop for a minute again," she says. *This is depressing.* I keep paddling.

Then it happens—the first powerboat speeds past us on the right, racing down the river, and here comes the wake.

"Lori!" I shout. "Rudder right!" She grabs the paddle off the gunwales, puts it in the water and points toward the wave. I pull hard to get up some speed and then do pry strokes to turn us perpendicular to the riverbanks and head us into the wave. We make it just as the wake hits the bow, lifts it, rushes under us, lifts the stern, and smacks both bow and stern on the water as it goes through.

"Rats!" I say as I use a few pry strokes to turn us ninety degrees into the direction of the current again, following the powerboat in the *V* of its wake. "We have the right of way, but they can still swamp us as they go past."

"But they didn't!" she says. "We foiled the monster."

I laugh. "We sure did."

"I thought they were supposed to go five miles per hour or have no wake."

"They must be some of those scofflaw people who scoff at the law."

We paddle closer to the western shore now, and watch a large sailboat motor past. Its wake is small, and we hardly need to turn into it. However, soon I say, "Uh-oh. Here comes another stink boat." This one is bigger and more powerful than the one before and has a more dangerous wake. "Look out!"

We handle this one like experts but still feel a thrill as the wave pitches us up and down.

"Do you know it's quarter of three?" Lori asks. "Randy'll wonder what happened."

"I know. And he'll accuse us of loafing too. I can hear him now. 'What did you two do—stop and take a nap?'"

"What are we going to do? I can't paddle any harder."

"I have an idea. Let's get ourselves a little help."

We paddle out to the middle, right into the path of the powerboats.

"Here comes one," I say. "You keep your head down and pretend you're sick." I start waving my paddle from side to side over my head to flag it down. Lori bends over so her head is almost touching the deck. I think she doesn't want to look at the people. I hear the motor slowing, and the big white beast glides up beside us. It's the kind with an inboard motor, a railing and wrap-around windshield on top, and a kitchen, bunks, and bath below.

"What's the matter?" says the young, suntanned man wearing a blue nautical captain's cap with a gold braid and insignia, tipped back jauntily on his head. "Need any help?"

"She's sick, and I need to get her down to the wharf as soon as I can. My buddy's waiting there with a car." A young woman in a bikini looks on sympathetically. *Out for a cruise in Daddy's boat?*

"Do you want to come aboard?" he asks. "We can tow the canoe behind us."

"How do you feel, Lori?" I ask. Then I tell the young captain, who is only a few years older than we are, "I'm just afraid she'll throw up again."

"I better not get aboard," Lori says.

"Could you just tow us behind you with us in the canoe?" I ask.

"Sure. I'll throw you a rope. Tie it to the front."

"Hey, thanks. We really appreciate this."

I let the boat drift forward and watch as the captain uncoils twenty feet of rope, ties one end to the back of the boat, and throws me the other one. I hand it to Lori, and the poor, sick girl ties it to the aluminum grommet at the point of the bow.

"Use two half hitches," I tell her.

She finishes and looks up at the captain.

"Okay?" he asks.

"Yes," she says.

He smiles. "You look like you're feeling a little better."

"A little," she says.

I wonder if he suspects something.

He climbs into the driver's seat, looks back, and slowly accelerates until the rope grows taut. Then he continues to speed up, and suddenly we find ourselves skimming along the water inside the *V* of wake with exhaust spewing into the air in front of us.

"Ugh!" Lori says.

The boat turns with the leftward bend in the river, and now the canoe is racing toward the right side wake. It's just like we're waterskiing, but I know that if we hit that wake sideways, we'll turn over. I shout, "Rudder left!" to Lori, and I start ruddering on the left side. We steer back into the center of the *V*. I look up, and the captain is pointing down at us to the girl in the bikini like a carny ride operator, and they're both laughing. Then I feel the boat speed up again, and the bottom of the canoe starts smacking the water like hands clapping: whap, whap, whap, whap . . . Spray hits my face, and I see a rainbow, while the exhaust makes me cough.

"He's mad!" I shout at Lori. Then, louder, to the captain, "Slow down! We'll capsize!" He looks back, nods, and does as I command, but just then turns sharply toward the wharf on the left, as our momentum takes us straight ahead. I shout, "Rudder left!" and frantically start prying on the left side to point ourselves toward the wharf, until the rope jerks us in that direction and nearly tips us over.

As the yacht approaches the wharf, the puerile madman swings sharply to the right, upriver, and slows to a stop. Now our movement takes us toward the wharf, until once again, the rope gets short. We cross the left wake, and I do a huge sweep stroke on the left side with all my might to turn the canoe to the right, parallel to the shore. The rope jerks us forward, I do a back stroke to bring us to a stop, and the roller coaster ride comes to a halt. Lori reaches up and unties the rope, and I shout, "Hey. Thanks for the ride. That was great!" *(you lousy juvenile delinquent bum)*. "What a kick!" I would not let on that he caused us the least concern.

He looks down at Lori and says, "I didn't make you feel sicker, did I? I just wanted to get you here fast."

Lori maintains the ruse, giving him a sour expression and saying, "I don't feel very good, but thanks for the quick trip."

"Anytime," he laughs, and he pulls the rope in, hand over hand, coiling it around his elbow as he goes. Then he guns the boat, and they wave, leaving us in another cloud of putrid exhaust—another big, disgusting motorboat fart.

We look up on the wharf, and there's Randy, sitting on the hood of the car, shaking his head and smiling.

"You missed it," I taunt, shaking my head. "You missed the best part of the trip."

"How did you get him to give you a ride?"

I told him the story.

"It was fun, but scary," Lori adds.

"I'm sorry you weren't with us, Clark."

And that's called turning a sow's ear into a silk purse. *Chalk up another one for me, Raandy.*

Back home, Lori gets out of the backseat, and I say, "I'll call you soon."

"I'm banking on it, Jeff." Can you believe that made me blush?

As Randy pulls away, he says, "What was that all about?"

"She's just interested in powerboat wakes, would you believe, you know, because we had to avoid some on the river, and I found something on it in the encyclopedia."

Another night of babysitting, with more money for my college fund, more time for Mom and Dad to go to another meeting at church, and yet another bedside demand: "Canoe story!"

"No," I beg. "Not another one. I won't do it."

"Yes!" Billy shouts. Then he starts plotting: "You have to do it, if you want us to go to sleep." Billy's developing. Pretty soon he'll be lying and scheming with the best of us.

"That's blackmail," I say.

"What's blackmail?"

"Never mind. Oh, well, let's see. Yes, I remember. One time I went canoeing on the wild Vermi-lion River out west. Vermi, you know, means worms in Latin. I learned that in Latin last year. And you know what a lion is. Well, this river was named after the fierce, bright-red, giant worms that wiggle along the bottom of the cliffs of Lorain County and have great big sharp teeth like lions. Water and rapids gush out of their mouths, and the rapids roar like lions. But I wasn't afraid of them. I ran up beside the water, tossed my canoe in, leaped into it, and started paddling as fast as I could down the river toward Lake Ee-rie. I was sure I could outrace worms. I paddled and paddled, and looked down, and there were a bunch of big steelhead trout with heads as hard as steel, and they were passing me in the water, leaping forward, trying to get away from the worms. And then, just when I thought I was safe, I looked back, and there they were: three giant red worms, all coming at me, faster than freight trains, with mouths as big as tunnels, and teeth as big as swords. I didn't know what to do. Ahead of me, I saw a big powerboat, a three-decker cabin cruiser with a huge *V* wave coming out of the back of it. I chased it down and paddled my canoe into the center of the *V*. They threw me a rope, and before I knew it, we were sailing up into the sky over Lake Ee-rie and back down again at Shale River Harbor, where I took the canoe out of the water and ran home. And that is the end of my canoe story."

"Is that true?" Jimmy asks. "Did that really happen?"

"You don't think I make these stories up, do you?"

That night I put a note on Brett's pillow: "Halfway there, big brother. Check your wallet. No excuses."

I get one back in the morning, while I'm in bed: "How're you going to make Shale River rise, dumbhead, do a rain dance?"

I lie back down, and my mind drifts to Lori saying, "I'm banking on it, Jeff." *And I'm banking on you.*

Worms on the Vermi-lion River

Chapter 8—Bad Loans

While Randy is caddying, Lori and I take the bus to First National Bank on Detroit Road. We're dressed up. She's in her calf-length plaid skirt and white blouse, and I've got on tan chinos, a blue-and-white sport shirt, and tennis shoes. We're both carrying spiral notebooks. We look like we're going to school, except it's summer.

"What are you going to ask him?" she asks nervously as we walk toward the building.

"Whether he makes house loans to Negroes."

"You're just going to come right out and ask him?"

"Are you crazy? No, no. I have to canoodle him first, like I always do to people."

"Canoodle? That's not an SAT word."

"Nope. It's just one of my favorites. It means to get your way with someone by coaxing or flattering them. I do it to people all the time. I practice it."

"You imp. But I thought it meant to make out with someone," she says with a sly grin.

"That's the other meaning, as in 'he tried to canoodle her into canoodling with him in the canoe.'"

She grins. "I'm on to you, Jeff."

"Yes, I know. But do you know what else? Buried inside that word is the word noodle, and you know what that means."

"A strip of dough?"

"That's one meaning. Another is 'head,' as in, 'That's using your noodle.'"

"Ah, yes."

"And the verb 'noodle' means to improvise a melody on a musical instrument or play around or think creatively.' Like 'noodling a plan to solve a problem.' There's a world of possibilities in these words."

"That's wonderful. But I still want to know what you're going to say to him."

"Don't worry. I'll use my noodle. We can just ask him about his job and take it from there. People love to talk about themselves."

We follow the receptionist down the hall and pass several offices where young men sit behind desks. Most are on the phone, speaking quietly. We enter an office at the end of the hall with a sign by the door, "Roger Compton – Branch Manager." It's a big room with dark wood halfway up on the walls, heavy mahogany furniture, up-high windows, thick carpeting. The walls are decorated with large photographs of a steel mill and Shale River Bridge, and two paintings of sailboats. The silence cries for sound.

Mr. Compton has on a double-breasted, charcoal-gray pinstriped suit, a white shirt with a starched collar, and a navy-blue tie with little gold diamonds on it. He is balding and pale with a sharp nose, large ears, and penetrating eyes. His mouth is wide, and he smiles constantly with his lips closed. I can smell his expensive cologne.

I step forward and shake hands, just like an A-person would do, and Lori follows my lead.

"I'm Jeff Klossen. This is Lori Matthews. . . . Nice offices you have here, sir."

"Thank you," he says, and invites us to sit down. "Now, what can I do for you? Miss Thornton said it was something about careers?"

"Yes sir, and thank you for seeing us today. Lori and I are spending some time this summer talking with people in different professions to see what they do. It's to help us decide what career we might like to go into and what education we should get. And naturally, we thought of banking."

"Very sensible. And it's a very good approach you're taking too," he says. "What questions do you have?"

"Can you tell us what you do in your job?" We open our notebooks and take out our pens.

"Certainly." He leans back. "As branch manager, I'm responsible for the operation of the branch. That includes hiring, training, and supervising the staff, and making sure they follow proper procedures. And I'm responsible for maintaining and increasing deposits at the bank. This includes working with senior staff to develop marketing programs to increase the number of customers we have. It also includes handling customer complaints. I approve the larger loan applications received by the loan officers, and handle any discrepancies in accounts and shortages in funds at the teller stations. . ." Blah, blah, blah, ". . . That's most of what I do."

"Sounds challenging, and like it's important work too," I say. "Taking care of people's money and making loans is really important. Do you enjoy it?"

"Yes."

"What education does someone need to do your job?"

"You should get a bachelor's degree in finance, economics, or a related field. Then you get additional training, once you are hired. Most managers start as tellers."

"How do you know whether to approve a loan application?" Lori asks.

"For a house or a business?"

"A house."

"Well, there are three key requirements. First is down payment. People must put down twenty percent of the purchase price plus closing costs. Second is income. People must have sufficient earnings to show that they will be able to make the monthly payments to the bank. Third is the appraisal. The house must be worth what the person wants to borrow. Our appraiser determines this by inspecting the house and seeing what similar homes in the area have sold for."

I'm nodding like a bobblehead doll.

"Are there different kinds of mortgages?" I ask.

"Oh, yes. Many. But basically, we have commercial loans for business, plus residential mortgage loans. Those can be conventional loans, which are usually for twenty years and are secured by a down payment, and FHA—the Federal Housing Administration—and the VA, which have a lower interest rate and down payment and are insured by the government."

"Interesting. Do you make many FHA loans?" I ask.

"Oh, yes. Most of our loans are conventional, but many are financed through FHA. FHA limits the amount that can be borrowed, so the program is really for lower-priced, smaller homes. Also, we rarely make them on new homes since they generally cost too much to meet FHA's requirements."

"There aren't that many small homes in Orchard Park, are there?"

"Oh, there are quite a few away from the lake."

"What are VA loans?" I ask.

"Veterans Administration loans. They're similar to FHA loans, but they're for veterans."

Lori changes the subject. "Are there many career opportunities for women in banking?"

He hesitates and then says, "Oh, yes. Many of our tellers and secretaries and accountants are women. But most of them resign to get married and have children before they can advance in their careers."

Then I look him in the eye and take the plunge. "Oh, one question I have is, have you ever had a Negro apply for a loan?"

He stiffens. "No. Negroes don't seem to buy homes on the West Side."

"Why do you think that is?"

His eyes squint, and his voice hardens. "I don't know. Why are you asking about this?"

"I'm just curious. Can you tell me . . . if a Negro did apply and met all the requirements, would you loan him the money?"

"Of course I would. We have no racial restrictions here. Now, if you'll excuse me." He rises to his feet. "I have some work to attend to." I can tell he's angry. But he never once changes his confident smile. We thank him graciously, shake hands again, and leave.

"Ha! We did it," I say on the way to the bus stop. "Canoodled him and dropped the big question—just like a water balloon." I whistle it down and make an explosive sound.

"Bravo, Mr. Jeff. But do you think he was telling the truth about never having had a Negro apply for a loan?"

"Probably," I say. "But you never know."

"He said that Negroes don't try to move here."

"Maybe that's true. Mom told me that some people wouldn't be nice to Negroes if they saw them moving in. Maybe Negroes don't want to move where people don't like them."

"So we really have no evidence that banks in Orchard Park won't loan money to Negroes, do we?" Lori says.

"No."

I reflect a moment. "Boy, he was getting really ticked at my questions. I hope he doesn't know Dad."

"What would your dad do if he found out?"

"Who knows. He might get mad and ground me. You know how parents are."

"I think our parents are different."

"What next?" she asks.

"Well, I think we're making some progress. Maybe some Negroes don't want to live here. Maybe they don't try to borrow money from the banks to buy homes here."

"Yes. And maybe banks won't lend money to them to buy here. We don't know," she says.

"I've been wondering whether builders will sell homes to them."

"Let's go ask one," she says.

"You are getting daring. But I bet you'll want me to do the asking."

"Of course."

Chapter 9—An Exclusive Development

The next morning, I borrow the car, and Lori and I drop in on Rick Schutz in the Wellington development. We decide it's too risky to go to the builder who built our own houses because he knows our parents. Lori is nervous.

"What are you going to say?" Lori asks in a breathless voice.

"You'll find out."

"This thing makes my stomach queasy. You're being so sneaky, and you haven't even planned what you're going to say."

"That's where the noodling part of the canoodling comes in. I improvise."

I turn onto the new street with the big sign, "Rocky Land Vineyards, An Exclusive Development." Below that it says, "Rick Schutz Homes."

The street is new, so the concrete is white. There's one house on each side a few lots down, and there's a white aluminum construction trailer on the left near the entrance and a late-model green Chevy pickup with a "Rick Schutz Homes" sign on the door. The morning sun makes sharp shadows of us on the street as we walk, and the air is starting to heat up.

"What do you think 'exclusive development' means?" I ask Lori.

"Do you think it means that some kinds of people are excluded . . . and can't buy homes here?" Lori asks.

We walk to the trailer. Wires run from the top to a utility pole, and I hear the hum of a window air conditioner. I climb the three narrow wooden steps, holding onto the steel angle railing, and then knock on the aluminum door. Lori waits at the bottom. After a minute, the door opens out; a big man with a bald head and red freckles appears. He has on a short-sleeve, red-checked shirt. From the sleeves, red-speckled arms and hands emerge. He looks like he could hammer me into wood like I was a nail. "Can I help you?" he asks in a deep, gruff voice.

"Mr. Schutz?"

"Yes?"

"I'm Jeff, and this is Lori. I called yesterday. We live in the neighborhood."

"Oh, yes. What did you want to talk about?"

"We're interested in learning about house building. It's for a summer project we're doing."

He looks down and sees Lori, checks his watch, and then looks back at me.

He shakes his head as if trying to decide whether to talk to us, but then says, "Okay. But just for a few minutes. Then I gotta go."

I thank him, and we go in. The trailer smells like stale cigarette smoke, but he's not smoking now.

At one end of the room is a desk. Near the wall at the other end is a big table with a kitchenette behind it. There's an ashtray on the table with lots of butts in it. Next to the table is a box full of tall rolls of paper—blueprints? On the side wall is a map showing the street, cul-de-sac, and building lots. Pictures of houses and floor plans decorate all the walls.

"We've seen some of your houses, Mr. Schutz," Lori says as he closes the trailer door. "They're really nice."

"I'm glad you like them. Let's go in here," he says, leading us into his office. The walls display more pictures of houses, photos of golfers, floor plans, and a big walleye mounted on a plaque. He moves behind his desk, which holds another full ashtray, and motions for us to sit down. I can see a pack of cigarettes in his pocket.

"Now, what do you want to know?" He cocks his head a little to the side and gives me a hard look, like he's a little suspicious or something.

"Thanks for seeing us. We're seniors at the high school, and we're going around talking to different people this summer about what they do for a living. It's part of our career planning, to help us decide what we want to do when we get older and what we should study in college."

"That sounds like a good idea," he says, nodding slowly.

"So, can you tell us what you do in a typical day?"

"Sure." He leans back with his hands behind his head, displaying impressive biceps. "Well, first thing in the morning, about six, I call all the subcontractors to make sure they're coming. Then I talk to my foreman about any changes the buyer wants in the house and what I want our crew to do that day. Subcontractors do most of the work. I only keep a small crew working, myself—just a few men."

I'm taking notes as fast as I can, and so is Lori.

"So I check with my foreman to make sure the subs are working and know what they're doing, then I walk around and look at the jobs."

"Sounds like you do a whole day's work before the rest of the world starts."

He smiles. "Yes. We start early. At seven, my secretary Cindy comes in. We talk about what the men are doing today, and I tell her when to schedule material deliveries. Then I go over bills with her and approve them for payment. She's a big help. She could run the business by herself. I also have to call the city whenever a job is ready for an inspection. The excavation, foundation, floor framing, walls, second floor, roof, rough electrical and plumbing, drywall, painting, and completed house—they all get inspected. I also call the city to put in the water and sewer lines when it's time for them, and the power company to hook up the electric. I call the bank to tell them we're ready for another payment, and to have them send out their inspector."

Timing. When to bring it up to catch him off guard. It's all timing. I don't want to change the subject now.

"And you do all this before nine," I say.

He chuckles. "Not quite."

I smile. "I thought you'd be out there swinging a hammer. But you have all these other things you have to do."

"That's right. I used to work on the job, but now I don't have time. I handle sales too. I meet with customers in the afternoon and evening to sell them houses, and do estimates on any changes they want. And then sometimes I have to go to some city-planning and zoning meetings."

"And you have a family too?"

"Oh yes. In my free time, I play with my kids, and on Sunday mornings I usually go to church, unless I'm playing golf. That'll give you some idea of what I do."

"Wow," I say. "I'm impressed!"

"Do you design the houses you build?" Lori asks.

"No. I leave that to the architects. Most of the houses are stock plans. I only offer ten designs, which can be reversed. They're all three- or four-bedroom homes at least eighteen hundred square feet on an unfinished basement with a two-car garage. I select the materials and put in the landscaping. I want all the houses to blend in together to make a nice neighborhood."

My mind is starting to drift. I start thinking of Lori again, but tear myself back.

"It sounds risky," I say.

"It is. You have to stay on your toes if you want to survive in this business."

"So can people make changes to the plans?" Lori asks.

"Yes, a few, but I have to charge extra for changes, and that can be expensive. I have to get quotes from the subs, and put them all together, and then add on my markup for all the time I have to take doing estimates, and ordering different materials, and changing the plans, and sometimes getting the city inspector to approve them, and then giving special instructions to the workers."

"It's complicated, isn't it?" I say.

"Yes, it is."

"How did you prepare yourself to do this work, as far as school and so on?" I ask.

"I mainly learned from my dad. He was a builder too. I worked on his jobs and helped him in the office. I picked up most of the practical skills from him: carpentry and masonry and wiring and plumbing and so on. I can do it all. But I did go to college for a couple of years to learn accounting. And I took a banking course. And the real estate test—that took a lot of studying."

He looks at his watch and stands up. "I'm sorry. I have to go to a closing now. Any last questions?"

"So you own all this land?" I ask.

Now he's turning his head to the side like he's trying to hear what's going on in my mind, and he starts stroking his lips, moving his thumb and forefinger together and apart, back and forth. *Probably wants a smoke.* "No. John McCormack owns the land. He bought it from a farmer, Mr. Wellington. McCormack and I work together. He developed the land—put in the streets and sewers. I do the building on his land. Then we both sell the house to the customer."

"And I was curious, what does the sign mean, 'Exclusive Development?'" His eyebrows go up, and then he frowns.

"It's an exclusive development because people can't come in, and buy a lot, and put up whatever they want. They have to buy from us, and I control the design and location of the houses, and the sizes of the houses, the plans, and the materials. People know that if they buy here, their neighbors will be buying one of these twelve designs, and using the good materials that I pick. There won't be any cheap materials used. They know that nobody can put up fences or outbuildings here or raise pigs in the backyard. Basically, their neighbors won't be able to do anything that will reduce the value of their property, and they won't be able to either."

"Are any of the home loans FHA or VA?"

"No. Not here. These homes are too expensive."

He's shuffling his feet now, anxious to wave us out the door. This is my last chance.

"So if a Negro family came in and wanted to buy, would you sell to them?"

"Negroes?" He glares at me and starts speaking faster and tapping his desk with his forefinger. "Let me explain something to you. Negroes lower property values, too, just like if someone built a shack in the middle of the neighborhood, or started raising livestock, or repairing cars. Neighbors would want to move out, and they'd sell their homes for less than they were worth, and that would lower the value of everyone's homes. And, face it, if I sold to a Negro, I'd be cutting my throat—no one else would buy a house from me. No, if I sold to a Negro, property values would go down, and everybody loses. Everybody loses. McCormack wouldn't approve the sale anyway."

We nod and act dumb.

"But Negroes wouldn't try to buy here, anyway. It wouldn't happen. They know they couldn't get a loan. The banks wouldn't give them one because they want this development to succeed. The banks don't want property values to go down because of people moving out."

"But if the Negro family had their own financing, would you sell to them then?"

Now he turns sour. "What are you kids after? Haven't you been listening? If a Negro family moved in here, I couldn't sell any more houses. I'd go belly up. . . . No. I wouldn't do it. I would never sell to Negroes, and it's not because I'm prejudiced against them. I knew lots of them in college, and we got along fine. But white people don't want to live next to Negroes."

"Isn't there some law that says you'd have to sell to them?" Lori asks.

"No, there isn't," he says, pounding the desk with his fist. "McCormack owns this land, and he can sell it to anyone he damn well pleases." He stands abruptly, sending a wave of fear through me; he looks like he might take a punch at me. Then he looks around for his briefcase, picks it up, checks his pocket for his pack of cigarettes, and says, "I gotta go."

I try to put on some charm as I wriggle to my feet. "Yeah, I can see how you have to help people keep up their property values so they don't lose money. People work too hard for their money. And a house is a big investment."

"And you're in business to help people," Lori says, "help them get a nice house . . . for their families."

"That's right," he growls.

He ushers us out. We thank him and leave, and I see him giving my car a hard look as he gets into his truck.

He follows us out of the development. It makes me nervous. "I bet he's reading my plate number," I say, glancing into the rear-view mirror.

"You're just paranoid."

"Probably."

"What'll we do next?" I ask on the way back. "We can't canoe Shale River, that's for sure."

"We'll be out of town next week. We're going to my grandparents' in Iowa. Flying out."

"Great. Have fun. Meanwhile, I'm stuck here."

Chapter 10—Come On, Rain!

Lori's away, and Randy's caddying all the time. It's just like the Fourth of July weekend, only longer. I've got to get my mind off my investigation. I've got to canoe Shale River! But the water is barely up to your ankles. Usually we get this weather in August, but it isn't even the end of July. The breeze is like blast-furnace exhaust, and there's never any rain. I raise my arms to the sky and shout, "Come on, rain!" but all we get is drought. If I knew a rain dance like Brett mentioned in his note, I'd do it.

Waiting for high water is like asking grass to grow, and right now, it isn't growing at all—it's just getting brown. People don't want their lawns cut once a week anymore. They keep telling me to come back next week. Everyone is watering to try to keep it alive. I ask the ones who aren't doing it if I can water for them (i.e., move the sprinklers around while I read). They figure they can do it themselves, at night, when there's less evaporation. But they have lots of other things to do, so sometimes it doesn't get done. I tell them that once it dies, crabgrass takes over and they'll never have a nice lawn again. Of course, all I really want is to make it grow so I can cut it for them, but there are no takers.

Boring, boring, boring.

So what do I do? I sleep a lot. I know it's time to get up when it gets hot in my room and I start to sweat. That means the sun is beating down on the southeastern wall, and that means it's ten thirty or eleven. The reason I sleep so late is because I have to. It's the only way I can get a decent night's sleep after staying up late listening to the Indians lose. They always lose. The Yankees are killing everyone this year, as usual, and the Indians will be lucky to win as many games as they lose. But they still have a bunch of guys batting close to .300, like Jimmy Pearsall and Tito Francona and Vic Power. And they hit homers too. I like it when Jim Perry pitches. He mows 'em down. He might win twenty games this year.

"Get up!" shouts the drill sergeant. She can't stand it any longer. "Get out of bed! Do something! Go get some exercise." She has physically invaded my realm, and I'm afraid she may come and shake me out of bed or hit me with her broom. She's tidying up in preparation for Helen coming tomorrow and is holding it diagonally across her body like a rifle at port arms.

"It's too hot."

"Mow some lawns."

"Nobody's grass is growing."

"Go swimming!" she thunders.

"Where?"

"In the lake."

"You want me to die, don't you."

She slams the broom onto the rug like a walking stick to emphasize her point: "Go to a museum."

"I've seen them all."

Her voice drops in pitch. "Then go to the zoo."

"It smells like animal droppings," I whine.

She pounds the broom on the floor. "Visit Lori."

"She's in Iowa."

"What about Randy?"

"He's caddying."

She juts out her chin. "Read a book."

"I don't have any."

She shrugs. "Go to the library."

"I won't be ready in time to go with you."

Now she bends her head toward me, so she can bore into me, and speaks slowly: "You can ride your bike and get some exercise."

"I think I have a flat."

"Walk, then!"

"It's too hot."

"Oh!" she hollers and turns and stomps off, broom in hand. I thought for sure she had meant to sweep me out of the house with it.

This is why they sent me to the north woods last summer. Mom just can't take it. She doesn't have enough stick-to-it-ivity like that spider does in *So Dear to My Heart*. She's not persistent enough. She lacks perseverance and tenacity. She gives up too easily.

I love to torment her. It breaks the boredom.

What really sets her off is when she catches me watching soap operas. I can't tell which one I like best—*As the World Turns*, *The Guiding Light*, or *Young Doctor Malone*. Catching me doing that brings forth a scorching, searing, scalding scolding that comes from the depths of her soul. It almost makes her cry.

After a couple days of battling with my mother like we were two prizefighters and listening to her threats to bring Dad into it, I start to get bored with the fight. I'm the one who lacks stick-to-it-ivity. I decide I must take action. The only thing I've been doing is babysitting the two wild men while Mom goes shopping or works at the library and when she and Dad go out at night.

So at lunch, I say, "Okay, boys. How about a canoe story?" I don't know why I'm volunteering. I must be crazy. Maybe to smooth things over a little with Mom.

The three of them are having tomato soup and toasted cheese sandwiches for lunch. I'm having them for breakfast.

"Yes," they shout. "Canoe story!"

"A canoe story? What's that?" Mom asks.

"Just little stories I tell them."

I'm not even finished eating when I start in. "One time I picked up my canoe in the backyard, lifted it over my head, and ran down into Shale River Valley to the river. I looked at it and was really disappointed. It was so shallow you could walk across it without getting your feet wet, if you stepped on the right stones. I couldn't canoe in that. But then I had an idea. I remembered up at the river museum seeing a little brown critter swimming in the water, and I heard him slap his flat tail on the water when he heard me coming. It was a beaver. So I went up there and looked around and saw one and decided to engage him in conversation.

"'Mr. Beaver,' I said. 'Can I talk to you for a minute?'

"'What about?' he asked.

"'I need your help. I don't have any place to canoe.'

"'Tho how can I help you?' I noticed he had a slight lisp, probably because of those great big buckteeth he had for chewing down trees.

"'I was wondering if you could build a dam for me and make a lake for me to canoe in.'

"'Maybe. I have thome buddies who could help me. But we only work at night.'

"'What is it, a second job for you?'

"'Yeah. My first job is thleeping! I do that all day long.'

"'Me too,' I said. 'I'm nocturnal myself.'

"That night, I camped in the valley by a meadow near the big golf course. Soon I saw a whole army of beavers swimming down the river toward me, coming to build the dam. They went to work, cutting down trees with their big buckteeth, dragging them out to the river, hauling them down to where they were building the dam, and piling them up, until the dam went all the way across the valley. As soon as they finished, the water began filling up the valley, over the meadow, over the golf course, and into the woods.

"I put my canoe into the water and paddled out into the middle of the new lake, right above the thirteenth hole of the golf course, and I said, 'Thank you very much. Any charge?'

"'No charge. We built thome new homes for ourthelveth, too. We call them lodgeth.'

"Just then we looked up and saw a giant steelhead trout come charging down toward us. It was just like the ones I saw up in the Vermi-lion River, only this one was as big as a car. He was really angry that the beavers had blocked his route to Lake Ee-rie. That's where he lived when he wasn't making baby trout upstream in Shale River. You know, the momma trout lays eggs in the stones and the poppa trout fertilizes them, and pretty soon little baby trout come out of the eggs and swim away. We were really afraid, because this poppa trout was so big and had that great big steel head to clobber us with.

"Then that fish started banging his head into the dam. He was going to break it and let all the water out!

"Mr. Beaver whistled through his two front teeth and said to me, 'I better go get the other ninety-nine beaverth tho we can fight this monthter.'

"'Wait,' I said. 'Let's talk to him first.'

"'If you think it will do any good, but thith one ith acting pretty violent. He wantth war.'

"I waved to the fish and asked, 'Mr. Trout. Why do you want to break the beavers' dam?'

"He said, 'Because I have to get through it to swim to the lake. I always do that. That's where I live when I'm not making baby fish.'

"'So that's your only problem? You need a way to get around this dam?'

"'You betcher, Chester.'

"I look at the beaver. 'Can't you make him one of those fish ladders so he can get around the dam?'

"'I'm not climbing up and down any dumb ladder,' said the trout. 'I don't even have any feet to put on the rungs.'

"'No, no, no, no, no . . . ' I said. 'A fish ladder doesn't have any rungs. It has rock stairs with water going over them. You can splash up and down it like crazy. You'll love it. Salmon do.'

"'I've heard about salmon, although I've never met one. But if they can do it, I can do it.'

"Right after that, those beavers got busy building the ladder. It took them less than an hour to gather those rocks and build that ladder. And to test it, the steelhead went flopping down the steps, and came back up, and went back and forth a few times just because he was having so much fun. His fish mouth was even smiling.

"I got in my canoe and paddled all around the lake that night in the moonlight. It was lovely. And when the sun started to come up, the beavers all went into their lodges to go to sleep, and I paddled to shore, picked up my canoe, and ran home before Dad and the other angry golfers arrived to find that the beavers had built a lake all over their golf course. And that is the end of my canoe story."

And that's about the only way I can think of to canoe on Shale River—hire some beavers to build a dam. Otherwise, if it doesn't rain, I'm out a hundred bucks.

Chapter 11—Left or Right?

Yay! The drought is over. Some showers have arrived, and the grass is growing again. It's August now, and strangely, not quite as hot as July.

Lori's back, but she's doing a lot of babysitting. Randy's caddying, and I mow lawns all day, even some that don't really need it. I want to get them caught up before the weather front comes in. The newspaper says it might rain on Saturday or Sunday, and I don't want to get behind. It's a lot harder to mow if the grass is long and wet.

Late Friday night, the deluge starts. It pours all day Saturday. Dad's mad because he can't play golf. "Why can't it rain during the week?" he moans to Mom.

"You probably committed too many sins," she kids.

They go to a movie Saturday night so I can earn more money for college. *Yeah, sure.*

It continues till dawn, and Sunday morning, it's raining so hard that we stay home from church.

Late in the afternoon, it starts to let up. I borrow the car for an hour and drive down Shalecliff Lane—the steep road into the valley—and turn right onto Valley Road. I can't go far before I come to a "Road Closed" sign on a sawhorse barricade with two flashing lights. I drive around it, park by the side of the road, walk as close as I can to the ford, and look. The river is a different animal now—a sprawling, splashing brown thing that has crawled up its banks four or five feet, flooding woods and ball fields and roaring as it mauls everything in its path and charges over the ford. *This may be the time.* Just as I imagined, there's a waterfall about a foot and a half high on the downside of the ford. The trough at the base, where the current reverses and goes upstream, is only a couple of feet wide, measuring from the ford. If we dig fast, we'll go right over it and won't get caught by it—as long as we keep heading downstream. But if we get turned sideways to it somehow, it could tip us over and start tumbling us. At last! Danger! Excitement! A little thrill from the mighty Shale River.

I get back in the car and drive north along the road, toward the lake. The road is passable, but at one place, a stream has overflowed a culvert and taken a path over the road to reach the river. It looks like the water is only a few inches deep, but I'm not going to risk going through it. My trip is over.

I turn around and drive up out of the valley and along the top into downtown, to the Westview Hotel. I park and walk onto the bridge and look south. *Wow!* The river is twice its normal width. It has inundated the park where the marina is, and the building itself is on an island. I cross traffic and look the other way to where the water is surging into the lake. I look down under the bridge to where they used to build those wooden sub chasers in World War I and out to the tip of the yacht club on Dead Man's Island. The water there has jumped the stone walls on the west side. Wooden docks have floated up their steel poles with the rising water, but they're still attached to the wall on the side. Yachts dangle from them like gems on a necklace. One dock has broken off and is hanging from another at an odd angle and may be preparing to voyage into the lake.

I follow the road along the valley and turn down Old Lorain Road, passing under the Lorain Road Bridge, the steel arches of which soar a hundred feet over the river. At the bottom, the water covers Valley Road under the big bridge to the left, and another barricade blocks the way. Straight ahead, the steel trussed bridge and road across it, which goes by Little Met Golf Course and up to Fairwood Hospital, are still high and dry. We could make a stop there.

I go back up the hill to Lorain Road, turn left along the valley and left again back into the valley toward Big Met Golf Course. Valley Road is dry there, but I can see it's flooded at both ends of the golf course—more blinking lights. This intersection is dry, but it's too far from the river to use to change paddlers.

Back on top, I make a few lefts and take the road into the valley toward the stables and the Mastic Woods Golf Course. This road crosses Valley Road and the river and continues up the hill into Cleveland. The water here is only a few feet under the bridge, and I can see that some of the horse trails along the river are submerged. *I hope they were able to get the horses to higher ground.* Farther south, water covers Valley Road.

This intersection might be a good place to put in. Randy and I could race down the river, jump a few of those fords, and Lori could pick us up at Shalecliff Lane. It looks like about six miles on the map.

I hop back in, beat it back home, and call Randy and Lori.

"River's up," I tell Randy. "It's perfect."

"I might as well go canoeing," he says. "The course will be mush. No one'll be out there."

We meet in his garage, as usual, and Randy starts out with an ultimatum. "I'm not going two-thirds of the way this time, kids. If you want a trip, I'm gonna paddle the whole way. If Lori wants to go, you two can each get halvsies."

"Dammit, Clark," I say.

Then Lori pipes in, "Well, I do want to go." *Of course she does.*

"It might be a rough trip for you." Randy tells her. "Are you sure? I'd feel better about going with Klossen. Everyone knows that flooded rivers are dangerous. You never know what you'll run into."

"I don't think she can hack it," I say. *I can't believe I'm saying this.* "She won't know what to do." *But I can get nasty when I'm fighting for something for me.* "You'll turn it over, Lori. Then you'll both end up in the drink."

Lori throws me a really nasty look. "I will not." Then she says, "And I won't drive if I can't paddle."

"That's great," Randy says to me. "Now she's going on strike."

Eventually, I give in, as usual, and all I've done by arguing is to make Lori mad at me and prove to Randy once again that I'm a twisting worm.

"If we start at Mastick Road, Old Lorain Road might be about halfway," he says.

"Yeah," I say. "But if we do break it in half, I want the leg from there to Shalecliff Lane. That water's got to be faster. The river's in a narrower gorge and swings around an oxbow where Hog's Back Lane comes down from Lakeshore. I think the first leg through the golf courses would be safer for Lori."

"You just want more kicks," Lori says. "But that's okay. I'll take the first leg."

I see Randy, standing there with that smug look on his face. He holds all the cards, and I think, *Loser. Loser. Loser. I'm a weak-kneed loser!* Then I think about Lori: *She wins too. . . . But at least I got the best half of the trip. . . . But doing it her dad's way, I would have paddled two-thirds of the way. Darn Randy, anyhow.*

That night, the rain continues, but all that's left in the morning is drizzle. We load up at about eight in our ponchos, and drive to the Mastick Road put-in. On the way, I start to worry a little about the river and decide they need some advice.

"Listen," I tell them. "If you come to one of those fords, make sure you go over it at right angles to the ford and stay in the main current. If you let the water sweep you sideways, it'll flip the canoe on its side at the edge of the ford, and then you'll get thrown out and stuck in the trough on the other side of the ford."

"Thanks, professor," Randy says.

"You think I'm kidding. The current reverses in the trough and goes around and around, and you won't be able to get out of it. It'll just keep tumbling you like you were a log, and you'll have to catch a breath when your body's facing up. You won't be able to get out of it unless you dive down under the wave on the downstream side of the trough, and you won't be able to do that if you're wearing a life jacket. So you'll have to hold your breath and take the jacket off while you're turning over and then dive straight down under that wave before you can come back to the surface in the downstream current and then try to swim or float to one of the banks." Lori's eyes widen. "I'm serious, Lori. That's what my canoeing book says."

"That's another reason I don't wear a life jacket," Randy says.

"But what if we capsize and you hit your head on a rock?" Lori asks. "You'll need a life jacket to help you float so you don't drown."

"Nah. Not me. I'll take my chances without it."

"Me too," I say. *I'm as tough as he is.* "But listen. I'm not through. When we're going over a ford, we've gotta dig hard, and I mean hard, so the canoe has enough speed and forward momentum to go over the edge of the ford and over that trough and back into the downstream current without getting stuck."

"An object in motion tends to remain in motion," Randy says.

"And we want that to be forward motion, too," Lori says.

"Right," I say and look at her. "Do you still want to go?"

She looks at me with stony eyes. "You bet, Klossen."

I shake my head. "You asked for it."

When we arrive, we strip off our ponchos down to swimsuits and sweatshirts. We know we'll get wet anyway. We pull off by the bridle trail, walk out onto the bridge, and stare at the water. Through the mist it looks like muddy brown lava racing down a mountainside, full of leaves and trash, and carrying logs and trees it's torn from the banks. The dark gray cliffs on the eastern side of the valley look silently down at us.

"What a monster!" I shout.

We return to the car, untie the canoe, carry it down a grassy bank to the river, and put it in. I hold the stern rope, and the current drags the bow forward to the bank. Lori climbs into the bow, and I hand Randy the rope. Lori pushes off with her paddle against the bank, and Randy, holding the gunnels, gives the canoe a forward shove and steps in.

"See you at the bridge at Old Lorain Road," I yell, just to make sure they don't get lost.

Then, with a few strokes, they're into the flow.

I ride the brake down the hill past the first arch of the Lorain Road Bridge and park on the side of the road in front of the steel truss bridge on Old Lorain Road. I can see blinking lights and floodwater over Valley Road on both sides of the bridge a hundred yards down. It doesn't look deep, but I'm not going to drive into it. I don't want to lose Randy's clunker. . . . I stand on the old bridge and look down between the angled steel webs at the molten chocolate boiling and spitting, racing toward me, under me, and on downstream.

The river is well below the bridge. On the western side, I climb down the rocks to the water at a place where they can pull in to make the switch.

This time, I'm not too worried about them stopping somewhere and making out. I think the river will keep them busy. But after an hour, I begin to worry. Then, here they come, gliding along the bank on the opposite side. I holler and wave, but they decide to get out over there, right at the base of the bridge. Lori steps out, stops the canoe, and wraps the rope around a bush. Randy follows her out of the canoe. They pull the bow up on the bank and fasten the rope more securely to a tree. Meanwhile, I climb up the rocks, drive across the bridge, and meet them coming up on the other side.

"How was it?" I ask.

Lori is effusive. "Great!"

"Did you go over any fords?"

"One," she says, "and we did just as you said. We went right for it, dug hard, and went right over it—the ford and the trough. It was a blast!"

"Were there any big rocks or trees or rapids or anything?"

"Just lots of choppy water and waves," she says, "and fallen trees along the banks. We stayed away from them."

"I can't say we were always in control," Randy says. "Sometimes we drifted sideways and went where it wanted to take us."

"And she did okay, Randy?"

"Yes. Just like last time. She did better than you would have."

"Yeah, yeah."

Lori smiles at him adoringly, and I can hardly stand it.

"Okay. Well, tell me when you're ready to go again."

Lori opens the picnic basket in the car and feeds us each a fried-egg-and-bacon sandwich, which we suck down with cups of hot chocolate from a red thermos. We yak, and she tells every detail of their trip. Then Randy says, "Let's go," and we climb down the rocks, get in, kneel on our life jackets, and push off.

I feel the power of the river as it sweeps us along, and soon we see the arches of the Lorain Road Bridge soaring above us. Water has flooded the valley here, leaving the concrete foundation of one arch on an island. We sweep around it to the right below a high cliff, then cross the valley to the cliffs on the west side, then move back again through woods to the cliffs on the east side.

"This is the life," I say, my paddle across the gunwales.

"We have to paddle enough to keep going in the right direction," he says. I told *him* that, but he makes it sound like he originated the thought.

We hug the cliffs and approach our first ford, where Valley Road crosses the river.

"Dig!" I yell, and we move back to the center.

We strain mightily, ride over it fast, near the center, and I feel the sudden plunge downward in my stomach and feel the spray as the bow dips into the water and crashes through the wave on the other side of the trough. I rudder briefly to correct our course.

"Yeah!" I bellow. It's over in an instant, and again we're doing an easy float on the back of the brown beast.

The valley narrows, with cliffs on both sides, and we start into the oxbow. The water gets choppy, fills the valley, and covers the road. We hug the cliffs on the inside of the bend to make sure we don't drift off into the shallows on the outside of the bend where the river has deposited a bunch of trash, wood, and trees, each with a tangle of submerged branches and roots.

"Ford!" I shout, looking ahead, and we start stroking hard.

Then the stern begins to move forward—the current is taking us sideways—just the right direction for flipping us at the ford.

"Paddle on the left!" Randy shouts, and we both do. He starts doing pry strokes to correct our course, and only in the last few seconds are we able to put our backs into pulling forward. Again we sail over the lip of the little dam, plunge downward and over the trough, and bounce back up into the main current.

"Yes!" I shout. "We did it again."

"You better believe it. We're pros!"

"Ha!"

We go through a long, straight, narrow stretch with cliffs on both sides, and the water gets choppy again. It's dropping fast and is deeper in the canyon. We both paddle so we can exceed the speed of the current. We speed past Hog's Back Lane and start around another horseshoe bend, this one in the other direction and up against high cliffs on the Orchard Park side. The water keeps moving fast. We pull vigorously, making constant corrections to our course.

"What a ride!" I holler.

Around the bend, I can make out the final ford, just before our takeout point at Shalecliff Lane. But between it and us, fifty yards ahead, lies a small tree in the middle of the river. Its stump is on the left, and a couple of big branches with leaves on them jut up on the right at low angles to the river. Water rushes around it on both sides, and it soon will be upon us.

"Which way, Klossen—to the left or right?"

"To the right," I say, full of confidence and good humor.

We heave powerfully with both paddles on the left side, fighting the current to get around it, but not making enough headway: it keeps coming toward us.

When it's twenty yards ahead, Randy yells, "Rudder right!"

I flip over to the right side and rudder while he strokes hard on the left. Then I start doing pry strokes to try to pull us over. In the last seconds, as the tree looms ahead, he switches sides and begins ruddering too. But we aren't going fast enough to move the canoe. All it does is swing the canoe sideways. The bow strikes the trunk first; then the stern swings around and hits. And then? Then we don't move. Water swirls to our front and back and under us, and we don't move. We're caught on a strainer.

"Hell," Randy says.

"Rats," I add.

We push hard with our paddles against the trunk, trying to move the canoe forward around the right side of the tree, but the canoe does not budge. We push and push, and then give up. Then we think.

"Maybe we can get out on the trunk and lighten up the canoe. We can hold onto that branch there," I say, pointing to the thick branch angling into the air, "and then we can take the rope and pull the canoe forward. Heck, we're so close to the takeout, we can probably jump in and swim to the ford. But I'm putting on my life jacket, just in case."

"Not me."

"Hard-ass."

"What if we go into the water and it gets snagged on a branch? It could hold you right under."

"Oh, right. What are the odds of that?"

We gingerly climb out and stand on the trunk, holding the ropes and paddles. The canoe floats upward as we lighten its load.

"Okay," I say. "Let's pull it."

I stand on the trunk, lean against a big branch, and pull forward on the bow rope. Randy pulls in the same direction on the stern rope. We give it our all, and the stubborn thing doesn't move.

I look over at the riverbank on the other side of the ford and see Lori standing there looking at us. "Hell. There's Lori. Look at her, Clark."

"I bet she's having a good laugh."

"Yeah."

"So whadda we do now, oh great leader?"

"You finally admitted it. I am the leader."

"Yeah. That means, 'You got us into this mess. Now get us out.'"

"Maybe we can rock it a little, and pull it along the trunk with our hands."

"We can try it."

We squat on the trunk and reach across to the outside gunwale and start rocking it and pulling it in the direction of the bow. It's not moving, so we rock it some more, and then more and more, and then . . . *uh-oh* . . . a little water comes over the gunwale, and then a whole lot of water comes over it. The canoe turns sideways to the current. Then we squat on the stump and listen to the rivets popping as the current folds the canoe in half.

"Damn!" I shout, and Randy uses some stronger language.

"You owe me a canoe, Klossen."

"Whaddaya mean? We both made the decisions here and both executed them."

"No. You made the decision. You said, 'Go right!'"

"Yeah, but you went along with it."

"Take responsibility for your actions, great leader. . . . "

The discussion continues, with the same amount of progress as we made pulling on the canoe, until it runs out of gas.

We try pulling on the folded carcass one last time.

"It's no use," I say.

"So now what?" he asks, resuming his role of faithful follower.

"We might as well leave it until the river goes down, and come back and see if we can get it and bend it back."

"But what do we do now?"

"I guess we just jump in and swim to shore."

We walk out the trunk, holding onto the sloping branch.

"Try to keep your head above water," he says.

"Don't go over the ford. It's only thirty yards away. You might get trapped in the trough."

"Right."

He jumps in with a splash, comes up hollering with the cold shock, and starts racing toward the bank, which he hits just above the ford. He crawls up the bank, stands up, and looks at Lori and then at me. *I gotta do that?* I think.

"Your turn, Klossen," he shouts. "Do it!"

Darn. I don't know if I can. And do I wear my life jacket or not?

I jump in with it on, and start crawling as fast as I can. The water's freezing. No leisurely backstroke now. But just like Randy on Hinckley Lake, the jacket holds me back. *I'll never make it.*

I'm swept onto the ford. I raise my head and gulp a big breath just as I hit the falls, and I'm thrust over the edge. My head falls first, into the water at the bottom, and my body and feet follow. Then, just as the book said, I'm tumbling backward to the current, right in the trough, and I can't seem to get out of it. So, as the book instructed, I unhook my jacket, let it go, and dive for the bottom, sweeping my arms to my sides, frog-kicking, then flutter-kicking. I swim downstream, underwater, and then rise to the top and gasp for air. I bounce along in the choppy waves for a while, and then renew my crawl to get to shore, where Randy and Lori pull me out.

"I told you not to wear that life jacket, but you wouldn't listen."

"Oh, Jeff," Lori says, as she gives me a hug. "Thank heavens you made it."

She electrifies me.

Randy puts his arm around my shoulder. "Yeah. Good going." I can't believe it.

"What are you going to do about the canoe?" Lori asks.

"We'll just have to leave it and come back after the water goes down," Randy says. "But it's gone. It's dead in the water."

"Kaput. Finis. The end," I add.

"The end of our canoe adventures," he says. "That's for sure. And I'm out one canoe."

"I'm really sorry about that, Randy."

"Sorry. Is that all you can say? It was your fault. You said, 'Go right,' so we went right. We would've been okay if we'd gone left. But no, I let you take us the wrong way, and you destroyed my canoe. You did, and you know it."

"It was an accident, Randy. You know that," I say.

"Everything will be just fine when you buy me a new one."

"What? You're crazy if you think I'll buy you a new canoe. You knew we were taking a chance with it. You knew it was a dangerous river. But you went anyway. That's just the way the cookie crumbles."

Rats. You're out a canoe, but I'm out a hundred dollars – from Brett!

Chapter 12—Scrap Metal

"Dad's really mad," Randy tells us. We're meeting outside his garage again. "I knew he would be. First he said, 'I thought you knew how to canoe.' Then, 'It's Garth's canoe, you know. I bought it for him, you borrowed it, you wrecked it, and you can get him another one just like it. . . . And do it before he comes home next month.'

"Then he asked, 'Is that friend of yours going to help pay for it?' I said yes. And then he said, 'You better get that wreck back out when the water goes down. It's worth a lot of money to a junk dealer because it's all aluminum. Don't you let anyone else get it.'"

"I'll hop on it," I said. "As soon as the river goes down a little, we can get it out. You know, maybe the damage isn't as bad as we think. We'll see."

I talk to Lori later. She had told her parents the whole story. They felt really sad about it. Her mom said it was too bad because we'd had so much fun with it.

I was a little vague with my parents. "We had an accident with the canoe. It got banged up pretty bad."

"Oh?" Dad says. "Is it still seaworthy?"

Sure. It only leaks over both ends when you hold it up in the middle and fill it with water. I'm glad parents can't read minds.

"Yeah, mainly," I say, "but we'll have to test it before we take it out again." *That's true in part; first we have to work on it, and then we have to test it.*

The rain stops that night, but the river rises some more the next day. I monitor it twice a day, confirm that the metal corpse is still washed up against the little tree, and wonder how the heck it could have happened.

On Saturday, the river starts to go down, and on late Sunday afternoon, Randy and I pick up Lori and drive down Shalecliff Lane into the park. We're wearing our swimsuits. We park near the ford, which still has a few inches of water flowing over it, and look past it to our broken hulk.

"Well, here goes nothing," I say.

The three of us start wading in with me carrying Randy's hundred-foot coil of stout rope. The water is little more than two feet deep now. It pushes against our legs, but we're able to keep our balance. When we reach the canoe, Randy gets on one end, and Lori and I, the other, and we try to push it off the tree. It still doesn't budge. It's like it's glued or screwed or something.

"Darn!" I say. "Half of it's out of the water, and it still won't move."

We try rocking it, and it moves a little, but not enough.

"Okay," I say. "Let's try the rope."

We put it through the bow grommet and tie it fast with two half hitches, and then walk the rope out into the water. Randy puts it over his shoulder while Lori and I try to pull it along with both hands. We tug and tug, but make no progress.

"Let's try the car," Randy says.

We take the end of the rope to the car, which Randy reparks parallel to the rope. We tie the rope around the bumper, again fastening it with two half hitches, and then get in the car.

"I hope the rope doesn't break," Lori says.

"Take it easy," I caution.

He puts it in first, and slowly edges forward. The rope gets tauter and tauter in a straight line from the canoe.

"It's moving," Lori says, looking out the back window, and we watch the canoe start floating down the river. The rope stops it at the ford, and we get out and pull the metal body to shore. Water rushes out of the stern as we pull it up on the bank.

"Hell," Randy says. "We won't even be able to get it on the car, it's so bent up." We lay it on its side on the road. It's folded, inside out, into a wide *V*.

"Let's see what we can do with it," I say. "Let's turn it upside down. You two hold the bow and stern and keep it from falling over, and I'll sit on it. Don't let it move."

I sit on it, but nothing happens. I bounce on it, it turns over, and I end up sitting on the ground."

"Hold it up, you two!" I growl. "Are you weaklings?"

"I'm trying!" Lori snaps.

We pull it up again, and this time, Randy bends his legs and back and puts his thighs against it and really holds it, and Lori gets a better grip. This time I start bouncing on it as hard as I can, and it starts to straighten out.

"It's moving," I holler.

Lori has to put her end on the ground, but Randy holds his up. I keep bouncing until it's nearly flat with me sitting in it; then I stand up, climb up on it, bend over, and start jumping on it until it flattens some more. Unfortunately, the center thwart has come loose and the sides are only up a foot.

"The keel is broken," Randy says.

"It's not quite seaworthy yet," I say.

"What?" he shouts. "You think we can make it right? Is that what you think? Do you know how to weld aluminum? That keel has to be welded. And the thwart has to be rescrewed. The screws ripped through the aluminum."

Lori just stands there shaking her head.

"Maybe we can find someone to do it."

We load the carcass onto the car, and it's spread so much that it goes almost to the side edges of the rooftop carrier. We tie it down and drive to his house. Luckily, his parents aren't home.

"Let's put it in the backyard," Randy says. "I don't want anyone to see it."

Randy and I carry it around the house, lay it on the ground, and look at it again.

"There's no way we can get this back the way it was," he says.

"Well, let's give it a try. Let's turn it upside down over a log or something."

We go into the woods behind his house, and Lori helps us pull out a dead tree, about four inches in diameter, and lay it on the ground. We put the canoe over it. Then Randy sits on the bow, and I sit on the stern, and we start bouncing. It works. The bottom straightens out.

"That's a start," Lori says.

"Now all we have to do is fix the sides."

We turn it on its side, and the three of us sit on the gunwale and bounce. The side moves a little, but refuses to assume its former shape.

"What if we hammer it? With a sledgehammer. Got one?"

"Yeah. A twenty-pounder."

He goes around the house into the garage and returns, while Lori and I stand around like we're in a hospital surgical unit watching a dying patient.

Randy and I tip the canoe on its side, and the two of them hold it while I start banging on it with the long-handle sledgehammer—hard, harder, and then as hard as I can—swinging in arcs over my head and down onto the suffering beast. Twang! Twang! I feel bad about it. It doesn't deserve this punishment, this torture!

"Give up, Klossen. It ain't gonna work. We would need a big vice to crush it sideways. Where would we get that?"

I think a minute. "We've got the car. We can use it to push the sides together."

We carry it around to the front of the house, prop the ends on two lawn chairs against the corner of the brick wall, keel down, and Randy starts slowly backing into it, pushing it with the bumper.

"It's bending," Lori says. Then Randy lurches the car and bends the sides too far. I yell, "Stop," throwing up my hands, but it's too late. He has crushed it much too far.

He hops out and looks. "Hell!" he says. "Now what do we do?"

We take it down to the ground. Fortunately, the chairs and the brick are not damaged. But the sides of the canoe are bent inward at different angles, and the loose thwart is resting on top.

"Now all we have to do is spread it a foot."

"It'll never work, Klossen."

"If we had something like a big wedge we could drive in there. . . . "

"Forget it, Klossen. This thing is a total wreck. We'll never get the sides bent out at the right angle. And they'll never be high enough. They're all flattened. And if we could do that, we'd still have to find someplace to get the keel welded. And look. There's a hole in the bottom where the keel broke. What do we put in there, chewing gum? And re-screw the thwart somehow? This is not possible. This canoe is totaled. Gone! This canoe is scrap metal."

I give up. "You're right."

Lori suggests that we have a moment of silence for the death of our friend, and we bow our heads. It really has been our friend.

"Amen," she says.

"So be it," I say.

We carry it back behind the house.

"At least we can sell it for scrap," Randy says.

I pass Brett on the way to dinner that night. He's on his way to visit Annie. "I heard about your little accident. Too bad, too sad," he sighs, like he's standing over my coffin, gloating. "You might as well pay me now."

"It's not Labor Day yet, brat."

Scrap. It's not scrap. All we need is for someone who knows what he's doing and has the right tools to bend it out and weld it. I need to call a place that sells canoes. They'll know where we can take it to have the work done. The next morning, I look in the phone book under canoes. Nothing there. Under boats and canoes, I find Lake Erie Boating in Vermilion and call them.

"I have a problem. I turned my aluminum canoe inside out, and I'm looking for someone who can bend it back and re-weld the keel and patch the hole."

Silence. Then awe. "You did what?"

I tell him the story.

"God. Where did it happen?"

"On Shale River."

"Shale River? It's just a stream."

"On Thursday it was a raging torrent. I had to jump off the tree into the water and was lucky to get out alive."

"I never would have thought of it getting that big."

"Big and mean. So can you help me?"

"No. We just sell boats and canoes. You might try Erie Marina and Boat Service over in Lorain. They do welding and repairs."

"Thanks."

"Good luck."

I think they will remember my call.

I call Erie Marina. The man sounds like he feels sorry for me. "There's not much you can do with a canoe like that. You can jump on it and try to hammer it out. It would take hours and hours, and then you could never get it right. It would cost a fortune for us to do it for you, plus the welding. You could try doing it yourself, but like I say, you'd probably never get it right. You might as well call it a total loss and sell it for scrap."

Thus begins our early August depression. I ask myself, is this how the summer will end? Is this right? My goal languishing unachieved—to canoe all navigable lakes and waterways in the area? Undeterred, I resolve to look for a used canoe.

Later, I check the phone book and find several places dealing with scrap metal. I call one.

"Do you buy aluminum?"

"Yeah," comes the gruff voice.

"What do you pay for it?"

"The going price is twenty cents a pound."

I gasp. "Is that all?"

"You can check around. Everyone pays about the same. What've you got?"

"It's really good aluminum—a wrecked canoe. What can you pay for it?"

"Like I said, twenty cents a pound. How much does it weigh?"

"About eighty pounds."

"Let's see. Eighty pounds at twenty cents a pound. That'd be sixteen dollars."

"Sixteen dollars! Is that all it's worth?"

"That's all it's worth to me. Bring it in in four-foot pieces. And does it have any wood or anything in it?"

"It has blocks of foam in both ends for flotation."

"They gotta come out."

"I don't have any way of cutting it up or taking out the foam. Can you do it?"

"Yeah, but it'll cost you."

"How much?"

"Oh, I don't know. It might take two men two hours. I'll have to charge you ten dollars."

"Ten dollars! So you can only give me six dollars for the canoe?"

"That's it. You can check around, but that's all I can give you."

"Okay. Thanks." *Darn!*

I tell Randy.

"Six dollars!" he moans, "for a six-hundred-dollar canoe? Dad'll kill me. Garth'll kill me. I'll get more for it than that." He starts making his own calls, and the story is the same—twenty cents a pound. But he doesn't tell them about the foam in the ends.

Two days later we load the deceased on top of the car and take it to the dealer (of his choice), Anchor Scrap Metal. It's near a railroad yard off Fulton Avenue. Piles of junk cars, crushed cars, and separated metals line both sides of a roadway. A huge magnet hanging from a crane mounted on tracks waits to be used while a rubber-tire loader with big pincers on the front carries cars into a large metal building with a sign on one corner that says "Office." The three of us go in and stand at the counter. A short man with a fat belly and bulging muscles wearing a T-shirt and chewing on a cigar comes up and looks at us with no expression.

Randy says, "I called earlier. We have that aluminum canoe."

"Yeah. Twenty cents a pound. Bring it to the door. We need to take out the foam."

"Is there an extra charge for that?" I ask.

"Yeah. Five dollars an hour."

Randy looks at me and shakes his head.

"Do you want to take out the foam and bring it back?" the man asks.

"No," Randy says quickly.

"Okay. Drive it up here by the big door." He pushes a button on a microphone and starts talking. We can hear it on the loudspeakers in the back of the building. "Ralph and Joe to the front. Bring wrecking bars and a big sledge."

We drive up and take the hulk off the car. Two men in long-sleeve work shirts and gloves walk up, one young with a broad back, the other middle-aged and wiry. Both are wearing goggles around their necks and carrying the tools.

Ralph and Joe attack the bow and stern bulkheads where they meet the bottom of the canoe, and in ten minutes, break the welds with the bars and hammers, bend the bulkheads up, jerk out the foam, and throw it in a Dumpster while the office man looks on. Then they pick up the canoe, carry it into the building, return in a few minutes with a printed ticket, and give it to the office man.

"Sixty-eight pounds," he says, "times twenty cents is thirteen dollars and sixty cents, minus twenty minutes at five dollars is a dollar sixty-six; comes to eleven dollars and ninety-three cents."

"Hell," Randy says, shaking his head. "I can't believe it."

"That's all it's worth, bud. Sorry."

He takes a ten, a one, and ninety-three cents from a drawer under the counter and hands it to Randy. We thank him and leave.

"We didn't cut it up into four-foot pieces. At least he didn't charge for that," I say.

That night I start checking the phone book under "Used Boats and Canoes," and make some calls, but the prices are too high. Dealers get their cut, I guess. Then I start searching the newspaper classifieds every day, and every day there's nothing. I've got to get my mind off it.

Cleaning day. "Get up!" roars the drill sergeant. "Clean up this room! Helen will be here in half an hour. This room's a mess. I will not have Helen come in here until it's cleaned up. Now get up. You have lawns to mow, and I need you to babysit this afternoon. Get up!"

I sit up in bed, rub my eyes, throw my feet over the side, and go to work.

Now it's Helen's turn. She knocks and booms! "Mr. Jeff? When will this room be ready for me?"

"Just a minute, just a minute." I race around, picking up, and then fling the door open and say good morning with a grin. Then I get out of her way as she drags in the canister vacuum.

"Say, Helen, can I ask you a question?"

Suspicion crosses her face. "What about?"

"Can you tell me why no Negroes live in Orchard Park?"

"Why do you want to know that?"

"I'm just curious."

"What makes you think we Negroes would want to live in Orchard Park?"

Of course they'd want to live here. "Well. It's a nice place. Nice houses and people. Great schools. Good roads, police and fire departments, and recreation department. Good shopping at the mall. Lots of things to do."

"Those are things we want. But what Negroes do you think could afford to live here?"

"Oh, I bet lots could afford it. A lot of our houses are pretty small, away from the lake."

"But the taxes are high."

"I bet lots of Negro doctors and lawyers and professionals could afford it."

"But, Jeff," she says, shaking her head and looking out the window. "Our families all live on the East Side. And you don't have any Negro churches here, or soul-food restaurants, or clubs, or beauty shops or anything. Where would we get our hair done? Our folks would have to go back to the city to find our kind and the things we're comfortable with, honey." I sit and nod. "And a lot of Negroes aren't comfortable around white people. And a lot of white folk aren't comfortable around us. I don't think they'd make us feel welcome. Why would we want to live where people don't want us?"

What a shock. They don't want to live near us either. Funny. A lot of Negroes work with white people, but they don't want to live near them? Is there something wrong with us? And a lot of white people believe that a single Negro family lowers property values in the neighborhood. That's why they have to be all white.

I'm dying to see Lori alone. I call her up after dinner and ask her if I can come over. I tell her we need to talk about integration some more, and about what we're going to do next. She says, "Sure. My parents are going to a concert, and I don't have any babysitting, so I'm free." Her voice has a sly sound and is a little breathy. I've gotta say, it turns me on.

I tell Mom and Dad I have to go to Randy's. They don't need to know where I'm really going.

Lori opens the door and smiles. Scottie's on the back porch. He barks until Lori shouts! "It's okay, Scottie."

She's wearing a blouse and shorts. We sit on the sofa, and she asks if I want a Coke. I say sure, and she hops up. She returns and hands it to me.

"Here you are, sir."

Now she takes me by surprise. She jumps on the sofa beside me, puts an arm over my shoulder, and says, "Now. What did you want to talk about?" I look at her mouth, and she looks at mine, and we start kissing, on and on, until I almost lose consciousness. We come up for air when a car door slams outside, and she says, "Quick. Sit up. Pick up that magazine. Look like you're reading. Tell them I'm in the bathroom."

Her parents come in and I ask how the concert was, and so on. The toilet flushes, and Lori emerges, straightened, and we continue our discussion. Her dad looks at me with his squinty eyes, like "I know what you're up to, bud." But they eventually drift away, and Lori positions herself on the other end of the sofa.

We talk about the canoe, and I tell her about searching the newspaper classifieds every day. "There's nothing," I say. Then I tell her what Helen said about Negroes not wanting to live with whites.

She's asks, "But is it true? We've got to talk to some more people and see what they say."

"Right. Corroborate the information."

"Yay. Ten points for that word. But who next?"

Chapter 13—Dr. Wallace and Edgewater Park

"I got us an appointment for tomorrow afternoon at three," I tell her over the phone. "Can you come?"

"I'll have to ask, but I'm sure I can," she says eagerly. "Where's the appointment?"

"Western Reserve Historical Society . . . with Dr. Conroy Wallace. He's a Western Reserve history professor and a historian for the Society."

"Let's go early so we can walk around the lagoon in front of the art museum . . . across from Severance Hall. And we can have a picnic on the museum steps by that Rodin statue of *The Thinker*."

"Maybe he can help us think," I say in a rational tone, hiding the fire she's lit inside me.

"Yes. And afterward, maybe we could drive through Rockefeller Park too. . . . "

"Yeah." I'm starting to blaze.

"I'd love to stop there and look at some of the wildlife," she says, "but it's probably not safe there now."

"Oh. You mean . . . "

"Yeah. The whole area is Negro now," she says.

"Maybe we could stop at Edgewater Park on the way back, and watch some submarine races."

"In broad daylight? People only watch them at night . . . when they're making out," she says slyly.

"Yes, but you can't see the submarines at night and you can't see them in daylight, so what's the difference?"

"I get it."

I take a chance. "I bet we can find some woods there."

"I'll bring a blanket."

Oooh. Let's go now and skip the appointment.

We walk up the steps under a high stone arch and into the main entrance. I tell the guard at the desk that we're here to see Dr. Wallace and have a three o'clock appointment. He makes a call, and soon a short man with a full brown beard and a paisley tie walks through the door and gives us a warm smile. He's in his early forties, I'd say, and has a medium build and thinning brown hair.

"Dr. Wallace?" I ask.

"Yes. And you're Mr. Klossen? And Miss—"

"Matthews," Lori says. "Lori Matthews."

We follow him into the library reading room—a large space with a high ceiling guarded on all sides by Greek columns with curlicues on top. Dark wood reading tables and chairs fill the center of the room, and on three sides are library stacks, two stories high. A librarian sits behind a counter on the left. We follow Dr. Wallace down an aisle between the stacks and the offices, turn left, go to the end, and read the plaque on the heavy oak door: "Dr. Conroy Wallace—History."

"And what brings you two to Western Reserve Historical Society in the middle of the summer—some sort of a report or something?"

"No," I say. "We live on the West Side, in Orchard Park, and we're just curious. We want to learn why there are no Negroes living there, or on most of the West Side, for that matter."

"Ah. Good question. I think it will keep us busy for the next hour. That's when my next appointment is. And you were right to consult a historian on this matter. The answers start deep in the past." He smiles, but taps nervously on his desk with his pen.

"So, I will give you a sixty-minute course on the racial migrations in Cleveland. But first let me suggest a book to you—*Forbidden Neighbors: A Study of Prejudice in Housing* by Charles Abrams, and, of course, *An American Dilemma* by Gunnar Myrdal."

"I brought a map of Cleveland if that will help."

"Good. Let's spread it out here on that table."

The next hour is nonstop talk. Lori takes notes, and I just try to absorb everything. First, he tells us all about how the Irish and Germans came to Cleveland around 1830 to build the Ohio and Erie Canal that went from the Ohio River to Cleveland. The canal made Cleveland a major port on the Great Lakes. Thousands of immigrants worked loading and unloading boats. Then railroads replaced the canals, and they employed more immigrant labor building and maintaining them. Before the Civil War, the city began to grow into a manufacturing center, mostly in the flats along the river. Refineries and factories made oil products, iron, steel, lake freighters, railroad rails, trucks, carriages, and other products.

"Were there many Negroes then?" I ask.

"Not many."

"Where did they live?"

"Mostly spread throughout the white areas on the East Side, although some lived in one area downtown—here." He circles the area with his pencil.

"Any on the West Side?"

"Very few."

"You say there weren't many Negroes in Cleveland then," Lori says, "but there are a lot of them now. When did they come?"

"They came in the Great Migrations. The first was during World War I, from 1914–1918. Our young men were fighting overseas. Immigration stopped, and factory owners needed more workers, so they went south and recruited Negroes to work in the factories. Thousands came, and they continued to come in the twenties and thirties.

"During World War II, from 1940–45, we had the second Great Migration. Thousands more came, but there was nowhere for them to live, so they ended up squeezing into houses in white areas. But whites didn't want to live near poor, rural Negroes and were afraid of crime and afraid their property values would go down. So they tried to keep the Negroes out of their neighborhoods. 'Whites only' became the unofficial policy of the Real Estate Board, and owners began putting restrictive covenants in deeds saying that the property could never be sold to Negroes. White people even tried violence and the threat of violence to keep Negroes out—bombings and fires and shootings."

Lori pales. "Really?"

"I'm afraid so."

"And all this happened on the East Side," I say. "Why didn't Negroes move to the West Side too?"

"Two reasons, mainly: first, the Cuyahoga River industrial zone was a natural barrier; and second, new arrivals tended to settle near the other Negroes living in the downtown area on the east side of the river."

"What direction did they go?" Lori asks.

He draws a large arrow on the map showing the direction of the movement.

"The Negro population moved to the east and southeast. It wasn't that they wanted to live with white people necessarily; they just wanted better housing for their families. They migrated like a chain with one link holding firmly to the one behind it, keeping a strong bond to their community while moving street by street. They were aided by block-busters—real estate salesmen who created panic among white people, scaring them into believing their property values would go down and crime would increase when Negroes moved in. The movement of whites out of the city was also assisted by trolleys and automobiles, which allowed people to live in the suburbs and work downtown."

Lori purses her lips, touches them with the point of the pencil, and asks, "Were some white people more willing to sell than others?"

I watch her as she speaks. *She's quite a girl.*

"Yes. On the East Side, immigrants from Great Britain, Russian Jews, and native-born Americans who were ready to move up to better neighborhoods were more amenable to selling. But the Poles, Czechs, Ukrainians, Hungarians, and Italians wanted to maintain their neighborhoods, and they offered stiff resistance.

"On the West Side, the Irish and Germans refused to sell. The Irish lived along the river here," (he draws circles around the areas). "They were tight-knit and would not let Negroes move in. They competed with Negroes for laboring jobs and were hostile to them. And the Poles, Ukrainians, Lithuanians, and Appalachian migrants on the West Side all kept Negroes out. You see, in Cleveland people have tended to live with others like themselves in many different ethnic neighborhoods: German, Irish, Czech, Slavic, Italian, Polish, Hungarian, Romanian, Ukrainian, Yugoslav, Russian, and Negro." He circles the concentrations on the map.

I'm starting to lose concentration. "Polian, Rokranian, Yugosian, Goslavian, and Negro," that's what I hear. Lucky for me, Lori's taking notes. . . .

Our hour is up.

"Thank you so much," Lori says as I fold up the map, now embroidered with ovals and arrows.

I shake his hand, thank him, and we leave.

On the way to the car, Lori says, "It's like everyone wants homogeneity—they like to live with people like themselves and stay away from people who are different."

"And that's why Orchard Park doesn't have Negroes."

"But after a few generations," she says, "most immigrants melt into the population, once they learn our language and customs."

"Yes, but Negroes don't melt in. They look different. And people don't understand them. And they're afraid of them. So we keep them out no matter what."

We stop at the street, watch cars pass, and cross into the parking lot.

"You know," I say, "America used to be a melting pot. But now we don't put different kinds of people in the pot and melt them together."

"No, people try to live just with people like themselves. We have all these ethnic neighborhoods, and each group tries to stick together and keep other kinds of people out."

"Birds of a feather flock together."

"Yes."

My mind soars to thousands of starlings I saw settling into a grove one evening and then rising in a cloud and swirling, rolling, and turning in synchronized waves. What a sight!

She looks at me quizzically. "Jeff. Are you there?"

"Sorry."

"But don't you think it's like that all over the world? People stay together in their own countries and villages. And they're separated from the other ones by language, and religion, and race."

"Yeah. In their own tribes. Just like animals—lions and zebras and buffalo and giraffes; they all stay with their own kind too. Ants and wasps too. And they're always fighting each other."

"But we're not animals," she protests. "We're people."

"Yes. And like I say—we're all of one blood. Black and white and brown and yellow."

"All the same species."

"Yeah, except we white people think we're better and smarter than colored people, and if we mix with colored people, the white race will get dumber."

"That's what Hitler thought, too," she says. "He thought his Aryan race was superior to other races, and he wanted to keep it pure."

We reach the car, and she bumps up against me as I open the door for her. I give her a sideways hug, and when I get in, she scoots over next to me on the seat. My blood is racing, and my thoughts about Negroes are over. Anyway, our brains are worn out now with too much thinking.

We drive through Rockefeller Park to the Shoreway and head west by Lakefront Airport, through downtown, and over the Flats to the park. I keep one arm around her and steer with the other.

We turn off at Edgewater Park. I take the road to the high part away from the big beach and stop near the steep stairs. "I'll race you to the bottom and back," I say. *That'll calm me down.*

"Can't you read the sign? 'Danger: Hazardous and Steep Areas. No Swimming—No Diving.'"

"There're only about a hundred steps."

"And no handrail."

"Come on," I say. "We can do it. I dare you."

"You go first. I'll watch."

I see a vision of me tumbling down the stairs into a heap of broken bones, that followed by one of me climbing almost to the top, missing a step, falling forward, and sliding to the bottom—hitting my chin on every step.

"There. I'm already back. Faster than the speed of light. You probably didn't even see me do it. Now it's your turn."

"Sure."

We're quiet. Then she says, "Why don't you park over there, and we can take a walk through the woods."

I say nothing, just move the car. She gets out and picks up the blanket from the backseat, and we start walking along the path. I put my arm around her waist, and we bump along. She's shorter than I am, and her hip fits nicely below mine.

We come to some big oaks. Between them, large bushes line the path, and among them I see a small space. "In there," I whisper. I hold back the branches. The clearing is big enough for the blanket, but nothing else. We look all around, and it seems well hidden. She nods, and I follow her. After spreading the blanket, she drops on her knees, rolls onto her back, and holds out her arms. And then we are woven together, our hands stroking and caressing. We deep kiss (I'm used to those braces now and like the way they feel). My mind drifts into oblivion and everything else fades away, until I hear someone walking by on the path above us, about ten feet away. I put my hand over her mouth, and we wait. The sound fades.

"We better go," she whispers. She sits up cross-legged, runs her fingers through her hair, pulls out a twig or two, and straightens her blouse.

I can hardly contain myself. "You're so wonderful, Lori. I—I love you."

She looks into my eyes. "You're sweet, Jeff."

We fold up the blanket, hurry to the car, and drive away.

After that I have only one thing on my mind. We try to plan another tryst on the way home. It can't be tonight or tomorrow. But it'll have to be soon.

At home, I lie on my bed, and force my mind to think about canoeing—shooting rapids past boulders and haystacks—pulling and straining every muscle. . . . I think of Brett. I have to get two more trips together or I lose a hundred bucks. We still have to do the lower Cuyahoga River and Lake Erie. Maybe we can do them both at once. If only we had a canoe.

My mind veers to our probe and what Helen said. Do Negroes not want to live here or are they kept out—by bankers and builders, and who else? I call Lori and try to keep my mind on business.

Chapter 14—Mr. Clark and Birds of a Feather

"Do you think real estate people tell them they don't have any homes for sale here . . . and that they should look in other towns?" I ask Lori on the phone.

"I don't know. Maybe we should talk to one and see what he says."

"Who?"

"I don't know any," she says.

"Well, there is Randy's father. Do you think Randy would mind if we talked to his dad about careers in real estate?"

She pauses. "I guess not. But are you going to just come right out and ask his dad? I don't think he'll tell you anything if you do."

"I would never do that. You know me."

The next day, Mom's using the car, so Lori and I get on the Detroit Road bus and get off at Mr. Clark's real estate office near the Westview Hotel. We ask the middle-aged receptionist if we can see him, and she calls him on the phone and then sends us back. He rises from his chair as we go in. He's a big man, like Randy, but heavier and stronger looking. He looks like he's lifted weights. But he still has Randy's big eyes and pointy chin. His desk has a brass nameplate with "Gerald Clark" inscribed in gold letters, and a small American flag. He leans over it and shakes my hand.

"What can I do for you, Jeff?"

"Hi. You know Lori, don't you?"

"Sure. You live up the street," he says to her. She nods. "You go canoeing with Randy."

"Yes."

"I was sorry to hear about your wreck. I hope you can do something about replacing the canoe. It's Garth's, and he's coming home in a few weeks."

"Yes, sir. I keep checking the classified ads in the paper to find a good used one."

"Good. Now, what can I do for you?"

"Well, Lori and I aren't sure what job we want to do after college and how to prepare for it, so we decided to talk to some people about what they do and see if we can make some plans. Do you have a few minutes?"

"Sure. Have a seat." We all sit down. He relaxes and seems pleased that we're interested in what he does.

We ask him all kinds of questions. How he got into it. What he likes about it. What he doesn't like about it. What courses he would recommend we take, what degree to pursue, what certifications we would need. He says some economics and real estate appraisal courses and architecture or construction courses would be useful. The answers gush out of him like a stream into a lake. "And it's good to get some practical knowledge about how houses and buildings are built. I worked for a builder in the summer when I was in school."

"Anything else?" I ask.

"You have to be good with people. You have to find out what they can afford, and then see what's available that meets their needs and pocketbook."

"You know, one thing I've been wondering is why there aren't any Negroes in town," I say, popping the question at last. "Why is that?"

He stiffens and says, "I don't think they want to live here, Jeff."

"Have any ever come to you looking for a house?"

"Actually, no. I never had any."

"That's surprising," I say. "This is such a nice town. Great schools. Close to downtown. The houses aren't too expensive. . . ."

"I think they're happier living with their own people, Jeff, over on the East Side."

"Do you think they bring down property values?" Lori asks.

He frowns. I can see he's starting to get irritated. "I know that some people don't care for them and don't want to live next to them, and if those people try to sell their houses, they might not get as much money as they should because Negroes live next to them. So yes, I'd say your property values do go down if you have some move in next to you."

"Do you feel it's part of your job to try to help people keep their property values up?" I ask.

Now he's mad. "You sound like you want Negroes here. Do you want what happened in Hough on the East Side to happen here? In ten years, sixty thousand Negroes forced forty thousand white people out of their homes in those Hough neighborhoods, squeezing all their children and relatives into those white homes. There was panic selling and blockbusting and bombings and cross burnings and everybody racing to get whatever money they could and get out. And the same thing happened over in Glenville. Is that what you want to happen to Orchard Park? Do you want Orchard Park to become all Negro? It can happen here. Do you want them to ruin this town too?"

I keep shaking my head. "No, sir, no, sir."

The interview ends abruptly. "You know, I'd like to keep answering your questions, but I have to make a living, and I need to get back to work."

We thank him, shake hands again, and leave.

Later, Lori and I talk to Randy in his garage.

"You sure ticked off my dad," he says. "What'd you say to him?"

"We just asked him why there weren't any Negroes in Orchard Park."

"What'd he say?"

"He just said they didn't want to live here."

"And that made him mad?"

"I don't know. I asked him if any had ever come to his office looking for a house. He said no, and I said that that was surprising because Orchard Park is such a nice place to live. Maybe it sounded like I didn't believe him."

"Well, did you?"

"I don't know."

He puffs up his chest and tenses his back like he's posing for a swimming picture and says, "So! What you're saying is that you think my dad's a liar."

"I didn't say that. You said that."

"Why, you . . . "

He takes a step toward me, fists clenched. I tense up, preparing myself, but Lori steps between us.

"Okay, boys. No fights. Come on. You're friends."

Randy backs off a step. "Negro lovers. What were you even doing there?"

"We already told you—we're trying to get information on different careers. We don't have our lives already planned out like you do, Randy." Randy wants to go to Case and become a mechanical engineer.

We were quiet for a long time after that, but I sensed that this wasn't the end of it.

After dinner that night, the phone rings. Someone picks it up. I'm lying on my back in bed reading the *Classics Illustrated* edition of *Dr. Jekyll and Mr. Hyde*.

Dad knocks twice, opens my door without waiting for a response, leans his head in, and says, "Jeff. That was Mr. Clark, Randy's dad. He's very angry. Something about you accusing him of trying to keep Negroes out of Orchard Park. What's going on?"

I sit up. "Lori and I were just interviewing him to learn what his job is like, Dad. You know, we're exploring different careers, and he sells real estate. And I was interested in what he would do if a Negro came into his office looking for a house, that's all. But it doesn't matter because he says Negroes never look for houses in Orchard Park."

"I don't want to hear about you stirring up anyone else with this kind of question, do you understand? If you do, there will be consequences. We've worked hard to get a good reputation in this community, and I don't want to see it ruined."

The master has spoken. "I understand. I won't ask any more real estate people about Negroes. I sure don't want to make anybody mad."

"All right."

We decide to see if we can find some more history about the West Side, so this time we take the bus to Fenn College downtown. Lori is wearing a pretty blue flowered skirt and white blouse. I'm sitting next to her, getting turned on just looking at her. I'd like to put my hand on her leg—try it at least—but there's a woman in the seat across the aisle who keeps glancing at us.

"Who are we going to talk to?" she asks.

"I don't have an appointment. We'll just have to canoodle our way in—use big words and act important."

"Okay, Mr. Big Shot. Just as long as you don't do the other kind of canoodling and start making out with the women."

We cross the Detroit-Superior Bridge to Public Square, change to the Euclid Avenue bus, get off at East Twenty-Fourth Street, and walk past Fenn Tower.

"Don't look up," I say. "You'll strain your neck." It's twenty stories high and full of classrooms, labs, and dorm rooms. We pass it, enter Stilwell Hall on the left, and walk into the library. It's typical: flat ceiling with fluorescent panels, stacks full of books, high windows lighting the aisles, and a central area with tables and chairs.

We walk past the desk like we own the place and find a table. Other students and some older people sit reading and taking notes. "Let's see what we can find."

"I'll check the card catalog," she says.

"I'll be in the history stacks."

Lori comes to my rescue soon with some call numbers while I'm still trying to find the Cleveland history section.

"A few look promising," she says.

We take out some general histories of Cleveland, carry them to the table, and start looking through them. There seems to be a lot of information about the canal and railroad and industry, but not much on ethnic groups.

While we're working, I see a tall man with dark hair in a brown suit and bow tie approach a library cart. He bends over and pulls out a book. I nod to Lori, and we approach him.

"Excuse me, sir," I say in an audible whisper. He straightens up and looks at me. "Are you the librarian?"

"Yes. I'm Mr. Wheeling."

"I'm Jeff Klossen, and this is Lori Matthews. We're working on a history project on ethnic groups in Cleveland, especially on the West Side."

"Oh?"

"We want to know how exclusive their communities are, how difficult it is for members of other groups to move into their neighborhoods, and how their members have assimilated into the community at large." Wow. I didn't know I knew so many big words.

He looks a little lost.

"We're especially interested in the Irish," Lori says.

"This sounds like a sociology project."

Oops. "It's both, sir."

"I know one study that might help you. It's called *Irish Americans and Their Communities of Cleveland* by Callahan and Hickey. It's in our Ethnic Groups room. Come with me."

We follow him into a small room. One wall contains books, and there are two tables and some chairs. He walks over, locates two books, and hands them to me. One is the Irish book, and the other is on Hungarian Communities.

"First dibs," says Lori, taking the Irish book.

I shrug at Lori and thank Mr. Wheeling.

"Just leave them on the table when you're done."

He leaves the room. "We're alone, Lori."

"Forget it, Klossen."

We read for an hour. She takes notes assiduously (that's another favorite SAT word of mine).

"Listen to this," she says, looking at her notes. "It says that on the East Side, the Irish were mostly concerned with moving up and out, but on the West Side, moving out of the Irish neighborhood was like giving up your heritage.

"There were two Irish Catholic parishes along the river on the West Side. The Yankee establishment let the Irish know that they were not welcome in other parts of town. The Irish were rough people and used to drink and fight a lot. They were laborers who spent all day shoveling iron ore and limestone and coal. The mother Irish parish on the West Side was St. Patrick Parish on Bridge Avenue. It was near the ore docks on Whiskey Island. And get this—Whiskey Island had thirteen saloons within less than a third of a square mile of land. The Irish loved to drink."

"They should have called it Saloon Island."

"He says the community there was very close. The pastor told his parishioners not to mix with native Americans or Germans, and Catholics were to marry only other Catholics, preferably Irish.

"Wow."

"Just north of this was St. Malachi Parish. The two communities together were called 'The Angle.' This one included the shacks on Irishtown Bend on the river. It was a true Irish ghetto, too—close-knit and poor, much poorer than the Irish neighborhoods on the East Side. And it stayed together for a century, from 1850 until after World War II. Since 1950, though, they've been moving out to the suburbs. But even so, many of the West Side

Irish who now live in Cleveland's western suburbs are related to one another and are aware of their relationships. It says that weddings and funerals and wakes are partly for the gathering of the clans."

"I like the way you say that, Lori."

"What?"

"Anything."

"Concentrate, Klossen. Listen to this. It says, 'On the East Side, the Irish were willing to sell their homes to Negroes when they moved, but on the West Side, the Irish considered that a betrayal of their neighbors and community . . . and they still do. And those West Side neighborhoods changed slowly because they were communities that were built around their church parish.'"

I add, "It's like we said when we were with Dr. Wallace—it looks like the Irish and the other ethnic groups blocked the movement of Negroes into the West Side."

"Birds of a feather flocking together," Lori says.

"Especially on the West Side."

On the bus on the way back, I start mulling things over and say, "You know, we might be at the end of this search, Lori."

"Let's make a list." She takes out her notebook, and we start reviewing the reasons again.

I start: "People won't sell their homes to Negroes because they don't want their neighbors to get mad at them for making their property values go down. That's one. And Helen said most Negroes don't want to live near us because they wouldn't feel welcome, and there wouldn't be any Negro churches and shops for them. That's two."

"Right," she says. "And don't forget 'birds of a feather' and that the Irish and Germans and other ethnic groups kept Negroes out of the West Side." She writes them down.

"White people feel like they are better than Negroes, and don't want their children to marry Negroes and have kids that aren't white. That's what my dad thinks." I see her jotting down "white superiority" and "intermarriage."

"Oh, and remember," she says, "the Negro migration moved like a chain to the east and southeast."

"Yeah. And Mr. Schutz said that builders and developers won't sell to Negroes because no one would buy homes in their development; and banks won't lend money to Negroes in an all-white development because it would make property values go down and they'd lose money."

We're both silent. Then I look at her. "Can you think of anything else?"

She shrugs her shoulders and shakes her head.

"I think those are the main reasons, Lori."

She nods. "I think so."

"You know, people might as well put out 'Whites Only' signs on the roads into town. That's the way it is. But it doesn't have to be this way. We don't have to keep living in a prison."

She smiles at me and shakes her head. "So what are you going to do, Klossen? Fight all these people to get them to change things? Or just move out? And go to college and find some group you like and never come back."

"Like I said before, we've got to do something to open this town to Negroes. We've got to try. The A-people won't do it. We've got to."

"What can we do?"

"I don't know. But we know what we're up against."

Chapter 15—Zonk, Becky, and the Piranhas

That's when the phone calls start—at least one a day. It rings, you pick it up, and there's silence. When Mom answers, she demands, "Who is this?" But it does no good. After more silence, there's a click. It's driving her crazy, and it's a little scary.

I get mad once and yell, "Go to hell!" and hang up. I shouldn't do that. I shouldn't let the caller know that he's getting to me.

I call Lori and talk to her about it, and she says they've been getting some too.

"I don't suppose it has anything to do with our interviews," she says.

"I bet it does. It could be any of those people."

"Or Randy? He was upset."

Canoes. I check the classifieds every morning. It's getting near the end of the summer. Surely some people will want to sell their boats now.

Saturday morning, I find one: "For sale: $100—Aluminum canoe—18′ with paddles, some dents and dings. No calls from dealers or services." It lists a Lakeshore number.

A hundred bucks, I think. *That's ten or twenty lawns. I don't want to spend a hundred bucks. But everything else is more. A new one's almost a thousand. What'll I get for a hundred? Dents and dings. Great. But I'll look. Maybe I can get the guy to come down.*

I dial the number. He answers in a nasal voice, and says I'm the third call he's had. I don't know if he's lying or not. I ask if I can see it. He gives me his address in Lakeshore and directions and tells me to be sure to bring the money. He won't hold it unless I pay for it.

I don't have a hundred bucks cash. All I can find is thirty. I ask Mom if I can borrow twenty, and the car. I have to tell her I want to look at a canoe, and it costs a hundred dollars.

"What happened to the other one?"

"Oh, you know, we had that wreck in Shale River, and now it leaks too much. . ." *now that we turned it inside out and the scrap dealer cut it up and crushed it!*

She tells me to get her purse, and gives me the money and keys.

"Is Randy going to share the cost?" she asks.

"Oh, yes, I'm sure he will. But he's caddying—I'll have to ask him tonight. But I have to see the guy with the canoe right now. It's the only one in the paper anywhere near that price. He might sell it to someone else."

"I hope it's a good one."

I drive over. The house is an older two-story with a big front porch, near Shale River Reservation. I couldn't miss the house. He's got the canoe right in the front yard with a sign on it, "$100.00." I park on the street and hop out. There's no one there yet, thank goodness. I don't want to get into a bidding war.

I walk up and start looking at it. It's upside down, so I can see most of the bottom. The ad wasn't lying. It has lots of dings and dents, none of which are too bad. *It has personality.* There are a lot of scrapes, but no patches, so no holes. And it's a gray color. I see where epoxy has been applied in three places along the keel seam and to some of the rivets. I start reaching up to turn it over when a tall, wiry old man with gray hair approaches. He hasn't shaved yet, and his face is tan and wrinkled. He's wearing a brown fedora that has been crushed, twisted, rolled, and stuffed a million times, faded jeans, a loose long-sleeve plaid shirt, and worn-out tennies. He looks to me like he's ready to hit the waves.

"You didn't waste any time," he says.

"Hi, Mr. Zonk."

"And you are . . . ?"

"Jeff Klossen. Am I the first customer?"

"Two guys in a car stopped, but they left before I could talk to them. So what do you think?"

"You told the truth about the dents and dings."

"I might as well. People are going to see it. I don't want to waste their time."

"Does it leak?"

"Does *she* leak. Her name's Becky. And yes, she has a leak. But it's slow. Just lay some strips on the bottom to lay your gear on and sponge her out every once in a while, and she does fine."

"Becky, huh? Can I see the inside?"

"Sure."

We turn it over on its back, and I look in. It's clean. It looks all right.

"Do these paddles go with it?" I ask, pointing to two old wooden paddles on the ground.

"Yeah." He picks one up and stands it up next to me, and sizes up my height and arms. "Looks like they'll fit you."

"So where've you gone canoeing?" I ask.

"All over—rivers and lakes in Ohio, Pennsylvania, West Virginia, Canada. How about you?"

"Lake Temagami in Ontario and all the rivers and lakes around here. But we had a little accident in Shale River." I tell him about it.

"Too bad. Those strainers can be bad." Then he looks me in the eye. "So, do you want to buy her?"

"I think so, sir. But can you take fifty dollars for her? That's all I've got."

He turns away, shaking his head. "No, no, no. A hundred is more than a fair price. You've seen the other prices in the paper, haven't you?"

"But this one does have a lot of dents in it, and it does leak."

"Just a little."

"Will you take sixty for it?"

"Oh. I get it. You're trying to beat me down."

"I only have fifty, but I may be able to get a little more from my buddy."

"The price is a hundred bucks."

"How about seventy?" He starts to walk away and I follow him. "We're buying it together, and I don't think he'll go over seventy with that leak and the dents and scrapes. I can try to talk him into a hundred, but I don't think he'll go that high. I would myself, but he's a lot tougher than I am. He'll laugh in my face when he sees this canoe."

He turns his head, but keeps walking toward the house. "I told you what the price is."

"Eighty bucks and you've got a deal. He'll never go over that."

He stops, turns around, and looks at me. "Why don't you go get him and bring him here so he can take a look?"

"I would, but he's working today. I can probably get him to come over this evening."

"It'll probably be sold by then, at this price."

"Maybe I could just put some money down, and then if he okays it, we can give you the rest then. How 'bout I put down twenty dollars."

He shakes his head. "That's not near enough. And the price is still a hundred dollars. Do you want it or not?"

"Can I put thirty down?"

"No."

"Forty?"

"You're getting close."

"Okay. I'll give you fifty dollars now and the rest when we pick it up."

He nods. "It's a deal."

"Can I get a receipt for the fifty?"

"Yeah, I'll write one out."

"And if I can't come up with the other fifty, I get my money back, right?"

That made him mad. "No, you don't get it back. If you can't get the rest of the money today, you're out of luck. I keep the fifty."

"How is that fair?"

"Listen. I can probably sell old Becky three or four times today while I'm waiting for you."

He gives me the receipt, noting that if I can't come up with the other fifty by eight o'clock, he keeps my deposit. We shake on it, and I go home. Some negotiation.

I don't want to talk to Randy about it. First of all, we'll get back into the argument about whose fault the wreck was and who should pay for the replacement and who owns it after we buy it. Right now, I don't care if he wins that one. We did wreck his brother's canoe after all. But then when he sees Becky and her dents and dings, he'll tell me I made a bad deal and he won't want to pay. But I've gotta have that last trip of the summer. I've got to. I have a bet to win.

It's six o'clock and drizzling. "I found a canoe," I tell him with an excited voice, wearing a great big smile.

"How much is it?"

"A hundred bucks. I put down fifty. Can you come up with the other fifty?"

Just like I thought, he wants to argue. "You want me to split the cost when you made us wreck?"

"Come on, Randy. You know it was just bad luck. A second earlier and we would've made it right around that tree."

"But you said, 'Go right.' You need to stand up like a man and accept responsibility for your actions."

"But you agreed with me that we should go right. Come on, Randy."

He shakes his head. "I don't know."

I start turning the screws. "Maybe Lori'll buy it with me. That way I can take the stern all the time and you and Lori can take halvsies on the trips." I am starting to get pissed, and he can tell.

"Okay. You win," he says. "I'll go look at it. But it better be good—as good as Garth's was."

"It's pretty good," I lie.

"And one other thing. I don't care if you do pay half. The canoe is Garth's—not yours or mine. Dad was really mad when we totaled it. He says he expects us to replace it before Garth comes home."

We get to Mr. Zonk's and walk up and look at it. Lori's tagging along, as usual.

"You said it was good," Randy says. "This thing's full of dents. It looks like someone's beat it with a sledgehammer. And look at all these scrapes and gouges on the bottom."

"It's not that bad," I say.

Mr. Zonk walks up and asks Randy, "What do you think?"

"I think it's one sad-looking canoe."

"She's seen a lot of white water and bounced off a lot of rocks and scraped over a lot of boulders and river bottoms, but Old Becky's still seaworthy. She'll get you where you want to go. Treat her right, and she'll be nice to you."

"I see epoxy on the keel in a couple of places. Does it leak?"

"Does *she* leak? Yes. There's a little seepage, but it's real slow. You can take care of it by wiping it with a sponge every once in a while. And you can probably fix the leak yourself. I'll throw in this epoxy kit. And here's a rubber mallet you can use for pounding out any new dents you get."

Randy shakes his head and turns around and starts back to the car.

"What? You're not going to buy it?" Lori says.

"Randy, if we walk away, I lose my fifty dollar deposit."

"That's your problem."

"Randy . . . ," Lori pleads. "We want to go canoeing again."

"And we won't find anything near as good for the price. All the other ones in the paper are two or three hundred dollars or more. Come on. Let's take it." He's still shaking his head.

"What? Are you worried about what Garth will say? Listen. He won't care. He doesn't even use it anymore."

"It's no skin off my back if you take her or don't," Zonk says. "If you walk away, I keep the fifty, and I have two other buyers lined up who say they'll take her for a hundred. All I have to do is call them. I can probably even take their highest bid."

"Come on, Randy. Let's try it."

"What guarantee do you give with this thing?" Randy asks Zonk.

He looks Randy in the eye and squints. "I guarantee it'll leak."

"What?"

"Come on, Randy," Lori says.

"Can I think about it until tomorrow?"

"Oh. You want to look at some other ones. Sure. But I can't guarantee she'll still be here. And then your buddy's out fifty bucks."

"Okay, okay. We'll take it. But if the leak's worse than what you say, we'll be back."

Now it's Zonk's turn to shake his head in disgust.

On the way home, I tell Randy about the phone calls we've been getting and say, "You don't know anything about them, do you?"

That pisses him off. "What? You think I've been making them?"

"I didn't say that."

He points his chin at me and looks down his nose. "You know, if you weren't asking people like my dad questions about Negroes, maybe you wouldn't be getting those calls."

"What people? What do you know about that? You heard that we were asking other people questions?"

"That's what my dad said." *Great. Word is getting around.* Lori looks a little worried.

It's unnerving.

"Why do you think the calls are about Negroes?" I ask.

"Why else would people be doing it." He won't look me in the eye.

"I think you know more than you're letting on."

They're in their PJs, ready for bed—Jimmy with his cowboy doll and Billy, his floppy-eared dog.

"Canoe story," Billy squeals, and Jimmy repeats the demand.

It's my job, so I plunge in. But what's this one about? All I can think of is leaks.

"One time I went into the backyard and picked up my canoe and raced down to Lake Erie and paddled to the end of the lake, over Niagara Falls, through Lake Ontario, out to the Atlantic Ocean, and down to Brazil. They have the longest river in the world there, the Amazon, although some people say the Nile River in Egypt is longer. I wanted to paddle up the Amazon into the jungle and see if I could see some spotted jaguar cats—they're as big as lions—and bright-colored parrots, and toucan birds with great big beaks, and huge anaconda snakes that will wrap themselves around you and hug you to death."

"Oooo," Billy says.

"So I started paddling up the river. It was really pretty, with all those big trees all around me. But suddenly I felt something bump the canoe, and I looked down, and there was a little hole in it, and water was spurting up through it like a fountain. Then I felt another bump, and there was another hole and another spout. I knew that if this kept happening, my canoe would slowly sink to the bottom of the river, and that would be the end of my trip. I looked over the edge of the canoe to see what was causing the leaks, and I saw a whole bunch of piranha fish—a school of them, thirty or forty, about two feet long. And all of them had that row of razor-sharp teeth on the bottom of their mouths. I knew that if the canoe went down, those fish would eat all the flesh off my bones. They'd eat off all my skin and fat and muscle, and my bones would just sink to the mud on the bottom of the river, and I'd never get home, dead or alive. I was really scared."

As usual, I pause to build suspense until Billy can't stand it any longer. "So what happened?"

"What happened?" Jimmy asks.

I take a deep breath, and explain, "Well, fortunately, I was chewing gum at the time—that juicy fruity kind—and I pulled some of it out of my mouth and stuck it in a hole, and it stopped the leak. Then I pulled out some more and put it in another hole. Then another. And another."

"You chew a lot of gum," Billy says.

"Yes, I do, when I'm canoeing, I like to chew a whole pack at one time."

"Five sticks!"

"It makes the flavor last longer."

"What happened next?"

"The holes started leaking again, so I had to put more gum in each one. Then they started leaking again, and I had to put gum in them again!"

"What happened then?" Jimmy asks.

"I ran out of gum, and the canoe started sinking down into the water. Slowly, the water kept climbing, just like I was in the bathtub. But this time the water went all the way over the top, and I started going down into the river."

Jimmy looks up at me like a cornered mouse and asks, "Did the fish eat you?"

"Silly. He's alive, isn't he?" Billy replies.

"I had water up to my waist, then to my chest, then my neck, my chin, my nose, my eyes, until I was all the way underwater. And I could see those piranha fish all lined up in rows like they were in school, all facing the same direction, all lying on their stomachs in the water, and all facing another piranha in front of them. That one was standing on its tail in front of them waving its fins. It was the schoolteacher! And I could see that all those piranha fish were chewing something. They were chewing my juicy fruity gum! And do you know what? I could hear the schoolteacher telling her students, 'Remember, never eat when you are chewing gum. You'll get food in your gum and gum in your food and that will be really ooey. Glooey-ooey, in fact, and you won't be able to swallow your food because you can never swallow gum; it'll stick to your intestines and you won't be able to poop. For instance,' she said, looking at me, 'You should never eat this canoeist while you're chewing gum. Do you want to spit out your gum and eat this canoeist?' She is chewing gum too.

"'No! Blub, blub,' they all shouted. 'We love his juicy fruity gum.'

"*Hurrah*! I said to myself.

"Then the teacher asked, 'Well, don't you think it would be nice to do something to thank him for his wonderful gum?'

"'Yes! Blub, blub,' they shouted.

"'Let's take him for a ride,' one said.

"'Where does he want to go?' another asked.

"Well, I told them I wanted to see the Amazon, and so they grabbed the rope from the front of the canoe and I got in, and they pulled me all the way up the river, so fast that the canoe went up to the top of the water and into the air. And I was able to see all kinds of things: toucans eating pecans, anaconda snakes hugging wild pigs, jagged-tooth jaguars lying in the trees, and parrots parroting everything, including each other, just like people do. (Parrots aren't very original; they talk just like everyone else talks.) Then we turned around and they flew me all the way back to the Atlantic Ocean. I thanked them and said good-bye. Then I went into a store and bought more gum, patched the holes in my canoe, and paddled back to Shale River. I ran home, and Mom made me a wonderful fish-stick dinner. I hoped they weren't made out of those nice piranha fish."

And I hope we don't run into any in Lake Erie.

Chapter 16—Up the Cuyahoga

"This is it. Today's the day," I tell Randy and Lori. "Our biggest test. The trip we'll all remember." This is the day we leave the land and enter the realm of Lake Erie.

We're all a little tense as we load the canoe onto Randy's car. It's seven o'clock, and the weather is gorgeous. Fluffy clouds hide part of the blue, and the sun is poking its way in and out and around them like a kitten under a blanket. The temperature is in the midsixties already and is expected to hit mideighties. But a breeze is blowing, and it's cooler out on the lake, so we're wearing light jackets over our swimsuits. We also have on our ball caps—mine touts the Indians, Randy, the Browns, and Lori, NASA.

The plan is to leave Shale River Harbor, follow the shoreline to Cleveland, go up the Cuyahoga, and return, if we aren't run over by a six-hundred-foot ore boat or burn up when the river catches fire. Yes, this will be a day to remember.

Randy seems quieter than usual. He's probably still ticked off about my talk with his dad.

We drive across Shale River Bridge into Lakeshore and turn right down the steep road into the valley to the marina. Randy and I carry the canoe to the boat ramp.

Lori hands Randy a life jacket: "Here."

"You know I'm not wearing that. You know how bad I swim with one of those on."

She offers one to me.

"If he won't wear one, I won't wear one."

"Oh! You guys are so stupid. Don't you know it gets rough out there? Well, I'm wearing mine." She slips the bright orange vest over her head, pulls the strap around her back, buckles it in front, and pulls it tight.

Randy and I put the canoe in the water and pull it sideways to the launch.

"I get the stern," I say.

"The hell you do. It's my canoe."

"Oh, yeah?" I say, raising my voice.

"Boys! Stop that right now. Jeff, you take stern on the way down, and Randy on the way back. And I'll take bow out to the breakwater and back."

"I'm not going," Randy says.

"Please, Randy," Lori teases.

She puts the life jackets and lunch bag in the canoe, and we climb in—her in the bow and me in the stern. Randy drags himself into the center and does a slow burn. Then we're gliding between high cliffs, under Shale River Bridge and the railroad bridge, and taking the East Channel past Yacht Club Island, where all the sailboats and powerboats are moored. Captains and crews are busily walking the docks, climbing in and out, bending, loading, rigging sails, and preparing to leave. One guy, though, is roaming the pier and talking to people with a beer in his hand.

"First one of the day," I say. "He probably isn't even going out. Just looking for a party."

Randy slumps down and pulls his cap over his face as we go by the club. He wants to be sure that no one sees that he's not in charge. That's the way it is with guys like him.

"I really should be paddling a third of the way," Lori says to Randy, "not just down to the breakwater. You're getting off easy."

"Look at it this way," I tell her. "When you're in the middle and we're paddling, you're the captain, and we're your crew. Right, Randy? We'll be doing all the work. We're your slaves. You'll be like Cleopatra on the Nile."

"But you guys get to make all the decisions—even the bad ones," she says.

"But you get to be the navigator and tour guide. Did you study up on the Cuyahoga?"

"Yes."

We pull in at the breakwater, and Lori and Randy change places.

"Don't worry," I tell her. "You can paddle again as soon as Randy gets tired, which won't be long. But you'll have to trade places with him. That means he'll have to stand up in the canoe and turn around and walk back and step over you while you go down on your knees. Then he'll have to turn around and step back over the center thwart and kneel down while you stand up and walk forward and step over the front seat and kneel down. And you'll have to do all this out in the lake while the waves are rocking and rolling us back and forth."

"I think I'll stay put, thanks," she says.

"We'll sleep well tonight," I say. "We have to paddle eight miles to the Cuyahoga and eight miles back, so the round trip is sixteen, plus going a few miles in the rivers at each end."

We round the breakwater and head east with the fickle sun in our eyes, infinite water on three sides, and cliffs on our right. I must admit that I have a twinge of fear as we move into the big water away from the shore. But the feeling dissipates when I see sailboats and yachts everywhere, even in the middle of the week. *A lot of people must be on vacation. Maybe a race is on.*

Lucky for us, the lake is calm. A southwesterly breeze nudges our backs, easing our journey, and waves from the northwest, about a foot and a half high, push us along. The air is bracing.

"Ah, this is the life," I say. "We should put up a sail."

"We don't have a poncho," Randy says. "Why didn't you think of that, Lori?" *He seems to be lightening up.*

"I don't know," she says. "But I can stand up if you want me to. I can be the sail."

We ride along, enjoying sky, sparkling water, and green shore around us.

"Tired yet?" I ask Randy.

"No, but I bet you are."

"He's a weakling," I tell Lori. "He gets tired quick. I knew we should have had you take the bow, Lori."

"Zip it, Klossen. We'll see who gets tired first. You just be sure you keep paddling back there and don't just rudder like you usually do."

"Also, Randy, be careful not to tip it over, because the water's polluted and we'll get polio," I warn.

"We've all had our shots."

"Thanks to Dr. Salk," Lori adds.

"But there're lots of other diseases we could get," I say.

We angle northeast into the waves, and then turn southeast with the waves behind us. The cliffs onshore make me think of that company that has all the ore boats: Cleveland-Cliffs. And we can see the high-rise apartments and mansions looking down on us from above. After an hour or so, we come around the bend that Lakeshore makes, and my heart jumps at the sight of the Cleveland skyline, dominated by the Terminal Tower, the tallest building outside of New York City. It's named for the railroad terminal under it. To its right is the smoke from the mills in the Flats.

"Look. There's a lake freighter heading in," I say. We're still a couple of hundred yards offshore with about four miles to go to the mouth of the river.

"We're going to follow it in?" Lori asks.

"Yep. Into the mouth of the monster," I hiss. "That's what that river is."

"Hey, deadweight," Randy says to Lori. I can see her bristle.

"I told you I would paddle, but you said it would throw the canoe out of balance if I paddled from the middle, and the J-strokes wouldn't work right, and . . . "

"Yeah, and we only have two paddles," he says. "So, Miss Queen of the Lake, how about passing me up something to drink."

"Just a minute." She pulls three plastic cups and the plastic gallon bottle from the bag, which she has tied to the center thwart. "Is water okay?"

"Sure," he says, "as long as it's cool."

I notice that the cups have strips of masking tape on them with our names written on them. She fills the one inscribed "Randy" three-quarters full and passes it up. He lays his paddle across the gunwales, reaches back, takes it with a "thanks," downs it in two gulps, and hands it back.

A wave hits us from the side and gives us a good roll. "Hell!" he hollers.

"You can start paddling again," I tell him.

"Are you sure we're allowed to go up that river?" Lori asks.

"It's a free country, isn't it?" Randy says.

"No," she and I say in a chorus.

"Not for teenagers," I say.

"Actually, they could have a million excuses not to let us in there," Randy says. "Like it's not safe for us to be around all those big boats."

"Or the water's unhealthy," Lori adds.

"Or the river might catch on fire."

"Listen," I say. "It's just like at the upper end of the Cuyahoga—we go until they stop us. And if they do, we play dumb. 'Oh, sorry, sir, we didn't know we weren't allowed in here. We'll leave right away. Sorry.'"

"Yeah, yeah, yeah. Mr. Big Talker," Randy says. "They'll say, 'You got a license for this boat?' Or they'll say, 'This boat's unsafe,' and make us get out."

We see Edgewater Park Beach on the right and the marina beside it. I think of my tryst with Lori. I wonder what she's thinking and wish I could make eye contact.

We're still about two miles from the mouth. Then it happens. Randy clips the top of a wave with his paddle and splashes Lori and me. She screams and I holler.

"Okay, Clark, if that's how you want to play it," I say, and I give him a good one right back, which also happens to get Lori since she's sitting between us. This time Randy makes an intentional sweep and aims a big stream my way.

"No!" Lori shouts. "You're getting me wet, and I'll have to sponge out all the water. And we can't have a water-fight out here in the lake. You'll tip us over for sure! And then we'll never get to the river."

Randy and I find some wisdom in her words.

"Truce?" I ask, and he answers, "Truce."

"You were just trying to save yourself, weren't you?" I ask her.

"That's right. Boys are such idiots. They have to have things spelled out for them."

We pass Edgewater Marina and start around Whiskey Island where a six-hundred-foot ore boat is being unloaded by four immense black clamshell shovels. They bend down and dig ore from the belly of the boat, lift it straight up, and dump it into elevated hopper cars, which carry it back onto land and dump it into railroad cars that take it to the mills. Or they drop it onto piles in an ore storage yard to reload in winter when the lake is frozen.

"Look at those things," I say, pointing to the shovels. "They look like black steel dinosaurs with long necks, bending down to feed in a marsh."

"Or big black dippy birds going down and up," Lori says.

"What are they called?" I ask.

"Huletts," she says. "They were invented by George Hulett of Ohio in the late eighteen hundreds. They're all around the lakes—over seventy of them. They revolutionized ore unloading."

"Thank you, Miss Brain," Randy says.

"You wanted to know, didn't you?" she snaps.

We come around the end of the breakwater where a small round lighthouse sits. It's white and has a steel walkway around the top and a white one-room cottage attached to it. Next we pass a small, low-slung, two-story, white building with a round observation tower. Out front is a large cross-shaped flagpole with ropes angling down from the ends of the cross piece to the bottom of the pole.

"What's that?" I ask.

"The coast guard station. That's where they fly the small-craft warnings—from that flagpole," Lori says.

"What are those diagonal ropes for that go up to the horizontal piece?"

"They're not ropes," Randy says. "They're halyards—the lines they use to raise the warning flags. And the horizontal piece at the top is called the yardarm. It's a nautical flagpole."

"I didn't know you were an expert on sailor slang. Batten down the hatches. She's beginnin' to blow. Hang him from the yardarm, mates."

"I've been sailing."

"Yes, but have you been into the underworld on the River Styx?" I ask. "That's where we're going now. I hope it doesn't burst into flames."

Lower Cuyahoga River—1960

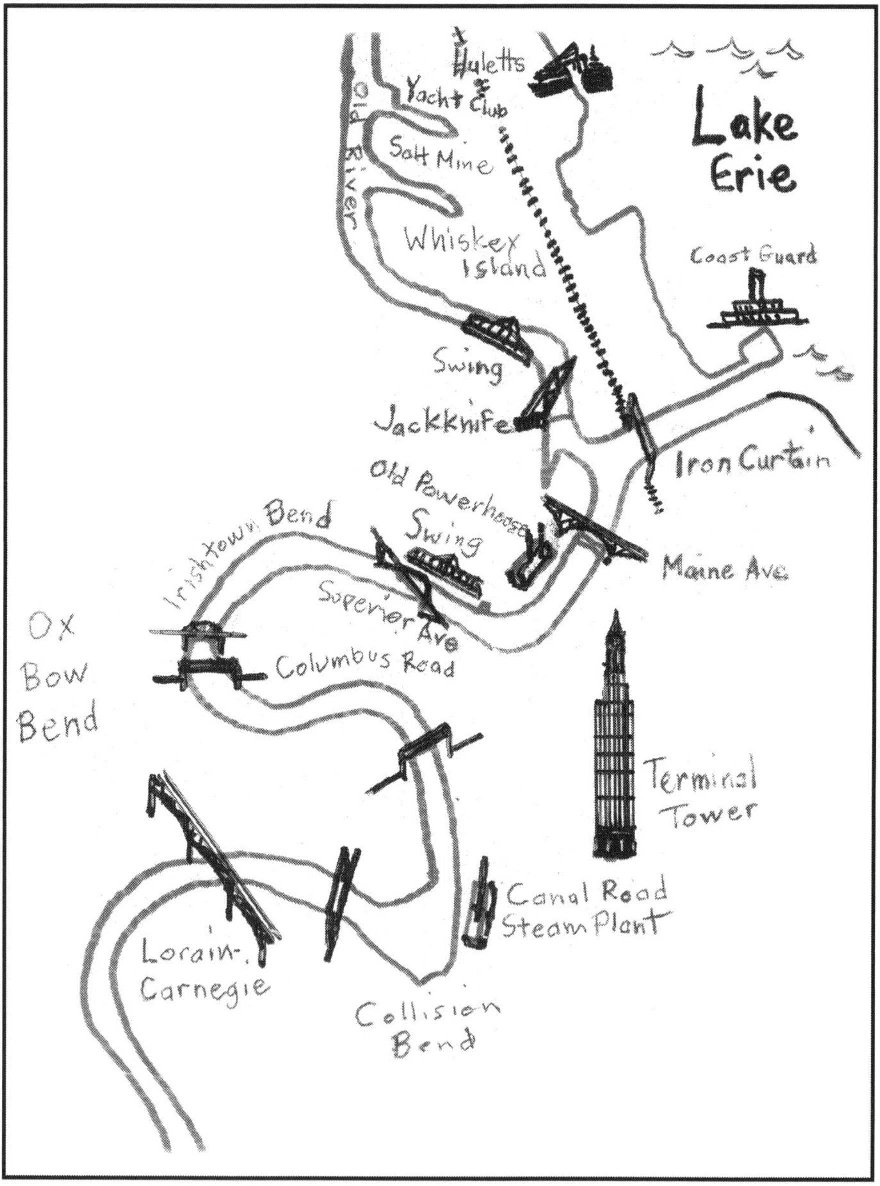

[sketch by AM]

Chapter 17—The Storm

"See that ahead?" I ask. "It's the smoke of Hades." It's rising and drifting to the east, and there's a faint smell of sulfur in the air.

"The Underworld," Lori says in a spooky voice. "Is that where you're taking us, Klossen?"

"You two are sick," Randy says.

Beyond the coast guard station, the water is flat with little current. In front of us is the first of the bridges that cross the river: a steel truss railroad bridge that goes straight up between two truss towers to let ore boats through and then comes back down to let the trains pass. It's down now.

"It's a low-level, vertical-lift, through-truss bridge," Lori says, "'low-level' because the bridge is down at the level of the river and has to get out of the way when a boat comes, 'vertical-lift' because it moves straight up and down to let the boats pass, and 'through-truss' because the train or cars drive right through a truss instead of on top of it."

"Jeesh," Randy says. "You know the technical terms for bridges?"

"Duck," I yell, as we approach it. "It's low level."

"It's not that low," Randy sneers.

"They call this one the Iron Curtain," Lori says. "It was just built, in 1956. When it's down, it keeps boats in or out, like the—"

"Iron Curtain!" Randy and I shout.

"Yes. It's part of the Nickel Plate Railroad Line that goes east along the lake to Buffalo and west through Orchard Park to Chicago."

"What's that paper you keep looking at?" Randy asks.

"It's a list of all the bridges down here and a map of the river. An engineer who works with my dad at NASA is a bridge nut. He gave a copy to my dad."

"Look at those two on the right," I say.

"That first one's a jackknife bridge—a low-level steel-truss bridge that goes up to one side of the river and stops at a sixty-degree angle when boats are coming and goes down for trains to cross. It was built in 1907."

"What's behind it?" Randy asks.

"It's a swing bridge: a low-level, through-truss bridge that swings in an arc out over the river at ground level."

"Wow," I say. "It swings around sideways to the other shore and you drive through it? Neat."

Next, we go under the Main Avenue Bridge. It connects the East and West Shoreway. It's way up in the air: a high-level viaduct. About a dozen steel-truss arches support the road as it crosses the Flats.

From here in the Flats, we have a good view of the Terminal Tower jutting into the sky up on the heights. The Flats are about a hundred feet below the heights.

"Uh-oh," Lori says. "Oil." The water has patches of color seeping over the blue surface.

"From the refineries and freighters," Randy says.

"And you don't see any birds or ducks now," I say. "The oil would kill them. We can thank the A-people for that."

Randy looks puzzled. Lori says, "He means the adults."

We round a bend and pass another swing bridge sitting beside the river.

"What's that?" I ask.

"Center Street Bridge," Lori says.

"And the building behind it?" I ask, pointing at a deserted brick structure with two smokestacks and high arched windows.

"The old powerhouse," she says. "They used to make electricity in there for the streetcars and trolleys. It's not used anymore."

"Where did you learn this stuff?" Randy asks.

"The library. You should go there sometime. I found a good book on the Flats."

Next, the river starts into Ox Bow Bend, a loop that turns south and then north. We go under the high level Detroit Avenue–Superior Avenue Bridge. None of us has ever seen it from underneath. It has a steel-truss arch that goes up over the road where it crosses the river; the rest of the road is supported underneath by a dozen or more concrete arches that bound across the Flats like a Roman aqueduct. It's a double-decker bridge. The lower one was for the streetcars, but they closed that part a few years ago.

"This is called Irishtown Bend. It's part of Ox Bow Bend," Lori says. A steep wooded bank comes down to the river from the city above; a couple of small, dilapidated houses about halfway up are engulfed by bushes and trees. "Those houses are about all that's left of the Irish immigrant community from the eighteen hundreds. Irishtown and Whiskey Island used to be all poor Irish."

"And they would never let Negroes move into their neighborhoods," I say.

"Damn good thing," Randy says.

Next, we go under the Columbus Road Bridge, another low-level, through-truss, vertical-lift bridge that goes up between two truss towers.

"By the way, Klossen, I'm still really mad that you called my dad a liar. I won't forget that."

"I did not," I say.

"Yeah."

"Are you sure you're not making those phone calls?"

"Screw you."

Lori ignores us. "This is the fourth permanent bridge to be built here, and this is where the riots took place."

"The Bridge War," I say, "between Ohio City up there on the West Side and the Clevelanders on the East Side. West-siders could get violent."

As we pass under the bridge and start around the ox bow, we see seven smokestacks sticking out of a long building. Beside them is a much bigger stack. Smoke pours from them and drifts up and to the east. The air has a strong smell of sulfur now, and the ground is covered with gray soot. Loud rumbling and clanking sounds fill the air, and we can hardly hear.

I shout, "That big stack is a blast furnace. It makes pig iron out of iron ore and limestone and coke. And those smaller ones are from open-hearth furnaces where they cook the pig iron and add other ingredients to turn it into steel."

"How do you know that?" Randy asks.

"Dad took us on a tour down here once."

The mill sits behind mountains of iron ore brought in on barges and ore boats. On the left is a long steel-truss bridge that sits on legs way up in the air.

"That bridge is for unloading ore," I say. "It's like the Huletts. It rolls along tracks on both sides of those ore piles and drops the ore onto the piles. They have to stockpile the ore so they can use it in winter when the lake and river freeze and they can't get ore boats in here."

Next to the mills is a smaller building with another eight smokestacks that are close together.

"I think those are coke ovens. They heat coal to make coke and collect the coke gas to burn in the blast furnace and open-hearth ovens."

We round the bend and head north now. From here we have a good view of the Terminal Tower again. Then we come to another vertical-lift, through-truss bridge.

The river curves to the right, almost due west, and widens. "This is called Collision Bend," Lori says.

"They must have had some crashes here," Randy says.

Beside the river on the east side is a building with three tall stacks sitting behind rows of railroad tracks.

"What's that?" he asks.

"It's the Canal Road Steam Generating Plant," Lori says. "It's old, but they still use it. It was built in the twenties. It supplies steam to heat downtown buildings and chilled water to cool them."

"Steam?" Randy asks. "They pipe steam under the streets to heat the buildings?"

"That's right, and cold water to cool them. It's called district heating and cooling. It's very efficient."

We keep turning and head south.

"Did anybody notice the water is dark brown now?" I ask.

"That's the oil on it," Lori says.

"Look at it," I say. "I could puke."

We look at our paddles, and they're beginning to turn brown.

"I'm glad it's not my canoe," I say. "You'll have a heck of a time getting it off the canoe, Randy."

"You're going to help me, slimeball."

We go under another bridge—vertical lift, through truss—wind to the left, and there it is, the gem of them all: the Lorain-Carnegie Bridge, built in 1932. It's high above the river and part of another viaduct. The road on top sits on a lot of steel-truss arches that gallop across the valley. But the amazing thing is that at both ends of the bridge on each side are forty-foot-high winged statues—the Guardians of Traffic—that look like Greek athletes, naked from the waist up, holding a car, wagon, or truck in their hands.

Lori starts dipping a cup into the water and skimming the surface. "It looks like the oil is over an inch thick here," she says.

"Oooo," I say. "Don't fall in. How would you like to have that oil all over you?"

"And they say that the only things that live in the water are worms that eat sewage," Lori reports.

"No, we definitely don't want to fall in."

We go under the bridge and look ahead. There are many more bridges, and in the distance, the new interstate, I-90—the next viaduct across the Flats. And we're slowly entering a brown fog—smoke from the refineries and mills—and the sulfur is starting to cut into my nostrils.

"P.U.! Rotten eggs," Lori says. "It's really starting to stink."

"Yeah," I say. "Do we really want to paddle way up there where those mills and refineries are?"

"The river could catch fire again," she warns. "It's done it lots of times, and there's oil all around us."

"It makes me mad how they pollute everything," I growl.

We look back toward the lake and see something coming toward us on the water—something gray and moving fast. It's flat and about twenty feet wide, and there's a tugboat behind it.

"What's that?" Lori asks.

"It must be a barge. Let's get over. I see a big wake behind the tug."

Randy digs and I steer us over to the side, and we grab onto the steel decking bulkhead that lines the riverbank. The barge is about half a football field long. We brace ourselves for the wake, and it rocks us nearly to the tipping point.

"Whoa," Randy shouts. "Down, boy."

We watch them go up the river and disappear around a bend.

"They were moving," he hollers.

"Yeah," I say. "I don't know how that tug can steer it from behind around all these bends and go so fast." I glance at my watch. "You know, it's starting to get late. Maybe we should go back."

"It's okay with me," Randy says. "I'll feel a lot safer, too, when I'm in the stern."

"I won't," I reply. "You just think you won't have to paddle as hard. And you don't even know where you're going. You'll probably take us down the wrong river."

"You're so full of it."

We spot a grassy place, pull in, climb out, and have a quick picnic. Then we turn the canoe over and dump out the water—it isn't much—trying to keep the oil off our hands. Randy climbs into the stern, and we start snaking our way toward the lake. Lori keeps track of the bridges.

We pass the steam plant on Collision Bend.

"Look out!" she shouts.

Bearing down on us from behind is the blunt nose of one of the ore boat behemoths—half a football field wide, over ten times as long as it is wide, five stories out of the water to the top of the cabins on the bow and three to the top of the main deck where the hatches are. There's another cabin structure over the engine room in the stern, built around a big black smokestack. The boat's guided by tugs on bow and stern, and they all sound warnings at us like a trio of foghorns.

"Okay, Clark. Let's see if we can outrun it," I yell.

"Let's go, Klossen. You and me." He steers it into the middle of the river, and we start paddling like crazy.

"No!" Lori screams. "You're idiots! They'll run us down."

We give it our best for about a minute. Then Randy looks back and shouts, "They're gaining on us. They're fifty yards back, Klossen."

"You're mad!" Lori shouts.

The warning horns blare again.

"They'll crunch us," Lori says.

"Okay, okay. I give up," I say. "We can't win, and they can't stop if they wanted to. Let's bag it, Clark. They're bigger than we are."

We tear to the eastern bank and grab the bulkhead. The tugboat wake bounces us back and forth but doesn't swamp us. Then we look up, craning our necks, as the monster—two football fields long—passes by fewer than thirty yards away, blasting its deep horn like a heavyweight bragging about a knockout. Looking almost straight up, we read the big sign on the side, "Cleveland Cliffs."

"What a blast," I say.

"Very punny," Lori says. "And now it's leaving us in its wake."

"It's shaped like a canoe," I say.

"A great big steel canoe," Randy says.

"Heading out to get another cargo."

We watch the rear tugboat pass and go out of sight around Ox Bow Bend.

"Well!" I say. "That was a kick."

"Idiots," says the queen. We ignore her.

"G below middle C," I say.

"What?" Randy asks.

"The pitch of the horn."

"You're crazy."

We continue on our way, passing the steel mill on the left and winding around the bend. When we pull under the Iron Curtain, Lori reports that she has counted one swing bridge, one jackknife, five vertical-lift, and four high-level bridges, eleven altogether, plus the jackknife and swing bridges over to Whiskey Island on the left. "There are lots more south of where we stopped—twenty-nine altogether in the Flats."

Now, again, we face the open lake and arrive at the coast guard station. "Uh-oh," I say. "The small-craft warning flag is up." A triangular red flag is flying on one of the halyards. "That means winds or gusts up to thirty-three knots may be coming."

"That's almost forty miles per hour," Randy says.

"The way it's waving, the wind is still from the southwest," I say.

"We'll be heading into it," he says.

"For eight miles," I say. "And the waves will be coming at us from the northwest and might catch us broadside."

I look at the lake. The sky is steel gray and grows progressively darker toward the horizon. The water's gray too, and white caps are starting to form. I can make out the stern of the ore boat as it charges into the abyss.

"Looks like a big storm is coming," I say. "We'll have to dig hard to beat it. Let's go."

"We're really going out there?" Lori asks.

"Sure," I say. "This is a test, our final exam. But the worst that can happen is we'll get blown back to shore."

"Aren't you going to wear your life jacket?"

I glance back at Randy. He's not wearing his, of course. "Nah. I need to kneel on it 'cause the bottom of the canoe hurts my bony knees."

"That's a good one," Randy says. "By the way, it'll help if you can stay low, Lori. It'll cut down our wind resistance." She bends down and puts her hands on the gunnels.

We head out into the wind, around the little lighthouse, and turn west toward Shale River Harbor, angling into the waves, cutting up through the crests, diving down to the troughs, and rising through the next crest. Randy does a short pry stroke on the right side in the stern, and I rudder right or dig hard on the left side to keep turning us into the waves. The canoe splashes through the tops of the waves, and they jostle us as they roll underneath and rock us side to side. Every stroke is arduous, every wave is different, and we always have to stay alert. There's no relaxing.

"The wind keeps blowing us away from shore," I shout. "We have to angle to the left."

Randy turns us, and then we try to ride the waves in. The wind is hitting us almost broadside.

"Pull hard," Randy shouts, and I do.

We make some progress toward the beach without turning over, but not much to the west.

"Better turn us back out," I say. He does, and we seem to do better.

Around Lakeshore hump, below the cliffs and a few hundred yards from shore, the wind picks up, and whitecaps appear all around us. Now we're cutting into four-foot waves, top to bottom, and pulling up from the troughs through curling tops fringed with white foam that sprays our faces. The sky is getting really dark, and lightning is stabbing the horizon in front of us. I paddle hard, sometimes pointing my paddle into the waves, but more often switching sides to get us through the turbulent waves.

"Rocking and rolling," I yell, and I give my paddle an extra-hard pull. The wooden paddle breaks in half just above the blade. I'm left with the shaft, while the flat blade floats away.

"My paddle," I yell. Randy reaches out and grabs the blade and hands it to Lori, who hands it to me. It's a clean break right above the blade.

"What do we do now?" she shouts through the wind.

Randy is struggling in the back.

I reach the blade down into the water, just as a wave bounces the canoe up.

"I can't paddle with it," I shout to Randy. "Just try to keep steering into the waves so we don't tip over."

"Damn!" he shouts, prying on almost every stroke.

We are making no progress. The wind continues to blow us away from shore, and waves keep trying to sink us.

I see a yacht coming our way, so I grab both pieces of the paddle and start waving them, but it doesn't see us and just cruises past. I search the water for other boats, but see none.

Now the sky is thundering. A fine rain commences, but soon turns into a downpour. Lori sponges water from the bottom, and begins using a cup.

The wind starts gusting, and the waves look like they're five feet high now.

"We've gotta run for shore," I say.

"It's worth a try," Randy says.

He turns the canoe with a couple of sweep strokes and starts digging, using his J-stroke to keep us going straight. Now we're riding down the troughs and up the crests, until we begin surfing on a crest. *What do we do now? Back-paddle? No.*

"Pull," I shout, and he does. The wave moves through, and the back of the canoe slides into the trough behind. He keeps paddling and pulls us up part of the way out of it, but loses power when he has to rudder to keep going straight.

Thunder booms. Lightning strikes near us. Then, in the darkness of the storm, as Randy tries to pull up out of a trough, water breaks over the stern, drenching him and rushing into the canoe. The stern drops in the water, forward motion slows, and a second wave swamps us. The canoe turns over, and we're in the water.

I don't know what happens next. Randy must have choked on some water. I look through the rain and see him flailing. I fight my way to him and wrap my arms around his chest to keep his head up. He grabs my shoulders and starts pushing me down into the water! *Why?* I catch a breath as he drives me under. Then I let go of him, grab his wrists, push them upward, go straight down deep, and swim away.

When I return to the top, gasping for air, I see neither of them.

Lightning hits the canoe with a thunderous explosion that blinds and deafens me, fills the air with ozone, and knocks me out. I wake up, gasping for air. As a wave carries me to its crest, I regain my sight, look back through the rain, and see the bottom of the stern sticking out of the water at an odd angle. But there's no sign of Randy and Lori.

Oh, God, no! No! I ride another wave down and up and view the same scene twice more, now blurred through tears. *Where are they? In the water? Did they drown?*

"Lori!" I shout into the rain and wind, but they suck up the sound like a sponge. "Randy!" There's no reply.

Another wave smashes over my face, and I sputter and turn over on my stomach. My feet sink, and my body goes vertical, and I have to start dog-paddling and flapping my arms to keep my head above the surface. The wind is baying.

God . . . save them. . . . Please!

Chapter 18—Searching

My legs and arms tire from pushing my head above the surface. I panic. *I've got to start swimming or I'll drown.*

I bring myself horizontal with two pulls of my arms and assume my backstroke position. My arms reach out and start pulling water to my sides as my legs begin their frog kick. First I'm paddling in the trough. Then the wave lifts me, and the crest rolls under me, and I start back down into the next trough. Whenever I see a wave's about to break over my head, I turn my head and hold my breath. But sometimes water gets in my nose, and I choke and cough and gasp for air and twist and start to sink. Then I have to pull hard with my arms to get level again.

One more time I look back through the rain and see the point of the canoe. Then no more.

The wind gets stronger and the waves even bigger—six feet high, eight feet, I don't know. *I have to keep pulling, or I'll never get to shore. They'll find my body in East Cleveland somewhere, or Erie, or Buffalo.*

The downpour continues, lightning flashes, gusts drive rain across the water and sting my face. I think about Lori and Randy and what good friends they've been. I pray some more. I hear Lori talking, "You tried . . . you tried to save Randy. See you in the next world." But Randy says, "You son of a bitch. You left me to sink to the bottom." Then I think about him trying to push my head under the water and wonder if it was intentional.

I keep fighting the waves, and it seems like they'll never end. But after an hour or more, a beach comes into sight. *Edgewa-*

ter Park? I turn onto my stomach and do a crawl stroke until my knees hit sand. I start moving on my hands and knees with waves breaking over me, smashing my back and pushing me sideways. I'm so tired and weak that I feel like falling on my stomach and giving up.

Ahead of me, through the rain, I see a tall figure draped in a green hooded poncho standing alone on the beach. I try to get up, but can't. Another wave knocks me flat. I gasp for air. My legs and back have no strength left. I rise to my knees again and just crawl. Inside the poncho hood, I see the face of a Negro man—young, I think. His brown legs and feet are bare. I get scared. *Negroes hate us. But I need help. There's nothing else I can do.* I reach out and rasp, "Help," and another wave knocks me down.

He runs into the surf and sticks out his hand. I don't know why—it's stupid, I guess—but that painting flashes through my mind—the one of God reaching out to Adam to give him life, where their fingers almost touch, the one Michelangelo painted on the ceiling of the Sistine Chapel in Rome. It's in one of Mom's art books.

He doesn't take my hand. He grabs my wrist, and I wonder if it's a trick. But he pulls, and I pull, and I struggle to my feet. I can tell he's strong. I take a few steps on rubbery legs and then stumble, and he grabs me under my arm; then I start to go down, and he reaches around my waist and pulls me up.

"Easy," he says.

We plod up the beach—wet sand under bare feet—and gradually I start to get my land legs back and begin moving on my own. Through the drear, I remember being with Lori in this park and being afraid we'd get caught by a passerby.

"Man, where'd you come from?" he asks. "You came out of that water like Darwin's lizard."

He's taken biology!

I tell him what happened and how I couldn't save my friends and swam to shore. Then I stop walking and start crying. "They're gone. Gone!"

"Maybe not. God acts in mysterious ways. He saved you, didn't he? You're lucky to be alive."

I choke back a sob. "And he helped you find me. . . . W-what are you doing here, anyway—alone . . . in the rain?"

"I was swimmin' and—"

"Swimming?" I look at the face inside the hood. "Don't you know the water's polluted?"

"I keep my mouth shut."

I laugh. He sounds like me. "How come you're alone?"

"A bunch of us saw the storm comin' in, and everyone else left, but I like all that flash and boom, so I stood and watched it. And then, there you were. You just crawled up in front of me. You scared me, coming up out of the water in a big thunderstorm with all that lightning and those big waves breaking over you. I thought you were a devil fish."

I shake my head. "Nope, just a man. . . . Hey, can we stop for a minute. I gotta rest." I take some deep breaths. "What's your name?"

"Walter. Walter Madison. What's yours?"

"Jeff Klossen."

"Glad it ain't Beelzebub."

I start shaking with the cold, and I remember Lori and Randy and break into sobs. "Listen, Walter. I gotta find them if they're still alive. I gotta help them. Can you help me look for them?"

"How? Drive you around?"

"You got a car?"

"Yeah."

"How 'bout you drive, and I walk along the beach till I can't walk any farther, and then I get in the car, just till we get to another place for me to walk. I've got to find them."

"Yeah, I'll do it." He smiles. "But you gotta sit in the front seat. I don't want anyone thinkin' I'm your chauffeur."

"I need to start walking right here. But let me see your car first so I know what to look for."

We slog on, leaving footprints in the wet sand, and start up the bank toward the parking lot. The grass is slippery and cold on my feet. I'm freezing. It's still raining a fine gray mist; I feel it on my face.

"You scared me too when I first saw you," I say.

"Why?"

"'Cause you're Negro."

"Why does that scare you?"

I look at him through the haze. "I don't know. I've never been around Negroes."

"I haven't been around many white folks either."

"Where do you live?"

"On East Sixty-Fifth near Central."

"I'm not sure where that is. We're always told to stay out of the East Side because it's dangerous. Negroes hate white people, and they'll beat us up and rob us and even use knives and guns to keep us out."

"That's what they say whites'll do to us if we go in your neighborhoods, and it's true. It happens lots of times. You'll beat us up. I know that."

I see a blue car in the distance. It must be his; it's the only one in the lot.

"We don't have any racial violence where I live," I say.

"Oh, yeah? Where's that?"

"Orchard Park."

"Lily-white Orchard Park. There's no racial violence there 'cause Negroes don't go there."

"You've never been there?"

"Just once, and I was ordered out by the police."

"Why?"

"They asked what I was doing there, and I told them I just wanted to see what it was like, and they said I better leave or they'd have to bring me in for questioning."

"They probably thought you were looking for a place to rob."

"'Cause I'm Negro."

At the parking lot, crushed gravel digs into my feet. We get to the car—a faded dark-blue four-door '49 Ford. The fenders and panels under the doors are rusted through in places. It looks like a two-hundred-dollar special.

Walter takes off his poncho, folds it up, and throws it in the backseat. He's as tall as I am, slender, muscular, and dark, with close-cut, kinky hair, and he's wearing a white T-shirt and swimsuit.

I'm still shaking. "Do you have a towel I can use?"

"On the backseat."

I grab it, dry off, and drape it over my shoulders.

He sits in the driver's seat and starts to put on his tennis shoes. They're old and low-cut.

"You don't have another pair of shoes, do you?" I ask. "I lost mine out there."

"No. Sorry."

I get a crazy idea: "You know we could do this a lot faster if you let me wear your shoes while you drive barefoot." He looks at me in surprise. "I'm not kidding. I'm gonna run into a lot of gravel and sharp stones that'll slow me down."

"Let me understand this. You want me to give you my shoes?"

"Listen. I've gotta find them. They might've washed up dead. Or they might've smashed into some sharp rocks or something and be lying there hurt and bloody and cold and in shock. I gotta find my friends and find them fast."

He pauses, shakes his head, and then slowly starts to take off his shoes. "Jesus. I can't believe I'm doin' this. For a white boy. I just can't believe it. Just don't call me a nigger. I'll kill you for that."

"Thanks, man. I really appreciate it."

"Leas' you didn't ask if I could look and you could drive." I have to laugh at that.

I lean against the car and put on his shoes. They fit pretty well. I thank him again. "You don't care if they get wet, do you?"

"Hell. I know you're gonna get them wet and muddy, and get tar all over them, and get them all cut up on sharp rocks, and ripped and everything, and then give them back and say thanks. No, I don't care at all." That makes me laugh again.

I hand him the towel. In this drizzle, it'll only get wet and heavy. Then I head back down to the water and start walking. I scour the long concave crescent of sand beach with my eyes and can see most of it pretty well. The sand stops at a low breakwater that goes by a big picnic area. It used to be the city dump; it caught fire and burned for years, and then they covered it with dirt and made it into the park.

The breakwater is several feet wide and made out of big, squared-off stones. Bushes grow over part of it. I pass them, and then I'm able to walk on top of the wall, which goes out to a far point and curves back. Soon I come to a *T*-shaped concrete fishing pier. I look under it and then go out to a part that's parallel to shore. I walk all along it, searching, but see nothing.

I continue on the breakwater and arrive at Edgewater Marina, which has hundreds of sailboats and powerboats tethered to docks on long wooden piers. Masts are everywhere. I pick my way over the rocks all the way to the opening where the boats go in and out—the neck of the bottle—and look to the other side, where the breakwater continues to another concrete fishing pier. I stop and ask myself, *Am I going to backtrack and walk all the way around the marina to get there? That'll take forever. I'm already wet with that stinking water. It'll take too much time to go around.*

I climb down into the water, roll onto my back with a splash, push off, swim the twenty yards or so across, and climb up the rocks on the other side. I trek over to where it meets the fishing pier, and then walk out to the end of the pier, looking on both sides, with water squishing in my shoes. To the east, I see the four Huletts unloading one of those enormous boats. The boat blocks my view. I can't see on the side of it facing the lake to tell if the canoe has drifted against it.

The nightmare hits me again. *What am I going to find? What if they're drowned and dead, their bodies washed up on rocks or against that boat?* I shake my head and push the vision from my mind.

I turn around and walk along the pier back to land, passing the wastewater treatment plant behind a high chain-link fence on the left and the public boat launch ramps on the right. When I arrive at the other side of the marina, I wonder where Walter is. I find him parked along the road with his head bent down, patiently waiting. I bang on the door. He looks up with a jolt. I smile, but his face is stone. He looks nervous. I wonder what he would say if a cop stopped and asked him what he was doing there.

"Hey, buddy," I ask, "can I have a ride?"

"We ain't buddies."

"We have to be. You saved my life."

"I did not."

I got in on the passenger side. I see him look at his shoes and then look up.

We turn left on Whiskey Island Drive and go around the wastewater plant.

"So you live on East Sixty-Fifth?" I ask.

"Yeah. In the projects—Central Terrace. It's just a couple of blocks from my church—Good Samaritan Baptist at East Sixty-Seventh and Quincy."

"How do you like Central Terrace?"

"It's public housing. You know—we got a small apartment. Most of our neighbors are on welfare. Mom's a nurse's aide at St. Vincent Hospital on Twenty-Second Street. She doesn't make much and has to pay bus fare to get there. So CT is the best we can do. But it's better than the old house we used to live in. It had rats and a coal stove heater in the living room, and it had only one bedroom for me and my mom and my brother."

"Did you have to sleep in the same bed?"

"Yeah. All three of us. But my brother and I were little then."

"Uh-huh."

"Now we still have one bedroom, but Mom has her own bed, and William and I sleep in a double bed. That's not bad. We get along. There aren't any rats, and we always have heat.

But there are still gangs and dope dealers and thieves to worry about. And sometimes the housing-authority police disrespect people and threaten to get them put out on the street. What about you?"

I'm embarrassed to say. "We have four bedrooms and a den. And we don't have to worry about crime, except that the kid up the street used to beat me up."

The road starts to get narrow.

"It's tough to be rich and white," he says.

"We're not rich."

"Oh, yeah?"

He hits a pothole. "Damn!"

I ask him, "Do you like school?"

"It's okay. And it's only a few blocks from CT."

"What school?"

"East Tech."

"Huh. I've heard of that. What are you going to do after high school?"

"College. I'm gonna be a doctor."

I control my surprise. "You have the grades for that?"

"Straight A's."

"Go, man."

"Where's your brother now?"

"He still lives with us. He's in the eighth grade."

I get out at a dirt path that runs along the chain-link fence. Across a big railroad yard, I see the Huletts taking bites of ore out of the boat, picking them up, carrying them back, and dumping them into a rail car. The whole operation is guarded by the fence. I walk along it most of the way to the lake, and then climb up and jump it and start walking down between the ore boat and the railroad cars. I feel small looking way up the side of the boat with these mechanical monsters towering over me. The clanking and grinding and buzzing of the machines are deafening, and the air is full of dust. The line of railroad cars curves endlessly around from Whiskey Island Road.

I watch the moving booms almost above me, but I don't want to get too close. I don't want those buckets hauling ore over my head to drop rocks on me. Anyway, I need to be looking on the other side of the ore boat, not this side. *How the hell am I going to get on the other side of the boat?*

Before long, a man in a dark-blue uniform with a gold badge trots up. "What are you doing here?!" he shouts over the racket. "You're not allowed here."

I raise my voice, and we begin a high-decibel conversation. I tell him about the wreck and that I'm looking for my friends. "Have you seen them?" I ask.

"No. But you can't go in there and look. We'll keep an eye out for them."

"Is there any way I can get on that boat and look over the side? I have to see if they're there."

"No, but I'll call the captain and ask him to have his crew look. I'll call the police and fire department, and the coast guard too, and alert them. You stay right here. Don't move."

He walks away, slips between two rail cars, and returns in a few minutes.

"The captain says they looked and there's no sign of them."

"Thanks for trying."

"Okay," he says, resuming his commanding voice. "Now you have to get out of here. No one's allowed in here. Come with me."

He leads me to a gate on Whiskey Island Drive, unlocks it, and lets me out.

"Hope your friends are all right," he says.

"Thanks."

He gets stern. "Don't come back in here. The next time we find you in here, we'll have you arrested for trespassing."

"Gotcha," I say. "Thanks for your help."

He looks at me. "Say—do you need a ride? I can probably get a police officer to help you."

"No thanks. I have a ride waiting for me, but I appreciate the offer."

I walk down the gravel road to the car and get in.

"No luck?" Walter asks. I shake my head. "Where now?"

"Let's keep going to the river."

We drive onto Whiskey Island. On the right, on the Old River—the part of the Cuyahoga they blocked off when they straightened the river—we pass Channel Marina with its boat storage racks, gas dock, picnic area, and boat slips. It's smaller than Edgewater—a third or so as big—but it's still full of yachts. Across the channel, we see tugboats waiting to guide the monster ore boats and barges to the mills.

Now the road disintegrates into one-lane dirt and gravel. It's full of jarring potholes—every one splashing muddy water onto Walter's car. "What in hell's name!" he says. "Why am I doing this, tearing up my car and getting it all muddy for some rich white boy?"

"Good deeds like this will help you get into heaven, Walter."

"There just better not be any white people up there."

"So you want it segregated, like Cleveland? The Supreme Court is against segregation."

"We black folk want the Almighty to deal justice to you people and send you the other way, that's all." Lucky for me, I see a hint of a smile on his face.

On the lake side, we go by a wooded area. Through the trees I see piles of trash and driftwood. It's a dump.

After a while, he says, "So you just want me to keep goin' down this sorry-ass cow path?"

"Just to the river. Can you do that? I can see that Iron Curtain railroad bridge up ahead. It's not far."

"It's not your car. What do you care?"

"But I've gotta get out here and walk. I can't see the shore from here. All you have to do is drive. You've got the easy part."

"You take me out in the middle of nowhere and then leave me alone so some white cop can come up and ask me what I'm doing here."

"I really appreciate this, Walter." I can't believe it. I think I'm making a Negro friend.

I push my way through wet, high grass and bushes and trees until I reach the lake. The beach here is coarse-gray sand, littered with driftwood trees and stumps. The sky and water are still gray. Occasional gusts hit me, but there are few whitecaps on the lake. Way ahead, I see the coast guard station on a breakwater projecting into the lake. I walk to it searching the driftwood. No sign of them here. At the breakwater, I look back toward the Iron Curtain and see that Walter is parked a short distance away just outside a wooden gate, which is apparently to keep cars from driving out to the station. I walk to the car, glance at the sign that says "Authorized Vehicles Only," lift the wooden bar, wave him through, and climb into the car.

"Who said we can go in here?"

"Come on. This is an emergency, Walter. I gotta find my friends."

"If anyone asks, I'm your chauffeur."

"But you said . . . "

"Sheeit. Things is different now."

We creep down the road toward the little white building with the observation tower and the cross-shaped flagpole. The Cuyahoga's on the right, and the woods are on the left. The land ends, and then we're just driving on the breakwater with the river on the right and the lake on the left. The road is barely ten feet wide, and there are heavy stone banks on both sides to hold back the water. We near the building and see the pole where the small-craft warning is still flying. We pull around the circle surrounding the pole and park at the main entrance.

"Come with me," I say. "Then they'll know you're with me." He nods.

Inside, a strong-looking man in his twenties wearing a white work uniform approaches us. He looks like he's ready to jump in a boat and make a rescue.

"Can I help you?" he asks, glancing at us, both in swimsuits, Walter's skin brown, mine white.

"I hope so. We're trying to find our friends. Our canoe capsized, and I don't know what happened to them."

"They're here," he says.

"Oh, thank God!"

"I'm Seaman Orinsky."

"Nice to meet you. I'm Jeff Klossen. This is Walter Madison. So are they okay?"

"Yes. Chief Petty Officer Klein checked their medical signs when we got them in here, and they seem to be okay—just tired." He leads us across the room. "Klein spotted them about an hour ago. They were almost at the dock before we saw them in all this rain."

"Was the canoe with them?"

"What's left of it. We had a hard time getting them up here because they wouldn't let go of it and wouldn't let go of each other either. We had to break their grips before we could reach down and haul them up."

"Do their parents know?"

"Yes. We called the girl's parents. Her mom's on the way. We also notified the newspapers and radio stations. They'll be interested in this story."

I ask where they are, and he leads us into another room—a relaxation room for the men—and there they are, Randy and Lori, sitting on a sofa, as close as they can be, skin against skin, with a wool blanket wrapped around them. She's studying his face.

Chapter 19—"I Don't Know How to Tell You This"

When she hears us at the door, she looks over and jumps up. "Jeff! You're alive." She runs to me and gives me a long, hard hug.

"Are you two okay?" I ask her.

"Yes, just exhausted. And I keep feeling like crying. Randy's okay, but he's really tired."

I notice Orinksy leaving the room, and I glance out the big windows at the forbidding gray lake. It makes me feel cold. The walls are like a government building—hard concrete painted white, with pictures of ships and coast guard rescue boats.

"We've been looking all over for you—me and Walter."

I introduce them all. Lori shakes Walter's hand, but Randy doesn't.

"Where did he come from?" Randy asks. I see Walter stiffen.

"Walter found me on Edgewater Beach and helped me out of the water. I was just about to give up and drown, and he saved me. Since then, he's been driving me around and helping me look for you two. Come on over and meet him."

"I don't have the energy," Randy says.

"Neither do I," Walter says. Then he looks at Lori. "Listen. I gotta go. You don't need a ride, now, do you?"

"No. My mom's coming," Lori says.

"Nice meeting you then."

I ask Orinsky for a pen and some paper, and Walter and I trade addresses and phone numbers.

"Let's keep in touch," I say. "And thanks for saving my life and driving me around, buddy. You're a great guy. I owe you." I feel close to him now, and I don't even know him. It's weird. I resist the urge to grab him and hug him. We shake hands, and I look him in the eye and say, "Maybe we can all get together sometime." Lori nods. Randy can't stand it, I guess. He just sits there and looks the other way.

The three other guardsmen come in and introduce themselves. One says, "A *Plain Dealer* reporter and photographer will be here in a few minutes. They want the story for the morning edition."

"Say, why don't you hang around awhile longer," I tell Walter. "You might get your picture in the paper. You're a big part of this story. And it'll look good on your college application."

He glances at his watch. "Okay. But just for ten minutes. Then I gotta go."

They arrive, and while the photographer is snapping pictures, the reporter grills Walter about the rescue. "I didn't do nothing," Walter says. "I just helped him get out of the water."

"I would have drowned if he hadn't have helped me," I say.

The reporter asks Walter where he lives and goes to school and what he wants to do when he graduates. Walter tells him and adds that he wants to go to medical school.

"That's quite an ambition, young man," the reporter says.

Then he asks me, "What did you learn from this experience?"

As usual, I say the first thing that comes to me: "Always bring an extra paddle."

"Is that all?"

"Well, you can't learn everything all at once."

In the car on the way home, Lori's mom asks what happened. I tell my version. Randy doesn't remember much about what happened after we capsized. Lori repeats her story, between sobs.

"We tipped over in the waves, and when I floated to the top of a wave, I looked over and saw Randy and Jeff. Randy was holding Jeff in a death grip. I think Randy was drowning. So I got behind him and grabbed his chin and pulled him away from Jeff and kept his head above the water. Then Jeff disappeared into the water. Randy was starting to go limp, so I reached around his neck across his chest to his armpit, grabbed his arm, and got under his body. I had on my life jacket. They didn't.

"Then I swam toward the canoe with my other hand and kicked like a frog. Randy started sputtering and coughing, so I knew he was alive. But before I could get to the canoe, the lightning struck it—blam!"

"Then what happened?" I ask.

"I don't know. Everything went black for a second, and I woke up with my body tingling."

"Yeah, me too."

"I couldn't hear a thing."

"Me neither."

"But somehow I was able to hold onto him."

"Amazing," I say.

"I kept swimming toward the canoe, thinking, *lightning won't strike the same place twice*. I still thought it would help keep us afloat."

"What about Randy?"

"Waves crashed over us a few times, and Randy kept coughing, but I could feel him getting stronger. And by the time we got to the canoe, he was alert."

"So you were able to hold onto it?"

"Yes. It was upside down in the water. Only the bottom of the bow showed, pointing up at an angle. I told Randy to grab it as I loosened my grip. He reached under and put his arm around the front thwart. I stayed behind him and put my arm over the same thwart, and then I wrapped my other arm around him and held onto the gunwale. I kept my arm around him to make sure he didn't slip off and go down."

"And that's how you made it here?"

"Yes. We drifted and bounced in the waves, and it got so cold I was shivering. But the canoe held us up, and the wind blew us here, and the men hauled us out. We were freezing and shaking like scared puppies."

"We looked at the canoe," I say. "It's amazing that it didn't sink. The lightning melted a hole two feet wide through the hull, down near the stern. It probably melted the flotation block too. But I guess the block in the bow held it up."

"How in the world did you know how to save him?" her mom asks. "You never had lifesaving lessons."

"I don't know, Mom. It just came to me."

"How'd you get so strong?" I ask.

"It must have been adrenalin."

I look over at Randy. He's next to me on the backseat half asleep. "Is that how it happened, Randy?"

"If she says so."

That night, I call Lori to see if she wants to get together. She starts to cry.

"Jeff, I don't know how to tell you this, but somehow, after saving Randy's life and after he and I were so close in the water for so long, with me holding his life in my arms for such a long time, I feel a bond with him now that I don't think will ever go away."

"What does that mean? You . . . you love him?"

"I love you, Jeff," she sobs. "I always will. But I'll never be able to separate myself from Randy, ever again."

"Damn, Lori. I can't believe it. I can't believe what you see in him."

"I'm sorry. I'm sorry. I can't help it. Just stop. Leave me alone—"

"Okay. Okay. Well, I guess I'll talk to you later."

I'm pissed. Randy. That jerk. How come it's always jerks that get the girls?

Oh, I still like you, Randy, even if you are a Neanderthal, even if you hate Negroes and think whites are the superior race, even if you did try to drown me out in the lake (maybe on purpose). But I'll get back at you. Don't worry.

Anyway, she won't be with you for long. She'll drop you like a sack of cement as soon as school starts, and kids find out you're going together and start ribbing you about going with a brain with straight hair who wears braces, and after they start getting mean about it. You'll get embarrassed, and the humiliation will spread to her like the flu, and the spell will be broken. She'll say bye-bye. Oh, yeah. She'll leave you, Randy, and I'll take her back with open arms. You bet I will.

The next morning, our picture is on the front page of the *Plain Dealer*—the four of us, each wrapped in a towel—followed by the story of the lightning strike and rescues by Walter and the Coast Guard.

We're in the kitchen—me and Mom and Dad and the two little gremlins. Mom is frying bacon and eggs. I love that smell. Dad is sitting at the breakfast table reading the paper. I already read it. I'm eating my grapefruit half.

"Well, I hope you learned a lesson," Dad says. "It says here that you said that the only lesson you learned was to take an extra paddle and that you weren't even wearing a life jacket. That was not smart. And that you went out on the lake when the small craft warnings were flying. That was idiotic. Were you trying to kill yourselves? You know, they fly those flags for a reason. When are you going to grow up, Jeff?"

I've had enough. I'm in a bad mood. I don't want to hear this. "You're right, Dad," I say. It's always best to agree with him. It makes his sails luff. He expects an argument and thinks, "What did you say?" Then his sail starts flapping and his compass spinning, and he doesn't know what to say next. So I leap in and point him in a new direction, "I was just lucky that Walter was there to save my life, Dad. Imagine. My life was saved by a Negro teenager from the slums." I have to bring that up, and I gotta keep rubbing it in (rub it in, rub it in).

"That's his picture in the paper, isn't it, with you and Lori and Randy and the coast guard sailors?"

I've got him now. I shake my head no. "You shouldn't call them sailors, Dad. They're not in the navy."

"What do you call them?"

"Guardsmen, Dad."

"Oh."

Now he forgets what he was going to say, which is always good.

Brett wanders in, sees me, and goes the other way.

"Where are you going, Brett? What's the matter? Don't want to talk to me?" He doesn't say a word. "I did it, Brett. Now it's time for you to pay up."

Dad asks, "Did what?"

"We made a little wager. I said I could canoe Hinckley Lake, the upper and lower Cuyahoga River, the Vermilion River, Lake Erie, and Shale River by Labor Day, and he bet me I couldn't."

"How much was the bet?" Dad asks.

"A hundred bucks."

"A hundred dollars! Oh, Jeff," Mom says.

"That makes me mad," Dad says. "You don't have the money to be throwing around on gambling."

"Don't worry, Dad. It wasn't a gamble. It was easy money."

"Sure," Brett says. "You idiots destroyed two canoes! Incredible. And you got unbelievably lucky when the drought ended and the rain gods raised Shale River for you. You really deserved to lose."

"What about the canoe?" Dad asks. "What are you going to do about that? Didn't it belong to Randy's brother?"

"Yes. We'll have to get another one. That's what I need the money for."

"Didn't you already pay fifty dollars to buy it in the first place?" Dad asks. I don't know who he heard that from.

"Yes."

"And then you wrecked it on its maiden voyage. Ha!" Brett says.

He pays me the next day, grudgingly, of course—counting out a hundred ones he got at the grocery store.

We start getting phone calls again. Dad picks one up in the kitchen, and from the living room I can hear him shouting, "Who is this? Who is this? I'll have the police put a tracer on this call. You're going to . . . " I can almost hear the click from where I am. "Jeff. You come here. Do you see what you've started? Do you see?"

I stand before him and face the music. "It must have been some nut who saw our picture in the paper and just got jealous of us." Alternate theories—that's all I need. "Or maybe some girl wanted to talk to me. I look pretty good in that swimsuit. Yeah, that's probably it."

"Humph. Or someone who didn't like you standing next to that Negro boy."

I diffused the issue, for a while, anyway. I wonder who was calling. I bet it was Randy or one of his friends, especially since Randy's dad was so mad.

After a few days, the disaster on the lake begins to fade. I tell the tale so many times that words begin to replace the memories, and the story gets stale and unreal, and recollections start floating around like ghosts, and I can hardly believe it happened. Then things seem to get back to normal. I keep thinking about Lori, and I can't help thinking about Walter and what divides blacks and whites.

I give him a call to see what he's doing. We talk for a while, and I ask if he wants to get together to shoot the breeze. He says okay and suggests we meet at the Soldiers' and Sailors' Civil War Monument on Public Square. I tell him I'll ask Lori to go too, but I don't say anything about her dropping me for racist Randy. He would surely think less of Lori.

If I can just keep Lori working with me, maybe she'll wise up and come back. I call her up and ask her if she'd like to go. "We need to break out of this prison and make friends with some people on the other side."

"The other side of what?"

"'The great divide.' Walter said that's what W. E. B. Dubois called it."

"Who?"

"That Negro leader who helped start the National Association for the Advancement of Colored People."

"Oh. Okay. I'll go. But this doesn't mean I'm going out with you, Jeff. I'm still going with Randy."

That meathead. "Yeah. I understand." I try not to picture them making out. And I try not to growl at her and tell her how stupid she's being.

Chapter 20—Freedom's Spirit

It's a bright Saturday morning and hasn't started to get hot yet. Lori and I take the bus to Public Square across from the Terminal Tower. The monument has a shaft about twelve stories high with a Statue of Freedom on top—a woman holding a shield. At the base is a square stone building with half-circle stained-glass windows under stone arches—three to a side. Bronze battle sculptures occupy each side of the building, and broad stairways, each with about a dozen curved steps, ascend from the sidewalks at the four street corners.

"I think this is an appropriate place for us to meet," I say. "I'm in favor of liberty and the freeing of teenage slaves."

"Freeing us from the A-people?" she asks, smiling.

"Right."

Walter comes. He's wearing an old Indians cap. We all sit down at the top of a stairway to talk and watch the pigeons and people strut by.

After some small talk, I ask, "What kind of work do you do?"

"I help a mechanic at a garage."

"Where'd you learn how to do that kind of work?" Lori asks, beating me to the punch.

"Just by helping him and watching and reading the manuals and ordering things for him."

"He pays you, right?" I ask.

"He does now, but not when I started a few years ago. I just hung around and helped him. But then when I started to get good at things—you know, brakes and tires and so on, so he could trust me—he started paying me and teaching me to do tune-ups and things."

"Cool. That's a lot better than what I do—mowing lawns."

"Then I learned enough to turn that wreck of mine into a car. And now I can make money and save it for what I want to do."

"You mean, go to college," Lori says.

"Yeah."

"Do you have a girl?" she asks.

"I don't have much time for dating, between school and work and helping Mom, but I go out once in a while."

We talk about the wreck, the newspaper article, our sudden fame, and how lucky—and unlucky—we were. Then I ask, "Say, Walter. I'm curious. You said your mom works. But where's your dad?"

"He got sick and died when I was a kid. Got lung cancer."

"Was he a smoker?"

"No, he wasn't. It could have come from dust in the mills. Who knows? He worked in the Flats."

I watch a bus start up, blasting a cloud of smoke from its rear end, and see a well-dressed family walk into Higbee's Department Store and some pigeons fly up out of the way of an approaching car.

We get tired of sitting and go down the stairs and make the circuit around the monument looking up at the four bronze sculptures: a cavalry grouping showing close-range fighting with pistols and sabers and a foundering horse; an infantry color guard with soldiers getting wounded; an artillery unit with a cannon and mortally wounded soldiers; a navy mortar group with a Negro sailor helping load the mortar.

I jog back up the stairs with the others in tow and plop down again.

"Pretty neat," I say.

"They make it easier to picture the war," Lori says.

A Negro man, about fifty, dressed in old pants and a long-sleeve shirt passes by at the bottom of the stairs, looks at us, scowls, and keeps walking.

"Walter, why is it that so many Negroes look like they hate white people?"

"Humph," he snorts. "Easy. They think white people are devils."

"What? All of us?"

"Yeah."

"Why?"

"Why? Well, first you make us your slaves for almost two hundred years. Then you keep us in our place with Jim Crow and segregation for a hundred years and make us do exactly what you tell us to do and lynch thousands of us and try to take away our right to vote. Then you exploit our labor with tenant farms and sharecropping, and keep us in crowded, rotten housing, and keep us from getting good educations and jobs, and refuse to pay us as much as you pay white people for doing the same work. There's a start."

"But I never did anything to Negroes. I had nothing to do with slavery or Jim Crow or any of that, and my family didn't either."

Walter sort of laughs, and his jaw tightens into a grim smile. He crosses his arms in a prosecutorial way, and says: "Let me ask you some questions."

"Shoot."

"Would your dad sell your house to a Negro?"

I shrug. I feel uncomfortable. "Uh, I don't know."

"What about you, Lori? Would your dad sell your house to a Negro family?"

She lifts her eyebrows and says, "I don't know either."

"Well, I'll tell you. No, they wouldn't. They wouldn't want to get threatened with violence. They wouldn't want to get all those threatening phone calls and crosses burned on their lawns and crowds of people out front carrying signs and shouting at them."

"What are you talking about?" I ask.

"They wouldn't want their neighbors to get mad at them for making their property values go down. 'Cause that's what they say—we always make people's property values go down."

I was curious: "Walter, let me ask you this—why do people think Negroes make property values go down?"

"Because white people won't live next to them, and they sell out at any price they can get because none of you wants to buy a house next to a Negro."

"So white people make their own property values go down," Lori says.

"Shit, yeah," he says, shaking his head in disgust. "Then you blame us! You even put restrictions in your deeds saying the house could never be sold to a Negro."

"What?"

"That's right. And the government supported them. The Federal Housing Administration wouldn't give Negroes FHA mortgages in white neighborhoods."

"You're kidding."

"Nope. And the FHA required deed restrictions that said the house could never be sold to Negroes or Jews. But they had to stop that in 1949 when the Supreme Court said the courts couldn't enforce the restrictions. But that's why so few Negroes have FHA loans."

"Where did you learn all this?"

"You've gotta be black to know these things."

"You know, Walter, we've been trying to figure out why there are no Negroes living in Orchard Park. We have great schools. No crowding. Nice houses. Not much crime."

"I just told you why. We've always wanted those things. But you wouldn't sell to us. And we don't want to live there anyway. Why would we want to live around people who want to keep us down? And what would we do for fun out in that white desert with no black people around—no brothers or chicks—and no black churches or barber shops or neighborhood clubs . . . and nightclubs and jazz clubs and Negro restaurants."

"You could just drive downtown or take a bus to get to them," I say.

He shakes his head. "Nah. We'd be turncoats—deserters. We wouldn't fit in downtown anymore."

I watch two more buses appear, belch their stinky exhaust, wheeze, grind to a stop, and pour people onto sidewalks.

The prosecution continues: "Let me ask you this, Jeff: would your dad give me a job?"

This one I deftly avoid. "He doesn't do the hiring where he works."

"He wouldn't if he could."

"I don't know. You're probably right." Dad thinks Negroes are inferior to whites, but he might think they make better laborers, so he might hire one.

"Another thing, Jeff. Would you let me date your sister?"

I parry with, "I don't have a sister."

"But you wouldn't if you did have one. You're just like all the rest. You're a white supremacist. We're not equal to you. You think you're better than we are and that you should rule us and always tell us what to do. And you want your descendants to be white. And you don't want us around. You wouldn't let us in your yacht club or country club. I don't think we'd be welcome in your church even. And you wouldn't let us move in next to you."

I give up. I don't know what to say. I glance across the street and watch two well-dressed black women enter Higbee's and other Negroes and white people pass by the Terminal Tower.

He won't stop. He looks at Lori. "What about you, Lori? Would you go out with me?"

"I'm going with Randy."

"Randy. He hates us. I thought you were with Jeff."

I blush and shake my head. "No."

"But if you weren't going with him."

"I'd have to get to know you a lot better, Walter."

"Yeah. Sure."

"Walter, if you dislike white people so much, how come you agreed to get together today?"

"I don't know. I thought I'd give you a try. You seemed nicer than most when I saw you at the coast guard station, and I thought maybe you weren't like all those other white folks."

"Well, are we?"

"I don't know yet." He tugs on his cap and looks around.

"Let's go inside the monument," he suggests. "It's a sacred place."

"Really? I've never been in it," I say.

"Me either," Lori adds.

We walk inside through heavy oak doors. We're the only ones there. The light is dim, and it takes a while for our eyes to adjust. It's a square room with a square central core. Chandeliers of incandescent globes light the four corners of the room, and lines of fluorescents are suspended from the ceiling. Around the outside, the stained-glass semicircles cast light. Brass guardrails encircle the exterior and the central square, three feet from the walls.

The outside walls are covered with names. "What are all those names?" Lori asks Walter. Her voice echoes off the hard walls and ceiling.

He whispers, "Those are the nine thousand folks from the county who fought to defend the Union and end slavery. Seventeen hundred of them were killed. I can feel their eyes looking out at us from those names."

"Seventeen hundred!" I gasp.

"Out of the 365,000 total northern soldiers killed and 260,000 total rebel soldiers dead."

"Hideous," Lori says in a hushed tone that nevertheless is echoed off the surfaces—as if many voices are repeating it.

Walking around the center core, we see four large bronze relief sculptures depicting the war. Walter especially wants to show us, "Emancipation of the Slave." In it, Lincoln is standing, breaking the chains of a kneeling slave, and handing him a rifle.

"This is what makes this place sacred—Mr. Lincoln setting us Negroes free." I can barely hear him. "This and that lady on top, holding that liberty shield. And all those men who fought and died to keep the Union together and end slavery. What a huge thing they did."

We study the russet faces, and he asks, "Can you feel the spirit in this room—freedom's spirit?"

"I think so," Lori says.

"It's thick in here," he says. "It comes down the shaft from that lady on top and out this sculpture and out all the eyes of the people who suffered and died."

I glance at the names, and they start to come alive. "Yes. I feel it. It's here."

We're transfixed.

"We have to let it out," he says.

We open the doors, and I feel it blowing past me like a wind. We close the doors behind us, let our eyes adjust to the glare, and sit.

"And here we are," he says, "and the question is, a hundred years after emancipation, are we free?"

"You . . . and us," I say.

"A hundred years after taking up arms and fighting for your freedom," Lori says.

"Yes. You know, two hundred thousand of us Negroes fought for the North—ten percent of the Union Army—and forty thousand died."

I didn't know that.

We're quiet. I stare down the limestone steps and say, "Hey, Walter, I was thinking. We have this foreign exchange program in Orchard Park, you know, where foreign students come live with our families for a year and go to school with us, and then our students go overseas and live with them for a year. Well, I was thinking we could start our own exchange program. Lori and I could go to your church some Sunday and meet your friends, and then you could come to Orchard Park and meet some of our friends. And maybe we could do it more than once. That way we could start to start to bridge this gulf between the races."

"Let me get this straight—you want to try to integrate Orchard Park?"

"That's right. Do what I can."

"And my neighborhood too?"

"Yes. Build a bridge. Bring us together."

"You're out of your mind. You know, some of our folks might not like having white kids invade their church. We have to have someplace of our own, you know. A lot of Negro people really hate white people. And to tell you the truth, they might come after me for bringing you into the neighborhood."

"Come on, Walter. We've got to cross this gorge that these A-people have dug to keep us apart. What do you say?" I look him in the eye. "Can we visit your church or not? Do you have the guts to bring us in? And do you have the guts to visit us out in Orchard Park?"

His face gets mean, and he says, "You jive, white boy. If you can, I can."

I shake my head up and down in his face and bark, "Okay."

He looks down, and then looks up at me slyly, tilting his head. "How are you going to get there?"

"We can take the bus. Mom and Dad will be using the car to go to our church."

"Oh. 'Mom and Dad will be using the car.' Okay, rich kid. The bus stops three blocks from the church on Central, but you have to walk through the projects to get to the church. Are you sure you want to do that?"

"Why? Is it dangerous?"

"It's a high crime area even for us. There are bad characters down there, and you gotta know how to protect yourself. It seems like there's a robbery or a shooting every day. You might get mugged or beat up. Oh, and didn't I tell you how so many black people hate you white people and why?"

"Jeff. I'm not sure my parents will let me do this," Lori says.

"You mean it's not safe in broad daylight on a Sunday morning?" I ask Walter.

"I can't promise it is."

I stop talking, for once, and look around again. Maybe I'm crazy. Maybe I'll be taking Lori into another angry lake with a warning flag flying.

"I understand. I'll go by myself. But I'm not carrying any weapons. I'll have to trust in the Almighty."

"Damn you, Jeff," Walter says. "That's not good enough. Listen. I'll pick you up right here. I just hope no one sees us and trashes my car while we're in church. But I guess if that happened, someone else could give you a ride back here."

We say good-bye, and he heads up the street. Lori and I stand frozen in shock. "God, Lori. Will white people and Negroes ever get along?"

She looks down and says, "I don't know."

"So, do you want to go if Walter picks us up?"

"Yes, but I'll have to get permission."

From her parents, or Randy?

Chapter 21—Disobedience

"What did you do today?" Mom asks me enthusiastically. I'm too slow to think of something creative, so I spout out the truth and now must suffer another interrogation. "Lori and I went downtown to see Walter."

It's dinnertime. The tablecloth, placemats, and iced tea are on the table, Billy and Jimmy are seated on their phone books, Mom is passing her creation, which I love—beef stew seasoned with green olives and sherry from a vineyard in Dover—and Dad has already blessed it to our bodies.

"Oh?" he says. "Where did you meet him?"

"At Public Square, at the Civil War monument."

"What did you want to see him about?" he asks and forks a chunk of beef into his mouth.

"Oh, just to talk."

"About what?" Now he's violently grinding that piece of cow.

"Oh, the accident and stuff. And then we looked at all the statues on the monument."

"Is that all?"

"Well, no. We made plans for me and Lori to go to church with him on Sunday." *What self-destructive urge made me blurt that out?*

He cranes his neck at me and stares. "Church with him? Why?"

"I just want to learn more about him and Negro people and see if he and I can develop a friendship."

"Well . . . where does he go to church?"

"Good Samaritan Baptist." I don't tell him where it is. "We'll take the bus downtown again, and he'll pick us up at Public Square."

"Where is this church?"

Caught. "East Sixty-Seventh and Quincy."

"Quincy! That's one of the worst parts of the city!" He looks at Mom and shakes his head rapidly. "I don't want him and his girlfriend going down there by themselves with a Negro kid they don't even know."

I look at Mom to see if I can get some support, but she avoids my gaze.

"But Dad, it'll be broad daylight on a Sunday morning. And don't forget, this kid saved my life!"

"I don't care. You are not going down there, and that's that."

That's what he thinks.

Knowing me, Dad adds, "And if you go ahead and do it, you will lose your driving privileges. I mean it."

Great. The judge, warden, and jail guard has spoken.

The next morning, I ask him if I can see the deed to our house. I don't tell him I want to see if it has any deed restrictions on it.

"Our deed?"

"Yes. I'm curious about what one looks like. I've decided to see what I can learn about some different careers this summer, like law and banking and construction, and some others, and I know lawyers and bankers and builders all handle deeds a lot, so I thought I'd like to take a look at ours."

He stares at me suspiciously, and I look him straight back in the eye without a quiver, and then he seems to accept it, although he keeps squinting at me. "Well. That sounds like a good idea. I'll have to get it out of the safety deposit box at the bank."

"Thanks, Dad."

That night, he shows me the deed. I study it. At the top it says:

"VOL 6392 PAGE 274." Below that is: "Know all Men by these Presents That we, Ronald R. Williams and Raymond O. Schneider (both married) Who acquired titled Date____ Volume 6045 Page NO 87 for the consideration of Ten and No/100 Dollars ($10.00) received to our full satisfaction of Irvin O. Klossen and Rebecca M. Klossen, whose last mailing address is 1438 Contin Rd., Orchard Park, Ohio," Give, Grant, Bargain, Sell, and Convey unto the said Grantees, their heirs and assigns, the following described premises . . . [a surveyor's description of the lot]" . . . [and that the property] is "free from all encumbrances whatsoever except restrictions of record, zoning, ordinances of the City of Orchard Park, and taxes and assessments for the year 1947 and thereafter."

And then it was all signed and notarized on April 14, 1948. I can barely read it all, it's so boring. But then I think, *Wait. Restrictions of record? What are those?*

I take it to him. He's sitting in the blue chair in the living room reading the newspaper. "Hey, Dad. What does this mean: 'restrictions of record'? Do you know what they are?"

"As I understand it, it means that we can't build a barn on the property, or a liquor store, or raise farm animals, things like that. We can only use the land for a private residence."

"And the zoning ordinances?"

"We can't build anything within such-and-such distance from the street, and our neighbors, and the back of the lot. And it can't be too high, and it has to meet other requirements."

"Oh. And I was wondering, can you sell the property to anyone you want to?"

He looks at me funny, like "why are you asking that?" and says, "Yes. Of course."

"Thanks. That's interesting."

Dead end. No racial restrictions . . . I think.

It occurs to me that Lori might like to see it. She may see something I missed. "Say, do you mind if I show it to Lori? She's interested too."

"Just don't lose it," he says. "I'll be really angry if you lose it."

After dinner, I take it over and show it to her. She reads it and can't find anything either.

"It's just like ours," she says. "I couldn't find any racial restrictions in it either."

"And there's no evidence that FHA has kept Negroes out."

"So is this the end of our search?"

I raise my eyebrows and shrug. "I guess so."

"Until we learn something else."

The phone rings after dinner. "I'll get it," I holler. Mom's upstairs. I'm in the living room reading *Curious George* to the boys. I don't want to subject her to another silent phone call.

"Hello. Klossen residence. Jeff speaking." You probably can't believe I answer that formally. But that's the way I've been trained to answer my whole life, and it's hard to break a good habit, try as I might.

"Hey, Klossen. We have a problem."

Yeah, I know we do. "What now?"

"Garth's coming home, and he wants to take his canoe back to Colorado."

"Did you tell him it's already been made into aluminum foil?"

"Not funny, Jeff. We owe him a canoe. And he wants one that doesn't leak."

"Now wait. You owe him a canoe."

"But you're the one who said we could beat the storm back to Shale River Harbor, that we'd just have to dig hard."

"Yeah, so I'm to blame?"

"And you said that the worst that could happen was that we would get blown back to shore."

"Yeah, well you were in the stern, man. You could make the canoe go anywhere you wanted to. All I did was provide muscle up front."

"Until you broke your paddle. We might've made it back if you hadn't broken your paddle. That's another reason it was your fault: you broke your paddle."

"Well, it doesn't matter anyway—he's your brother, not mine. What do I care if he beats you up."

"My dad's really mad."

"That's too bad."

"Yeah, well he'll call your dad, and then he'll get mad."

"What else is new? Dads are A-people; they stick together, and they're always mad."

He's silent. I believe I have beaten him into submission. That's why the debate team at school has been so good for me. It's like fencing—parry and riposte.

"Come on, Jeff. I thought we were friends."

He's on his knees—begging. "Nah. Not anymore. First you try to drown me. Then you take my girl. You don't even have a canoe. How can you say we're friends?"

"You son of a gun. I really did think we were friends. I thought you'd help me with this. You have to admit, you were partly responsible for this wreck."

I guess I've jerked his chain enough. Now I have to end the charade. "Okay, okay, okay. I'll help you. But this time, I think you're the one who should have to find the canoe. Just look in the paper every morning, and when you see one you like, go look at it."

"But I work all day."

"Yeah. You sit around the caddy shack and wait for golfers. What do you think I do, sit around and watch soap operas?"

"I bet you have more time than I do."

"Listen, Randy, it wasn't my fault your brother's canoe got hit by lightning. It was an act of God."

"All I know is that we took his canoe out and trashed it—put a huge hole in it. And he wants a good one back."

"Well, you find one, and we can dicker over the price. This time the shoe's on the other foot."

"So that's the way you feel about it, Klossen?"

"That's the way I feel about it, Clark."

"By the way, I'd like you to stay away from Lori. We're going together, you know."

"I tell you what, Randy. I just changed my mind. I'll help you get another canoe if you break up with Lori. Is it a deal?"

"Why you . . . I never thought you'd bring her into this!"

I call her on the phone. "I've got to talk to you. When can I come over?"

"Randy's coming over tonight."

"Oh."

"Maybe tomorrow morning."

"Okay. How about at eleven. I have a couple of lawns to do first."

Eleven comes around and I go over. I'm all sweaty, but it doesn't matter anyway because we won't be messing around, not with her going with that insect Randy. She lets me in and looks at my perspiration. "Ooo. You are really wet."

She leads me to the water-resistant lawn furniture on the back porch.

"So what did you want to talk about?" she asks.

"Lots of things," I say, smiling and glancing at her lips. "But what I came over for was to tell you that my dad says that if I go down to Walter's church on Sunday, I'm grounded. What did your parents say?"

"They don't like the idea, but they say that I can go if you and Walter are with me. But they said they can't help me. They have some other things they have to do, so I'm on my own."

"At least they'll let you go. I still to have to do the disobedience-and-pay-the-price thing. But maybe they wouldn't let you go if they knew I'm not allowed to go. So is it still okay with you?"

"Yes. I just won't tell them. I want to cross the bridge too."

At six thirty Sunday morning, I unhook the screen on my first-floor window, slip out, and walk around the house to the garage end where I've left my bike. I pump away, turn up a neighbor's driveway and skirt his garage, staying close to the flower beds so the line the wheels make in the dew won't be noticeable—an old paperboy trick. Then I cut through the yards to the other street. I must look weird riding a bike in my navy sport coat, white shirt, tie, and shiny black dress shoes. I park in Lori's driveway, and she meets me at the front door wearing a longish dark-red pleated skirt, white blouse, bobby socks, black flats, and a round white hat the shape of a tuna-fish can. "Just a minute." She closes the door and soon appears by their garage walking her bike.

"You look . . . fetching this morning," I say.

"Don't start."

We pedal off in the early light and cool of the morning, up the ancient beach ridges of Lake Erie to Detroit Road and Center Ridge Road, and on to the bus stop at the shopping center. There we fasten our bike locks to the rack and wait in the shelter. After most of an hour, we board the bus. This time there are no people sitting across the aisle or in front or in back of us. It's perfect for canoodling, except for one thing.

"No," she says as she grabs my hand and removes it from her leg. "I told you I'm going with Randy!"

"Okay, okay."

Our relationship is the worst casualty of the lake disaster.

We get off at Public Square, walk to the monument, stand in front of Higbee's, and look around. After about ten minutes, Walter pulls up and we hop in, Lori in back.

"Hi," I say. "You're right on time."

"Actually, you're early, but that's good—I didn't have to park."

I tell him about my dad's ultimatum and how he probably tried to get the police to look for me. "But he won't remember your last name and doesn't know the kind of car you drive."

"Good."

He stays on Euclid for about a mile to East Twenty-Second Street and turns right.

"I want to show you where my Mom works. We have time. It's right on the way."

"At the hospital?"

"Yeah. St. Vincent's."

After half a dozen blocks we come to the Cuyahoga County Detention Center. "What's that, the jail?"

"Yeah. For juvenile delinquents. Some kids from my neighborhood are in there."

He turns left onto Central Avenue and says, "There's the hospital." It's a big old brick building on the right, four or five stories high.

"Is she working today?" Lori asks.

"No. We'll see her at church."

"Oh, good."

We go another mile or so, past some of the worst old run-down houses I've ever seen, turn right on East Fifty-Fifth Street, go a couple of long blocks, and come to a big brick building set back on a lawn.

"That's East Tech."

"It's big," I say. It's older than Orchard Park High, but looks in good condition.

Turning left onto Quincy, he drives ten blocks through another run-down section and past a cemetery. Then on the left, coming toward us, we see a steeple rising at least ten stories high into the sky.

"Is that it?" I ask.

"Yes. Good Samaritan."

"Wow. What a building!"... *Rising out of the slums.*

"I can't wait to see inside," Lori says.

He turns left and parks by the side of the church—a long brick wall with five arched stained-glass windows more than two stories high. Wide steps wrap around the front of the building and lead up to a central entrance below the steeple. A few people in church clothes stand on the sidewalk chatting. Others are walking toward the steps.

We enter a side door into a basement level and go up some worn marble stairs to the foyer. Two men in dark suits greet us enthusiastically. They ask who we are and where we're from. We say we're friends of Walter's from Orchard Park. They hand us programs, and an usher leads us into the sanctuary. The ceiling soars above us like a cathedral. It's supported by giant timber trusses, the bottoms of which slope upward, and the ceiling is clad with dark wood. Rows of pews face the front, which has a pulpit, altar, choir chairs, and a circular stained-glass window with the brass pipes of the organ standing below it. A baptistery is to the right. More than a dozen choir members in dark-red robes with long white sashes stand in front, facing us.

I notice that everyone in the church is black except Lori and me, and many people are looking at us. It takes my breath away and makes my knees a little weak; we're different—we're the minority. What are we doing here? Outsiders.

About a third of the pews are filled. Walter spots a woman up front waving at him. "There she is," he says, and asks the usher to seat us next to her. We walk down the center aisle toward her, a moderately plump woman with brown skin wearing a dark-blue dress and a broad-brimmed black hat with a blue ribbon bow on it.

Walter introduces us, and Lori moves into the row and shakes her hand; I reach over and do the same, and we exchange greetings.

The service begins with an organ prelude. Then we sing a hymn: "Come, Ye Thankful People, Come."

Reverend Henry calls for recognition of visitors, and Lori and I stand and turn to face the congregation. The church is more than half-full now.

"I'm Jeff Klossen and this is Lori Matthews. We live in Orchard Park. Walter saved me from drowning in Lake Erie last week after we had a canoeing accident. And he lent me his shoes so I could search for Lori and my other friend Randy along the shore down by Edgewater Park and Whiskey Island. He drove me from place to place and let me out. Walter is my Good Samaritan, and I want to meet everyone here today and thank you for helping make him who he is today."

During the offering, a man in the choir sings "In the Garden." Lori and I drop some bills on the plate. Then we all sing another hymn.

As if I hadn't embarrassed Walter enough, Rev Henry's sermon is on the namesake of the church, the Good Samaritan, and how we should always go out of our way to help others, even if they are different from us, people who are despised, criminals, or addicts—anyone in need. "God wants us to help these people and not just pass them by." He gets warmed up and repeats his phrases a lot, and people in the congregation call out "amen" and "yes, brother" and "yes, sir." He ends with a prayer asking God to help us help others.

That's about it. The whole thing is pretty familiar to me. It's not too different from our church, and quite similar to my grandparents' Baptist church, only more emotional.

At the end, Reverend Henry walks down the aisle to greet people at the door. Most file out while the organ is playing joyful music I don't know, but many come forward to greet Lori and me.

"Can you stay for our dinner?" Mrs. Madison asks.

I'm surprised. I look at Lori, and she nods.

"Sure," I say.

We go to the door to shake hands with Reverend Henry and then follow Walter and Mrs. Madison into the basement, where the smells of fried chicken and yams and collard greens and rolls are rich in the air. People have already filled half of the round tables. Walter goes to a table and tips up four chairs to save our places, shakes a few hands on the way, and then joins us in line.

We put some money in the donation basket and proceed to load our plates. The women behind the serving line smile and greet us. "Nice to have you, Mr. Klossen and Miss . . . uh . . . "

"Matthews," Lori replies. "Nice to be here. This food looks scrumptious."

We sit down to a fine meal. An old couple and a young woman join us. Walter introduces us. "This is Mr. and Mrs. Phelps," he says. "They've been members here since before I was born."

"It's nice to have you," the old man says.

"And this is Sarah Williams. Sarah and I are friends. We're kind of . . . going together."

"Nice to meet you," she says.

"Well, you've got a winner, here, Sarah." I say. "Hang onto him."

She just smiles, and then asks, "Are you and Lori going together?"

I blush. Damn. I always have to blush! "No. We're just friends. . . . Do you go to East Tech too?"

"Yes. I'm a year behind Walter. I'll be a junior this year."

I ask Mrs. Madison how she likes working in the hospital.

"It's hard work, but I like to help people. One of these years, though, I want to go to their nursing school. I can do more good if I'm a nurse like Mrs. Phelps was, and I'd make more money."

"What did Mr. Phelps do?"

"He used to work in the mills, like my husband did."

"My grandfather worked in a mill in Pittsburgh," I say. "It was a rolling mill. He lost the tips of two fingers once when his glove got caught in the rollers."

There's lots to talk about, and the chicken melts in my mouth, and so does everything else, especially the sweet potato pie for dessert.

Afterward, we say good-bye, and Walter and Sarah drive us back to Public Square.

"Next Saturday we're having our church picnic, from eleven to three. Can you two come?" I ask. "You can meet my family and some of my friends."

"Rich people."

"Not so rich."

"Sure," he says.

The pair look at each other. Sarah shrugs. "I'm not afraid if you're not."

"Can you come, Lori?" I ask. I really want her to come.

"I think so."

Randy won't mind, will he? I think it, but don't say it.

"How're you going to get us there," Walter asks, "past all those cops in Lakeshore and Orchard Park."

"Don't worry. I'll figure it out. I'll protect you."

"Yeah. Like on Whiskey Island. You left me parked on the road waiting for the cops to come arrest me while you took a walk on the beach. I didn't think you'd ever get back."

Lori falls asleep on the bus trip back, and I feel her head on my shoulder. I love it. I wish it could just stay there. But the ride ends. We get off, hop on our bikes, and ride home.

"I'm going to see if I can get a reporter and photographer from the *Herald* there Saturday," I say. "We can have more impact if we get a story in the paper."

"You're right."

"And I'll call Randy and see if he can come, so we can have everyone in the picture again."

"I'll talk to him too."

I don't know what she's thinking. "Just don't tell him that Walter's coming."

"No, I won't."

"Just tell him it'll be fun." She nods. "See you. It was great being with you."

"You too, Jeff," she says, looking up into my eyes.

I'm gonna get her yet.

I pedal home, taking the streets instead of cutting across the lawns. Now it's time to face the music.

Chapter 22—The Picnic

"Your father is furious." She looks like *she* could chew nails. "He wanted to go looking for you, but I wouldn't let him. Where were you?"

"At that church downtown."

"After all he's done for you, and you disobeyed him just like that? You know what this means. He's going to ground you."

"I know, Mom. But I had to go."

"And why is that?"

"You know why. I have to make friends with some people on the other side."

That seems to soften her a little. "Well . . . that's good, Jeff. . . . So . . . so how did it go?"

"It was a new world. The people were nice. The service was a lot like ours, really. We even sang some of the same hymns. Then we had dinner in the basement of the church—in their fellowship hall. Really good food—fried chicken and sweet potato pie for dessert. And the church is gorgeous. It's like ours, but a lot bigger, and it doesn't have any columns, just a really high steeple, maybe ten stories high, and high stained-glass windows on the sides. And it's right in the slums. I couldn't believe it."

"That's interesting. By the way, we had another call today. I wish they'd stop."

Dad's at the driving range, whacking balls. When he gets back, I'm in the living room reading a magazine; Mom's in the backyard with the boys. I stand up when I hear him coming. I want to meet him eye to eye. He walks into the room, and I can see he's mad. His eyes are pinched, his mouth's in a snarl, and he's gritting his teeth.

"You're grounded."

"But you said I would just lose my driving privileges."

He pauses. "That's what I mean."

"For how long?"

"Until I say so."

"Oh. Okay." The punishment sounds really bad, but I know it won't last. They need me to drive too much. He'll have second thoughts the first time I tell him I need gas for the lawnmower.

"Listen, Dad, I'm sorry I had to disobey you."

He points his chin at me. "Had to?"

I nod. "Yes. It's important to me to understand what Negroes are like, and we don't get the chance in Orchard Park."

"You're lucky you haven't been around them, and that your mother and I have been able to protect you from all their crime and laziness and lower-class morals."

"I think you're wrong about them. But I have to see for myself. I know one Negro who saved my life. You can be grateful to him for that."

He shakes his head. "He must be one in a million."

"Oh, I forgot to tell you. He and his friend Sarah are coming to the church picnic on Saturday. You'll get to meet them."

"Humph. Why would I want to meet them?"

"Because he saved my life, Dad."

"Well, don't blame me if they get snubbed."

"Is that what you're going to do?"

He looks me hard in the eye. "Don't be smart."

"Think of them as exchange students, Dad. They're here to get to know us and learn how we live, and so we can learn how they live."

"I have no interest in learning how slum kids live."

On Thursday I call the weekly newspaper, which I used to deliver before I started carrying the *Plain Dealer*. One of the reporters answers.

"I used to be one of your carriers a few years ago, and I'm also the boy who almost drowned in the canoeing accident a couple of weeks ago on Lake Erie."

"What's your name?"

"Jeff Klossen. I wanted to tell you that the Negro high school boy from Cleveland who saved my life is coming to our church picnic on Saturday to meet my family and my friends from church. The picnic's from eleven to three."

"Uh-huh."

"I thought it might make a good human interest story for you, especially since I used to deliver the paper. If you think so, you might want to send a photographer like the *Plain Dealer* did a couple weeks ago. One o'clock might be a good time to come."

"Hmm. We'll talk about it and see if someone's available."

My other call is to the police department on Friday.

"Police."

"Hi. My name's Jeff Klossen. I live in Orchard Park. I'm the guy who almost drowned a couple of weeks ago on Lake Erie when lightning hit our canoe."

"I heard about that."

"Our pictures were on the front page of the *Plain Dealer*."

"Oh, yes. You're the ones who weren't wearing life jackets."

"Yes, sir. I learned a lesson from that."

"And you didn't have a spare paddle."

"No, sir. We were up ship's creek with only one paddle."

He chuckles. "What can we do for you, Jeff?"

"I'm just calling to let you know that tomorrow that Negro guy who saved my life a couple of weeks ago, well, he and his girlfriend are going to be driving through town in an old blue Ford sedan at about eleven o'clock to go to our church picnic. Me and my girlfriend will be with them."

"Uh-huh."

"I'm worried that someone might suspect them of something since they obviously don't live here. I just want you to know that they have a legitimate reason for being here so you won't have to worry about them." So you won't stop us is what I really mean.

"Where's the picnic?"

"Oakwood Park."

"Okay. I'll spread the word. Thanks for the information."

My last call is to Randy.

"Hey, buddy. I was wondering if you'd like to come to our church picnic on Saturday afternoon over at Oakwood Park."

"Now why would I want to do that, Klossen?"

"Because a photographer from the *Herald* is going to be there taking pictures, and he wants to take a picture of us, the survivors of the lightning strike on the lake, and you'll have some fun and good food too. Lori said she would come."

"Humph. You've been spending a lot of time with her, Jeff. Taking her down to that slum church with all those Negroes. Now you're taking her to a picnic. What's going on? I've about had it with you."

It's mutual, buddy.

"There's nothing going on, Randy. I'm not taking her. She's just coming. Would I be asking you to come if there was something going on between us?" I'm Mr. Sincere. "So can you come? Mom's bringing her fried chicken, and we need you for the softball game. And you'll get your picture in the paper again."

"You know I have to work."

"Go out early and slip away later. It doesn't start till eleven."

"I'll think about it."

"Great."

Of course I don't tell him about Walter. He wouldn't come if I did. But if he does come and spend some time with Walter and Sarah, maybe he'll change his attitude about Negroes, at least a little, and that's what we've got to do with everyone, white and black. Then again, maybe he'll get pissed and put his racism on display for everyone and embarrass Lori. That's what I'd really like to see.

Saturday morning, Lori and I ride our bikes to the Lorain Road Bridge, which crosses Shale River Valley. The sun is half-way up in the sky, and the day is warming fast. We chain the frames to a railing and wait there for the dark-blue Ford. By taking Lorain Road, Walter will stay in Cleveland and never have to go into Lakeshore, and we'll only have to go through a short stretch of Fairwood to get into Orchard Park.

They arrive, and Sarah jumps out of the front passenger seat, gets in the back, and slides over. I climb in next to Walter, and Lori gets behind me. They're in shorts, short sleeves, and ball caps, just like us. Sarah looks cute. "So far, so good," I say. "Now Lori and I can ride shotgun all the way to the picnic. They won't get you, Walter, I promise."

"I'm not afraid of your cops."

We make it through Fairwood and halfway to the park in Orchard Park when we pass City Hall and the police station. Right away we hear the short growl of a siren and see blinking lights behind us.

"Hey, Jeff," Walter says, looking in the rear-view. "I thought you said you called the cops."

"I did. Somebody didn't get the word."

He pulls over and puts both hands on the steering wheel. "Put your hands on the dash, Jeff. Hands on the front seat, girls." He's been through this drill before.

The officer walks slowly up to the car, and orders, "License and registration."

Walter reaches across me for the glove compartment, retrieves the registration, and then pulls his wallet out from his front shorts pocket. The officer peruses them carefully and hands them back.

Then he bends down at the window and asks me, "What's your name?"

"Jeff Klossen."

"License, please."

"W-why?"

"License," he demands with steel in his voice.

I reach for my wallet and say, "Officer, I called the station yesterday and told them we were coming. They must not have told you. We're going to our church picnic. I'm Jeff Klossen. I live in Orchard Park. I go to the high school." I give my license to Walter, who passes it on. "I'm the one whose canoe got hit by lightning a couple of weeks ago, and Walter here saved my life. The story was in the *Plain Dealer*."

"We know who you are, Mr. Klossen. You and your girlfriend are the ones who've been asking all the questions about why there are no Negroes living in Orchard Park. I guess you decided to bring some in yourself, huh?"

"There's no law against that, is there?"

"No." He hands back my license.

I put it back in my wallet and then look at him and say, "Why did you want to see my ID?"

"We have to make sure you're who you say you are."

"Oh." *Yeah, sure.*

"You can go."

We drive away. I'm fuming.

"What was that all about, Jeff?" Lori asks. "Why did he stop us?"

"He just wanted to hassle us," I grumble.

"Now you know how we feel," Walter says.

"Sorry," I tell Walter and Sarah. "I thought I had everything arranged. I guess you want to forget the picnic now and go back."

Walter looks over the backseat at Sarah. She tells him, "I'm all right. We can keep going if you want."

"Okay, then, let's see how many more racists we can find."

We turn into the park, leave the car in the lot, and walk to the pavilion that shelters a dozen or so picnic tables. Over the building, an oak tree canopy provides cooling shade, and squirrels are chasing each other along the branches. I smell hamburgers frying on a charcoal grill and see smoke wafting upward.

Parents with children, some people older than my mom and dad, and some very old people sit at the tables. I see my family, and we walk their way. Mom and Dad are on one side of the table with the boys between them.

"Mom, Dad, this is Walter Madison and Sarah Williams.

"Nice to meet you," Mom says warmly, leaning up to shake their hands.

Dad looks up at Walter and grumbles, "Thanks for saving Jeff." I'm dumfounded, and I think Walter is too. Then Dad looks away.

"You're welcome, sir."

"Mom. They're brown," Billy says.

"Yes, dear. That's their color."

"Why are they brown?" Jimmy asks.

"People are different colors. Some are white, some brown, some yellowish, some reddish."

Reverend Thomas gets everyone's attention and says grace, and I ask if I can introduce my guests. He nods, and I say, "These are my friends Lori and Sarah and Walter. Walter saved my life down at Edgewater Beach and helped me look for Lori and our friend Randy after our canoe was struck by lightning. Please stop by and meet them."

"You may have had some divine help too, Jeff," Reverend Thomas says.

"I'm sure we did."

We sit down—Walter and me across from Dad, and Lori and Sarah across from Mom and the boys. It's nice sitting next to Lori. It's like she's part of the family. I sit close enough to accidentally touch her once in a while.

Mom has fixed fried chicken and potato salad, iced tea, and rolls. I guess she thought that Walter and Sarah would like chicken since their church served it.

"Walter plans to be a doctor," I tell Dad.

He tips his head back. "Oh? You must like to study."

"Yes, sir, especially science."

"That's a long row to hoe, becoming a doctor. And it's expensive to go to school for that long." *It sounds like Dad is trying to discourage him.*

"I know. I'll have to work my way through."

"Walter fixes cars."

"Do you? What do you . . . fix?"

"Right now, I do oil changes, tune-ups, tires, and brakes."

"Do you get paid?" *Come on, Dad.*

"Yes, sir. I work for a mechanic at a garage, and he pays me."

"That's good. You'll save a lot of money being able to do those things yourself."

"He started out by helping the mechanic for nothing until he learned how to do things," I say.

"On-the-job training—your own apprenticeship program," Dad says.

"Yes, sir."

I think Dad's impressed with Walter, a little at least. I look around at the other tables. Two people look over at our table as if they're curious but then look back. One woman has an angry look.

Reverend Thomas stops by and introduces himself, and then a few others come by.

"I wonder if Randy will come," I ask.

"Oh, is he coming?" Mom asks.

"I think so, if he can get out of the caddy shack. Oh, and a photographer from the *Herald* may come at around one. I thought it might make an interesting story for them since I used to be one of their paperboys."

"Does Randy know me and Sarah are here?" Walter asks.

"No. I thought we'd surprise him."

"He wouldn't come if he knew we were here, now would he?"

Not many people have come to say hello, so I say, "Let's go meet some people." I stand and drag Walter up. "I want everyone to get to know you."

"Come on, man. Maybe they don't want to meet us."

"You mean, maybe they don't know they want to meet you."

Lori and Sarah stand, and we start making the rounds, going to each table. I know most of the people. I've been going to church with them for years, singing in the choir, going to dinners and picnics and everything with them. I give them big smiles and introduce them by name, and most of them warm up to my guests. They're not going to be nasty to me, are they? Children do stare at Walter and Sarah, and some of the old people act nervous, and a few seem repelled—like magnets turned the wrong way. But on the whole, people are friendly.

We sit down again and get ready to feast on Mom's apple pie, when Randy pulls up to the table on his bike.

"You didn't say we'd have colored people here, Jeff,"

"What?" I ask in astonishment. "You say that right in front of them?"

"That makes me mad," Randy says.

"You're mad?" I say. "I'm the one who's mad."

Randy shakes his head at me. "Shithead. I'm not eating with colored people."

"Randy!" Lori says.

I can see that Walter is getting steamed.

"Sorry, Lori, Mr. and Mrs. Klossen," Randy says. "I don't believe in associating with Negroes from the slums. I'll have to see you another time."

"Why you—" Walter says, half rising off the bench. I put a hand on his shoulder to hold him down.

"But, Randy," Lori says. She's starting to cry.

"What about the newspaper photograph?" I ask.

"I don't want any more photographs of me in the paper with Negroes, thanks."

With that, he turns and wheels away.

I'm burning inside. "Sorry, Walter, Sarah. I didn't mean to put you through that. I thought that once he was here, he would be nice and join us and maybe even learn something."

"He's a racist bigot. You can't change them just like that," Walter says.

I notice that Dad is silent through all of this.

"Why is everyone so mad?" Billy asks. "Why is Lori crying?"

"Because some people can't be nice to other people," Mom explains.

"Like Randy?"

"Yes. He was really impolite to Walter and Sarah."

After lunch, there's a sack race for the kids. Billy tries, doesn't get the hang of it, and ends up crying. Then there's a softball game for the adults. Walter lets us know that he's not very good, but he joins in anyway. Dad does not. He claims he's not feeling well. *I wonder. Just too old?*

Halfway through the third inning, the reporter, a young woman, arrives with the photographer, an older man. The four of us gather for the picture.

"Walter here saved my life," I tell her. "He pulled me out of the water when I was drowning. But Randy Clark's not here."

"Who's he?" the reporter asks.

"He lives in Orchard Park too, and is a senior at OP High like us. He was in the canoe with Lori and me. Lori helped him keep his head above water until they washed up at the coast guard station."

"I understand you weren't wearing a life jacket when your canoe turned over. Is that true?"

"Yeah. I learned that lesson the hard way. Next time I'll have a vest on. We were really stupid. Accidents happen."

In the car after the picnic, the four of us promise to get together again soon. "I hope we can keep this friendship going," Lori says. "Maybe we can get together at my house sometime."

"Or mine," I say. "Then maybe at yours sometime, Walter."

"So you can see how poor black folk live. I don't know. Some of our neighbors might not want us bringing in white folks."

"Well, there are lots of places we can go and things we can do," Lori says.

"You can come to our church," I say. "And have Sunday dinner with us afterward at my house."

"That sounds like fun," Sarah says. Walter looks at her and nods.

"How did you like the picnic?" I ask him.

"Not too bad," he says, "except for your buddy Randy. I was getting ready to slug that SOB. He's a white supremacist. He's probably in the Klan."

"Sorry about him."

We part ways, and Lori and I ride home, down the ancient slopes toward the lake. In her driveway, I say, "Well, I think we did okay at the picnic today—you know—building bridges. It's a start, anyway." I don't mention Randy. I let her bring him up.

"I think so too, except for Randy. Oh! He made me so angry. I was so embarrassed. Can you imagine how Walter and Sarah must have felt?"

"Yeah. Maybe I shouldn't have sprung it on Randy the way I did. But he wouldn't have come if I'd told him that Walter was coming."

"I'm glad you surprised him. I learned so much more about him. He was so hateful."

"Yeah."

"I don't know how I can stay with him now, even if there are so many things I like about him. We're just too different. But I still feel like I want to be close to him, and help him, and keep saving him."

"You can't save him, Lori. And you can't help someone who won't be helped."

I reach out with one arm, and she joins me in an awkward little sideways hug, from bike to bike.

"At least we did something about our prison," I say.

"We did."

She leans up on her toes, gives me a little kiss on the cheek, and turns away.

At home, for dinner, we have split-pea soup and peanut butter crackers.

"Did you have fun at the picnic, boys?" I ask Billy and Jimmy.

"I didn't like that sack race," Billy says, scowling.

"Oh, we'll practice that. That'll be fun. You'll have a good time next year. Did you see anything on your hike?" Mom had taken them on the hike with the other little kids while we big people played ball.

"We saw a dead bird," Jimmy says. "It had ants on it."

"You didn't touch it, did you?" Dad asks. "It might have had a disease." They shake their heads.

"How did everyone like eating with Negroes?" I ask, looking at the boys.

"Fine," comes their chorus.

"Did you like them, Dad?" I ask.

"They were well behaved."

"I thought they were very nice, Jeff," Mom says.

"I'm sorry Randy was so ugly," I say. "I was really embarrassed."

"Yes," Mom says. "He was rude. I felt sorry for those kids."

"I don't know why you invited him," Dad says. "You know how he feels."

"I thought he would enjoy being with us and eating the food and playing ball and getting his picture in the paper. That's why."

"I guess you learned your lesson." *He always wants to teach me lessons.*

"Yes, I did. Oh, by the way, we plan to continue our student exchange. We're going to bring them to church and maybe to a party."

"I hope your friends at school don't object. I expect a lot of them feel like Randy does," Dad says. "They might shun you."

"You mean the ones who blindly follow their parents?"

"Jeff!" Mom says. "Respect!"

"Sorry."

"Jeff," Randy says on the phone that night, "That was a real cute trick you played, not telling me you were inviting colored people to the picnic and that I'd have to sit with them. You know I don't mix with those people." *I know, you stupid bigot.*

"I'm sorry you couldn't bring yourself to do it just once. You might have found out what nice people Walter and Sarah are."

"I really don't care how nice they are, Jeff. I don't want to associate with them. They have their world, and we have ours."

"'East is East, and West is West, and never the twain shall meet,' huh?"

"What?"

"That's Rudyard Kipling. He was talking about the East Indians and the British."

"Right. Well, anyway, that's not why I called—"

"'There is neither East nor West, Border, nor Breed, nor Birth,/ When two strong men stand face to face, though they come from the ends of the earth!'"

"Shut up and listen, asshole—" *Idiot.*

"I'm just saying that you wouldn't dare face Walter. Too chicken."

"The hell with you! Dammit! Listen!" I can see he's red in the face now. I can see, right through the telephone wires. "Garth came home last night, and he's not pissed about the canoe. All he wants is a hundred bucks to settle up. He wants to buy one in Colorado so he doesn't have to drive one across the country on the roof of his car. So—are you listening?"

"Yeah."

"So if the three of us kick in thirty-three bucks plus change, that'll do it. Lori should pony up' too. She's the one who demanded to be an equal partner."

"Right."

I still have a real bad taste in my mouth from the way the insect acted today. I really can't stand him. But I am glad he showed Lori and everyone else what a racist jerk he is. Now maybe she'll get some sense in her head and realize that—and come back to me.

Later that night, I answer the phone, and some man says "nigger lover," lets it sink in, and hangs up. It's scary. Like, what are they planning next? And who was it? Not Randy—I know his voice. One of his friends? Some adult? A friend of Randy's dad or the builder? The police? The newspaper? Someone from church? Could be anyone. I don't know. Then I get steamed up. Racists and cowards—that's what they are. The next call I get, I'm going to give the guy a piece of my mind.

I don't say a word about it to Mom and Dad. They'd be on me like hungry wolves.

I call Lori to tell her and find out if anyone has called her. No one has. "Do you still want to keep going with this exchange program?" I ask.

"Yes!" she says. "We can't quit now."

I'm surprised. I didn't know she was a fighter.

Chapter 23—Rolly

It's lunchtime. We're all sitting at the table finishing our egg salad sandwiches and chicken noodle soup. Billy shouts, "Canoe story!" and Jimmy chimes in. I'm feeling bored again, so I relent.

I can't think of anything. But then: "Well . . . one time I decided to go to Benny's Ribs and Wings in Lakeshore to buy some wings. So I ran past the Westview Hotel and across the Shale River Bridge, and I looked down over it, way down to Shale River and all those little sailboats and motorboats down there. And then I ran into the store carrying my canoe over my head—you know, the one I used to have. I had to duck to get through the door—and I told the Chinese lady who was working a crossword puzzle at the counter, 'I want to be fitted for wings for my canoe.'

"She frowned and said, 'Sorry. Only fried chicken wings.'

"So I said, 'But I want water wings.'

"'To put on children arms to make them float? We don't have.'

"'No, no, no. I want wings to make my canoe fly like a bird through the water.'

"'Through the water? Not above the water?'

"'Yes. Through the water.'

"'Oh, you want that kind water wings. Down the hall, door to the left.'

"'Thanks.'

"I ran down the hall, carrying the canoe over my head. I had to have the canoe, to make sure that the wings were properly fitted.

I ran through the door on the left and into the kitchen, where five Chinese chefs wearing tall white hats and white shirts and black aprons stood at black stoves with stainless steel tops making big pots of green tea and wonton soup and standing up on ladders dropping eggs into the egg drop soup, and chopping vegetables and meat with big cleaver knives, and rolling it all up in little pancakes made of eggs and flour to make egg rolls, and frying them in a big skillet on a big flaming stove, and turning and broiling a dead chicken on a spit and a whole pig with its eyes staring straight ahead like it was still alive and with a spit running through his mouth and out his rear end—both turning over low flames—and much, much more. And the head chef shouted to chefs up on the ladders, 'Drop eggs in soup, not on floor! You drop eggs on floor, you get down on knees and clean up fast. No rotten egg smell here.'

"The smell of soup and tea and cooking meat made my mouth water and my stomach growl, and I was just ready to ask if I couldn't just have a couple of egg rolls and some egg drop soup, when one chef said to me, 'Water wings?'

"'Yes,' I replied.

"He said, pointing, 'Through door and down stairs.'

"So I carried the canoe through the door and down some steep stairs that kept curving to the right and going and going, down and down. Finally, at the bottom, I found a tailor shop. An old Chinese woman stepped out from behind a table where she was measuring some cloth. There were big rolls of fabric of all colors behind her and big spools of colored thread and long, sharp scissors and a black sewing machine on the table.

"I said, 'I need water wings.'

"She replied, 'Ah, yes.'

"She picked up a measuring tape and said, 'Put canoe down.'

"I swung it down from over my head and laid it on the floor. Then she proceeded to measure it, stretching the tape across the canoe and then spreading her arms out wide and pulling the tape from fingertip to fingertip. Then she nodded and said, 'I have,' and she went through a door into another room and came out with two big wings under her arms that looked like eagle wings but were much bigger, and they were wiggling and squirming like they wanted to start flying right away. She walked over to the canoe and fastened the giant feathered things to the sides of the canoe.

"I asked, 'What do I owe you?'

"She said, 'You try. You like, you come back and pay later. But better get in canoe now.'

"As soon as I did, the wings started flapping, and off we went, through a big door and down a long tunnel, through another door and into the underwater world of eerie Lake Erie.

"I reached into my pocket and pulled out a big clothespin and put it on my nose to keep out the water so I didn't have to hold my nose all the time, because I didn't like to get water in my nose because the water was polluted. And then, I had to hold onto the sides of the canoe to keep from falling out while those wings powered us right through the water, very fast, past all kinds of fish, small and large. There was a smallmouth bass with a mouth so small" [I pucker my lips] "that it talks like this, and when it eats, it can only suck in spaghetti. And there was a rainbow trout with rainbows on its sides. And I heard a croaker croaking at me. And a sucker chased us and tried to kiss me!

"We came to the skeleton of a shipwreck—an old steamboat sent to the bottom by a fierce Lake Erie storm. Millions of mussels covered part of it—you know, they're like clams and oysters you've seen on the beach. And a school of minnows came out of the wreck. Then out came a great big shark. It was the rare freshwater bull shark that everyone talks about, and he came right at me, and tried to bite off my nose, but all he got was the clothespin, but that was bad enough, because that meant I had to let go of the canoe and hold my nose so I didn't get water in it.

"I used my paddle to guide the canoe to the top of the water so I could get some air, and when we broke through the surface, the water wings took us right up like a flying fish, and we flew way up into the sky and then glided around in circles, and then flew all the way up to the Hudson Bay, where I looked down and saw some polar bears, and then went down along the Rocky Mountains and through the Grand Canyon, and then across the Gulf of Mexico and around the tip of Florida, and all the way up to New York and right by the Empire State Building, and then flew back home. We swooped down like an eagle over Shale River Bridge and right back to Benny's Ribs and Wings. The wings folded back up, and we went sailing into the store and landed on the floor in front of the lady at the counter. She looked up with a bored expression, and then looked back down at her crossword puzzle, pointed down the hallway, and said, 'Down the stairs.'

"I ran the canoe back through the kitchen with the cooks and egg rolls and egg drop soup, and down the long, steep stairs, and into the tailor shop. I told the tailor that I had great fun with the wings, but I didn't want to keep them because someone else might want to use them. She said okay and told me how much money I owed her. I gave it to her and picked up my canoe, ran up the stairs, back through the kitchen with the Chinese cooks, out across the Shale River Bridge, and back to home sweet home. And that is the end of my canoe story."

I look at Billy and Jimmy. Both of them are asleep with their heads on their plates. Mom stands up from her stool, looks at me, and whispers, "Good story, Jeff, but too long." She picks up Jimmy, I pick up Billy, and we carry them upstairs for their naps.

Lori and I take the bus to East Ninth Street and walk down to the pier to meet Walter and Sarah. There are only a few cars near Captain Frank's Seafood House—the lunch crowd is mostly gone. Walter is parked a distance away. Today, he's going to show us some places around town. He and Sarah see us coming. She waves.

I ask him, "Are you going to buy us all lunch at Captain Frank's?"

"Sure. Right after you buy us all tickets for the cruise up the Cuyahoga, rich boy."

We walk out to the end of the pier and look around.

"It's a beautiful day," I say. Beyond the breakwater, I see the lake reflecting the deep-blue sky out to the horizon and half a dozen sailboats riding a warm, stiff breeze from the west. To the right is the airport, and to the left is Cleveland Municipal Stadium, where the Browns and Indians play.

"So what are you going to show us today?" I ask Walter.

"You'll see."

We drive out to East Sixty-Ninth and south to East Sixty-Ninth Place. I have to admit I feel nervous—a white face invading this black world. He stops at a gravel yard surrounded by a chain-link fence with half a dozen cars and a small concrete block building sandwiched between two old brick warehouses. It has two overhead doors, both open, that display lifts for raising cars. Parts and equipment are neatly arranged on two walls, some tires sit on shelves on another wall, and there's a faint odor of gasoline and rubber. To the left is an office area with a door and one window, which is guarded with steel bars. "This is where I work," Walter says. "Step outside and meet Mr. Bradley, my boss."

Mr. Bradley is putting brake pads on a wheel. He looks up and smiles. He's dark and bald, except around the ears, and starting to gray.

"Who's this here?" he asks Walter in friendly voice.

"These are two of the kids who almost drowned in that canoe accident two weeks ago, Mr. Bradley. This is Jeff, and this is Lori, and you've met Sarah before, I think."

"Yes. And Walter says you two live out in Orchard Park."

"Yes. Walter's the one who saved my life, and we wanted to meet some of his friends."

"Well, he's a friend of mine. He's a big help to me here at the garage. I don't know what I'll do without him when he goes off to college next year."

"Maybe I won't be going out of town, Mr. Bradley. Maybe I'll still be able to do some work here."

A new black Cadillac Fleetwood comes by and stops. Mr. Bradley looks up and stares. Faces in the front and back look at us, and it slowly moves on.

"That was that Adolph Morton," he tells Walter. "He probably wants to know what these white kids are doing down here. You better get them out of here."

"Right."

"Nice to meet you, Mr. Bradley."

"Same here," he says.

We get in the car and Walter drives off.

"Who's Adolph Morton?" I ask.

"A big drug dealer—a gang boss," Walter says, his eyes on the road. "I stay out of his way. But we better get you two out of the neighborhood. Some of these lowlifes may have seen you when you came to church. And now you're back again."

"How did he just happen to drive by when we were there?"

"I don't know. He's always driving around. Maybe one of his lieutenants saw us and called him. They have two-way radios in their cars."

"That's scary."

"Can we at least drive by where you live?" Lori asks.

"Sure. I shouldn't, but I will. It's just an apartment building."

We drive down Central past boarded-up storefronts, warehouses, vacant lots hiding trash in high grass, and old two-story houses with sagging porches, twisted siding, peeling paint, and broken windows. Sidewalks are black with soot, and air drifting into the car stinks of sulfur, tar, and garbage. A Negro woman and toddler come out of a house. I shudder. I can't believe that people live in there. We turn left at East Sixty-Seventh toward Walter's church. On both sides is a large development of three-story red brick apartments.

He pulls to the curb and stops. "This is it—Central Terrace. I won't take you in, but not because I'm ashamed of it. We have a nice, neat, clean home. I just don't think the neighbors would understand having white people come in."

"Afraid, huh?" I ask.

"For you and Lori."

"Maybe we better go," Lori says.

"Can't we just peek in and then go?" I ask.

He looks down and then over at me. "Okay. But I warned you."

He stops the car on the street in front of the apartment and looks all around.

Then he says, "You all stay in the car while I check it out. I want to be sure Rolly's not there."

"Who's Rolly?" I ask.

"Someone who wouldn't understand."

He leaves the motor running, motions for Sarah to get behind the wheel, gets out, goes up the outside stairs, and disappears through the door.

"Tell us about Rolly," I say to Sarah.

"He lives on the third floor. Walter and his brother and Mom live on the first. Rolly's a bully and a drunk. Sometimes he sells drugs, and sometimes he pimps. We try to stay away from him."

I'm looking out the window when I see a curtain move on the third floor above Walter's apartment.

Walter appears at the door and waves us to come in. We get out and walk quickly up the stairs and into the building. A hallway goes straight back and dead-ends. On the left, stairs lead to the upper levels. The door to Walter's apartment is on the right.

"Walter," I say, "when we were in the car, I saw the curtain move in the apartment on the third floor."

"We won't stay long."

We follow him into the living room. There's a faded tan upholstered sofa and a floor lamp on one wall, and an overstuffed chair and bookcase with an old encyclopedia and lamp on the opposite wall. I can smell someone frying something somewhere. Chicken? A small table with an unabridged dictionary and radio on it sits under a steel window covered by a white lace curtain, and a small TV is on a table in the corner. The sound of Sam Cooke singing about chain gangs drifts in from outside—"ugh . . . ah . . . ugh . . . ah"—and I can hear the floorboards squeak above us from people walking around, and an occasional muffled voice. *Walter must have a high power of concentration to block out the noise.* On the walls are pictures of a black Jesus, Franklin D. Roosevelt, and a picture with Walter and his mother, and I guess Walter's younger brother and father. At the other end of the room is a round table with four chairs, and a kitchenette with a small range, sink, and refrigerator. Across from it is a bathroom. We peer into it. It has a tub-shower, toilet, and wall-hung sink. You could sit on the toilet and wash your feet in the tub and your hands in the sink. The bedroom is nearly wall-to-wall beds—a double bed for Walter and his brother against the wall on the right, a single bed for his mom, straight ahead. *They must be crawling all over each other, bumping into each other, saying "excuse me" all the time.* There's one three-foot bureau and no closet. Clothes are hung on hooks on the wall and on the back of the door. There are two windows, so it's not dark.

"How do you keep everything so neat when you have so little space?" Lori asks.

"We have to keep it neat because it's small," Walter says.

"Do you have enough space for clothes?" I ask.

"We don't keep more than we need. We just keep washing and wearing them, and when they wear out, we buy some more."

"Where do you study?"

"In the living room and at the kitchen table."

"What if someone wants to watch TV?"

"We don't watch much TV, just the news sometimes. We don't have time. I usually don't get home until eight. Then I have to eat something fast and start my homework."

"'You're a better man than I am, Gunga Din!'" I say.

"Gunga who?"

"Never mind. I just meant that I could never keep up with your schedule. You're amazing. And you probably hear the neighbors' TVs while you study."

"It doesn't bother me. I'd miss it if it weren't there."

"Is your apartment like this?" Lori asks Sarah.

"Yes, just the same, but a lot messier. I have a brother too, and my dad's with us too, so Mom and Dad get the double bed, and my brother and I are in bunk beds, but those men are messy. They're not like the Madison men."

"Do you have the top bunk or the bottom one?"

"I'm older, so I get the bottom."

We open the door and step out, and there's Rolly coming down the stairs. He's dark and over six feet tall, like Walter and me, but he has bulging muscles, no neck, a round face, high cheeks, a sneer on his face, and hands clenched into fists. He looks like he could break us in half. I feel rigor mortis setting in.

He blocks our way and asks Walter in an almost whiny voice, "What're these crackas doin' here, Walter?"

I don't look at him. *"Never look a predator in the eye." Or is it "always look a predator in the eye." I can't remember.*

"They're the kids I helped save when lightning struck their canoe. They wanted to see where I live."

"Rich white kids."

"You'll never see them again, Rolly, I promise. Let us pass, please."

"Gimme your wallet," he says, looking at me.

Now I'm shaking. I can't stop.

"Don't give it to him, Jeff. Let us pass, Rolly, come on. They don't have any money. They took the bus to get here. They're not rich. Come on. They're good kids. You don't want to get in trouble."

"Trouble," he sneers. "You think I'll get in trouble, huh?"

"You know the cops'll come after you for robbing white kids. You'll get hard time for that. It's not like they were black."

"And you'd tell the cops I did it?"

"No, but they might. Come on, Rolly. Let us by."

There's a deathly pause. Then he inches out of our way. "Okay. But I better not ever see you back here," he says, looking at me. "Next time, you'll end up in the river, white boy. You too, girl."

We get in the car and drive away.

"I knew I shouldn't take you in there."

I'm still shaking. "I appreciate it, Walter." *I learned a lot. There's nothing like seeing things with your own eyes.*

On the way to Public Square, I ask him, "So what can I do to get on the good side of Rolly so I can come visit you?"

He shakes his head. "Humph. You don't give up, do you? The only way you could get on his good side would be to buy some of his coke or pot. Then you'd be a customer."

"Or have him get you a girl," Lori says. Sarah laughs out loud. "I'm just kidding. I would never force you to do something like that."

We get to the square, and I ask Walter, "How would you and Sarah like to come to church in Orchard Park on Sunday? Then have Sunday dinner at my house."

"What say, Sar? Do you want to see how rich people live?"

"Sure."

"Great," I say . . . *if Dad is hospitable.*

Chapter 24—The Sit-In

Walls have ears. I would never eavesdrop, but can I help it if I happen to hear them around a corner?

Dad says, "Right in our home? It's bad enough that Jeff goes to their slum church. Now he wants to bring these people into our church and home. We need to keep them in their place, not bring them here."

"Honey, these are kids just like I taught in school. We need to learn what their lives are like. This boy did save our son's life. We ought to learn why. He must have had a good Christian upbringing."

"We'll have to hide the silver . . . and your jewelry."

"My jewelry isn't worth much anyway. You know that."

"Don't expect me to say anything."

Sunday morning is another bright, beautiful day. Labor Day's only a week away. Summer's over, and then it's back to the grind.

Lori said she would come even though she doesn't go to church. It will be a learning experience for her too.

Mom and Dad and the boys and I pick her up. We squeeze the boys between us on the backseat. Brett has the day off and went with Annie to ride the Wild Mouse at Cedar Point.

Lori tells me that Randy's caddying. "I didn't tell him what we were doing. I hope he doesn't find out. I'd don't want him to embarrass us again today."

Why don't you just drop him, Lori?

She and I stand on the steps out front and wait while Mom and Dad and the boys go in.

Pretty soon we see Walter's old dark-blue Ford emerge from downtown Orchard Park. I wave my arms and walk to the street. He stops, and I see Sarah in the front passenger seat. I open the door and deposit her with Lori, then jump in and lead Walter to a parking place on the street beside the church. Then he and I join the ladies and go in. We're wearing khaki chinos, short-sleeve shirts, and no ties or coats, and the girls are in white blouses and pleated skirts.

"How'd you come?" I ask.

"I took Detroit Road all the way through Lakeshore and crossed the bridge into Orchard Park without being stopped."

"You were lucky."

I think the ushers and maybe everybody have been forewarned about what's going to happen. They understand that this is not an invasion or a sit-in. It's just the president of the youth group and his crazy student exchange program. Just relax, grin, and bear it, and wait for it to go away. The two ushers hand us programs.

I say, "Good morning, Mr. Bennett."

He says, "Hi, Jeff," smiles, and nods. "And who have we here?"

"These are my friends, Lori and Sarah and Walter."

"Welcome."

The church is about half-full, which is pretty good for summer. Most people are dressed casually—men are in shirts and ties with their coats folded on the seats beside them. Women are in summer dresses and hats.

I see Mom and Dad and the boys surrounded by people on the right, so I lead the way away from them to the front. No one sits there.

It's the usual summer service with no choir and a short sermon. Reverend Thomas preaches on helping others. Our paid soloist,

Mr. Stella, sings a moving rendition of "Create in Me a Clean Spirit, O God." I think I see him looking at me a couple of times and decide that I'm one of the sinners he's singing about. Then, we in the congregation get to stand up and exercise our lungs with "When Morning Gilds the Skies," "Faith of Our Fathers," and "All Creatures of Our God and King." During visitor recognition, Reverend Thomas introduces us, and we receive lots of smiles. At the end, the acolytes extinguish the candles, the organ begins a jubilant postlude, and we leave. Just like in Walter's church, people gather around us to meet Walter and Sarah and Lori. People we saw at the picnic smile and wave in recognition.

Outside, Lori and I get in with Walter and Sarah to drive to the house. On the way, they talk about how similar the service is to theirs, what a nice church it is, and the like. They never mention that our church is much smaller than theirs.

We pass the high school. "That's where we go," I say. "It's not as big as East Tech."

"Looks nice," Sarah says.

At home, Mom has prepared roast lamb with mint jelly, browned Irish potatoes, onions, green beans, gravy, brown-and-serve rolls and butter, and iced tea. The aroma is torturous; we're all starving. I help carry in the food from the kitchen. Dad prays, we pass the plates, he carves and serves the lamb, and we plunge in.

"What have you been working on at the garage lately?" Dad asks Walter.

"Mostly oil changes and tires, but a couple of brake jobs too. The tires are heavy, and Mr. Bradley likes me to do the heavy stuff."

Sarah and Walter say how much they enjoyed the service. "It was a lot like ours," Sarah says.

"You should see their church, Dad," I say. "It's much bigger than ours." I describe it for them.

I can tell he's not interested. I don't know whether it's their color or their poverty that puts him off the most.

"What a delicious meal, Mrs. Klossen," Walter says.

"Anyone for seconds?" she asks.

"Yes, please," I jump in, passing my plate to Dad. I don't want Walter to feel like he shouldn't ask. All four of us hand our plates down.

I glance at the living room window. Through reflections of light, I see the shadow of a face. "Someone's looking in the window," I say.

"What?" Dad asks.

"I saw someone looking in the window. Excuse me." I stand up, run to the window, and look out, but see no one.

"Are you sure?" Mom asks.

"I think so. But whoever it was is gone."

Lori looks apprehensive. "Maybe it was Randy."

Walter frowns.

I say, "So what if it was. If he had hung around, we could've invited him in for dessert. Speaking of dessert, what do we have, Mom?"

"You know what. Cherry pie."

"À la mode?" I ask.

"Of course. Who's going to scoop it?"

"Everyone," I say. "So everyone gets as much as he wants."

"I'll just have a small scoop, Jeff," Dad says.

The four of us walk to the kitchen, load up our pie, and return to the table. Lori gives Dad his plate. He thanks her.

When we finish, he lights up a Camel, and we all sit there wondering what to talk about.

Walter says, "This is a beautiful house you have here, Mr. Klossen."

"Thank you."

"I was wondering—if you wanted to sell it, and a Negro family asked to buy it, would you sell it to them?"

Oh, boy. Here we go.

Dad taps ash from his cigarette and says, "Walter, don't you think that Negroes would rather live with their own people?"

"I think some would. But I think some might want to get out here where there's no crime and gangs, and where they can put their children in fine schools and raise their children where they can be sure to get into good colleges."

"Don't you think there are places like this on the East Side where Negroes already live?"

"Maybe there are, but it's a free country, isn't it, Mr. Klossen? Shouldn't they be allowed to live where they want to live?"

"I suppose."

"So, Dad," I say, "what's your answer? Would you sell to the Negro family?"

"So my neighbors' property values would go down? No, I don't think I would."

"But the values would only go down if they panicked and sold their homes for less than they were worth."

"I can't determine how people feel about Negroes, Jeff. If they don't like Negroes, they're going to sell."

"Then isn't it their own problem if they lose money?"

"This is the end of this discussion, Jeff." He snuffs out his cigarette.

"Thanks for your honesty, Mr. Klossen," Walter says. *I know what he's thinking.*

Walter and Sarah thank Mom and Dad for dinner, and then Lori and I walk out with them to the car. We offer to drive with them to the edge of town, and they accept, so we ride with them past the diner into downtown Orchard Park.

Walter asks, "Say. I'm curious—does that diner serve Negroes?"

"Of course they do . . . I think," I say. "I don't know why it wouldn't."

"Maybe we could find out sometime," he says.

I smile. "What? Have our own sit-in, right here in Orchard Park?"

"Yeah. We could just sit there until they serve us. If they don't want to serve us, it'll be them making it a sit-in, not us. We just wouldn't move."

When they let us out, I say, "Man, Walter, you are a radical."

"I just want to see what you white folks out here are really like. So far, I think I have you figured pretty well."

"But people at church were friendly. You have to give them time."

"That's what you white people have been saying for a hundred years. How much time do you want?"

Lori and I walk home. It's just a couple of miles.

"I think we're making progress with our exchange," I say.

"Especially with Walter's confrontation," she says. "Frederick Douglass said there's no progress without struggle."

"Where did you learn that?" I ask.

"From his autobiography. You should read it."

"Maybe we'll make some more progress at the diner."

She nods.

I change the subject. "Say, I wonder if that was Randy at the window."

"I don't care if it was him. We need to change him too."

When we get to her house, I lean down, and she lets me give her a kiss on the cheek.

When I get home, Dad tells me, "I want you to stay away from that Negro boy, Jeff." *Sure, Dad.* "He's a bad influence."

"He's my friend, Dad. He saved my life. He's a hard-working Christian. He's going to be a doctor--"

"You heard me."

Dad and I don't speak about Walter after that.

Later in the afternoon, we get another obscene phone call, but this time Dad answers. (It had to happen sooner or later.) He comes thundering out of the kitchen, shouting, "Jeff! You get out here right now! Now people are calling us 'nigger lovers!' And . . . and it's all because of you bringing that colored boy and girl into town."

Slipping into the living room from my bedroom, I take a defensive position behind a chair. I've never known him to get violent, but this might drive him to it. "They're white supremacists, Dad. Just ignore them."

"Ignore them? The next thing they'll do is burn a cross on our lawn and set our house on fire."

"I'm sure they don't have the nerve to do that."

"From now on, you are forbidden from seeing those black kids, Jeff. Do you understand me?"

"Yes." *I understand, but it doesn't mean I'll obey.*

I talk to Walter later in the week. "Lori and I were wondering if you'd want to go to the diner on Saturday morning. Kind of early. Join the morning crowd."

"That sounds all right," he says. "I'll ask Mr. Bradley if I can get off. I'll tell him I can work in the afternoon."

Walter calls back. His boss wasn't happy, but he let him off. "I told him I had to go to the store for Mom."

Lori and I ride our bikes. We're waiting for Walter and Sarah in the parking lot at 8:00 a.m. They pull up at five after. There are a dozen cars spread around the building. He parks between two of them.

We say hello and discuss our plan. "The place has booths and counter stools," I say. "But I don't think we should hide in a booth. I think we should go for the counter right by the front door, just like they did at Woolworth's down in Greensboro. And that way no one has to seat us. We can just sit down."

"And remember, no one loses his temper no matter what happens," Lori says.

"Right," I say. "We all just sit there and keep quiet."

"That won't be easy for you, white boy," Walter says.

We walk in, me and Lori first. I glance around. There are stools at counters on each side of the cash register by the front door, booths by the windows, and some tables. Behind the register is the kitchen—open to view—where the cook is frying eggs and pancakes on a big grille. The aroma spikes my appetite.

A dozen or more people sit in booths. Two men occupy stools on our side of the diner and one on the other side. We find four stools together with our backs to the door, sit, pick up menus, and mind our business.

I see the waitress catch the attention of the cook and nod our way. A man with his elbows on the counter looks over at Walter and Sarah and stares. Conversation in the diner stops. From the back, I hear a man say, "What are they doing here?"

Apparently, the waitress doesn't know what to do. She just turns away and starts thumbing through a stack of sales slips.

We wait. Then the man near us puts his coffee cup down with a noisy jangle, slides off the stool, and walks toward the cash register. He's medium height, stocky, around thirty, and wears striped gray coveralls.

"Find another place to eat, niggers," he says.

Walter stiffens and turns his head toward the man but says nothing.

The waitress takes his slip and adds it up, and he pays and leaves.

I ask our group if they are ready to order. They nod. "We're ready to order," I say. This is the moment.

I see the cook shrug at the waitress. She walks over with her pad, sighs, and says, "What'll it be?"

I guess we're not in the segregated South. . . .

She takes our orders for eggs, bacon, pancakes, and coffee, and hangs the slip on a clip for the cook to retrieve.

A family comes to the cash register. The woman takes the two young children out while the man pays. He shakes his head and whispers to the waitress. I can't make out what he says. He throws us a hostile glance as he leaves.

The other man at the counter, who's dressed in a sport shirt and slacks, approaches us on the way to the register. He says, "Good morning."

We return the greeting.

"Where are you from?" he asks.

I tell him that Lori and I live here, and Walter and Sarah are visiting from Cleveland.

"Well, enjoy your food."

The rest of the meal is uneventful, until we go outside and discover that one of Walter's tires is flat.

"Look," he says, and I can see fury in his eyes. "Someone jammed a knife through the sidewall. Tire's no good now. I have to throw it away."

"I wonder who did it?" Sarah asks.

"Probably that cracka in the coveralls," Walter says.

I help him change the tire and put the bad one in the trunk.

"Now I know what people out here are like," he says bitterly. "We won't be coming back."

"But, Walter. We're not all racists."

"It's not just that I'm afraid of you rednecks. I'm also afraid of getting arrested by one of your white cops, and getting a record that'll keep me from getting a scholarship."

"Oh," I say.

"And my boss told me some of his customers are complaining about me having white friends. He told me I need to quit seeing you or get a new job. And Rolly told me I better not see you again."

"Phooey. I was going to invite you to our youth group at church."

"Why? You know, sometimes I think you're using us, Jeff."

"Darn right I am. And we've got to keep using each other until we can get these A-people to change, and all the Randys and Rollys and everyone like them."

He shakes his head. "That'll never happen, brother."

I'm feeling desperate. "Try to change his mind, Sarah. We have to stay in touch and keep getting together. Between our ghettos, if we have to, in the free spaces, like we did before. We're friends now."

They drive off. Lori waves.

I look down at her. "It's hard to change the world."

At bedtime, Billy demands, "Canoe story," for the umpteenth time.

"Okay. Put your heads on your pillows first." They do and I think.

"One time I picked up my canoe, lifted it over my head, and ran down the hill into Shale River Valley until I came to the river, only today it was different. Today, it was really wide. I don't know why. It hadn't been raining all that much. I couldn't even see across it. It looked more like Lake Erie than Shale River. I put the canoe down, stepped in the water, climbed in the canoe, pushed off, and started paddling. Well, I paddled and paddled and paddled and paddled. When I got to the other side, I pulled the canoe up on the muddy beach and looked all around. All I could see were old houses. They looked like they were getting ready to fall down. Their roofs were tipped and sagging. Windows were broken. Fences were overgrown with vines. Porch railings were falling off. How could people live in them? I wondered. They must not care about keeping them up. I wondered why.

"Then out of the houses, one by one, came these strange-looking creatures. They looked like people, but their skin was blueberry blue, and they had long, pointy noses, and their green hair stuck straight out in all directions. The men were wearing old, raggedy pants and shirts, and the women's clothes were torn and dirty. And when they saw me, they all got really mean looks on their faces. They made a circle around me, and I thought they were going to hurt me.

"I asked them, 'Why are you so mean to me?'

"An old man stepped up and said, 'Many years ago, when the river was smaller and the land was close together, some people on your side came over to our side and caught many of us and took us back to your side and made us do whatever they wanted us to. They made us their slaves.

"'Then the people on your side decided to let us go so we could do whatever we wanted to, but they kept us away from them. We couldn't go in the same stores or restaurants with them or the same hotels or schools or use the same bathrooms or live in the same neighborhoods or do anything together.'"

"Why?" Billy asks.

I ignore him. "The old man said, 'Then we noticed that the river was wider and getting wider all the time. And we blue people didn't want to be with the white people anyway. We didn't like them because of all the things they did to us and because they didn't like us, either, and still don't. They try to get away from us whenever they can. They move away if we move into their neighborhood. They're afraid of us, and they think they're better than we are. And that's where we are today. We blue people live on one side, and they live on the other. And most of them are afraid to come over here. They think we'll hurt them, and some of us might do that. And we're afraid to go over to their side for the same reason. So we stay away from each other. I guess we always will.'

"'I'm glad you didn't hurt me.'

"'We're glad you came for a visit,' a young woman says.

"'I'm glad too,' I say. 'But I have to go now. Can I come back?'

"'Yes,' said a tall blue man with green hair pointing out in all directions. 'Come back soon.'

"I thanked them and got in my canoe and started back. I turned and waved to them, and they waved back. And when I turned to look at the water ahead, I could see the other shore. It was a lot closer now than it was before. The river wasn't as wide. I quickly paddled back, pulled out my canoe, lifted it over my head, ran home, and went inside for something to eat. And that is the end of my canoe story."

"Can you take us to see them sometime?" Billy asks.

"Sometime."

Chapter 25—Signs

I ring the bell, and Lori comes to the door. Her parents are home, so she steps outside and leads me around the corner of the garage into the shade. It's late in the afternoon, but it's still hot.

"Now, what did you want to talk about?" she asks.

"I just wanted to rehash the summer. It's almost over, you know. . . . "

"Yes."

"And we did all the rivers and lakes around here and learned a lot about why there are no Negroes in Orchard Park. And then we started to break out of our racial prison. . . . "

"Things sure took a turn when we met Walter," she says.

"Yeah, but we probably won't be able to keep our exchange going, since Walter said he wouldn't do it anymore."

"He just proved to himself what he'd always thought about white people," she says glumly.

"No, I don't think that was it. I think he was afraid he'd get in trouble, and that would keep him from getting a scholarship."

"Oh, you're right."

"For a while, I wondered if it was Randy who stabbed that tire, but I knew he was working." *Or was he?*

"He might have done it, if he'd been there." She sounds a little bitter.

"But listen. There's something else I need help with."

She looks up at me. "What?"

"Summer's almost over, and I can't think of anything to do about this pollution stuff. That was one of my goals, you know, to do something about it. All I can think of is to start a 'save nature' group at church. But I wish I could do something now."

"Hmm. You know what, Jeff?" she says, and her voice sounds soft and warm and slow and sexy. "I had one thought about something we could do. But it's probably childish and irresponsible, so you might not like it."

I have to smile. "Me? You're out of your mind. That's my kind of thing. What's your idea?"

"Well, you know those 'No Swimming' signs you hate so much?"

"Yeah?"

"And the 'No Fishing' signs at Peninsula. The ones you say are the A-people telling us what not to do when they're the ones who pollute the water."

"Yeah," I say. "*We* didn't do anything wrong. The A-people killed the Cuyahoga and Lake Erie, and now they tell us we can't swim in them or fish in them. That's wrong."

"Yes. Well, I was thinking maybe we should talk back to them—tell them what *they* can't do anymore, like polluting the water."

"Lori Matthews. I've turned you into a rebel. You used to be such a sweet, quiet girl. Have you told Randy what you've been doing?"

"Yes. Last night. I told him about all the things we were doing with Walter and Sarah. I couldn't hide it anymore. And he got mad, and we had a big fight."

"Wow. Are you still going together?"

"No. We broke up."

"Oh my gosh."

Somehow I keep from cheering and shouting "it's about time!" and "I never knew what you saw in him anyway!" and insulting him for being a moron with worn-out racial and class biases, and chewing her out for her poor judgment in sticking with him. No, that might've been the end for me. I can see she's near tears, so I just put my arm around her, and she puts her head on my shoulder, and I kiss her hair and hold on to her.

After a while, she seems to recover. I restrain myself from saying, "I can't say I'm sorry it didn't work out." I just ask, "Are you okay?"

She says yes. Then, "You know, you were right. That was Randy spying on us when we were having dinner at your house. He told me so."

"I knew it. What about the phone calls? Did he make any of them?"

"Yes—the silent ones. And a friend of his made the obscene ones."

"Damn. I don't suppose he was trying to drown me out on the lake, was he—you know, because he thought I was accusing his dad of lying?"

"Oh, no, Jeff. That's just what drowning people do. They'll push you under to push themselves above the surface and save themselves. That's why you have to come at them from behind, so they don't take you down with them."

Suddenly, I feel a bit lonely. The canoeing's over, I've vanquished Randy, and Walter says he won't return to Orchard Park. I'll miss Randy and our competition—it was fun! Now we'll just pass in the school hallway again and hardly notice each other, him in his swimming world, me in dramatics and debate and the newspaper.

"I'll miss Walter and Sarah," Lori says.

"Oh, we'll see them again, don't worry—on neutral territory like Public Square or Ninth Street Pier. We won't let that friendship die." *And I'll never let my friendship die with the amazing Lori Matthews either. Oh, no.* "So what exactly do you have in mind with those signs? Knock them down?"

At 2:30 a.m., I unhook the latch on the screen and slip out my bedroom window. I walk by the neighbor's flower bed and cross the backyards, moving from bush to bush, and then go by a house on the other street and up to Lori's, avoiding the streetlights as much as I can. I go around by the screened porch in the back. She said she would be sleeping out. She does that sometimes.

"Lori!" I whisper through the screen. "Let's go."

She's dressed in dark clothes too—long-sleeves and jeans—and she smells like mosquito repellent. I have on a navy sweatshirt, jeans, and a cap, and I have a pouch fastened to my belt. Like nighttime burglars, we steal down the backyards to the end of the street where it crosses the railroad tracks, and follow the tracks east. The sky is cloudy and moonless, so we have to point our flashlights down as we step from tie to tie and hope no train comes. It's a long dark walk, but it's safer than the streets; we're less likely to be seen by the cops or people in houses. We pass the park where we had the picnic, and a lot of houses. Most people have garages and back yards separating them from the tracks, so they're not likely to see us.

It's three thirty when we reach the street where we turn north toward the lake. We've already decided that if a cop comes, we'll hold hands and just keep walking, but if he slows down, we'll run. We walk on the sidewalk side of the street away from the streetlights, but that doesn't help much.

Pretty soon, we cross the lake road. From there, it's only a couple of blocks to the park. It's the same one where we watched the fireworks and got caught in the thunderstorm.

Walking down the gravel road to the parking area, we see there's one small light on a pole near the stairs to the beach. Otherwise, it's pitch black. There's still no sign of cops anywhere. Maybe no one has seen us.

After crossing the parking lot, we walk up to the first sign, "Park Rules," which is under the light. I pull out the jar of black enamel paint and the artist's brush, hand it to Lori, and she goes to work. The first rule says "No Swimming" in three-quarter-inch letters. Through "Swimming," she paints a bold black strikeout line. Underneath it she prints "Polluting." That's the deal. The A-people don't have the right to pollute the water and then tell us we can't swim in it.

We walk down the little road to the beach using our flashlights to get to the other sign, the big one that shouts at us, "No Swimming." Then we see headlights flash into the parking lot.

"Quick," I say, pulling on her hand. "And get ready to run."

We turn off the flashlights, duck behind some bushes, and lie together motionless in the dark. The headlights circle the lot, shining first toward the lake, and then over our heads, and then sweeping around to face the entrance to the lot. The car door slams, and I see a flashlight beam searching the lot. It doesn't linger at the sign, thank goodness. It shines down the hill toward the beach, but we're pretty well hidden, and it sweeps right by us.

Why is he searching the park? Did he see our lights when he pulled in? Uh-oh. Here he comes. He's walking down the road to the beach. Lucky for us, the beam concentrates on the road and beach. I can read his mind: *Teenagers swimming, probably skinny-dipping.*

He's down on the beach now, probing the shrubby border. Lori and I take the opportunity to bury ourselves deeper into the foliage, and when he starts back up the road, his voyeur beam misses us. *They got away,* he thinks (I suppose). The car door slams, and we watch the headlights circle the lot, flash over our heads again, and reenter the street beyond.

We stay still, like hiding children, our bodies touching, and after a while, relax. In the quiet darkness, I smell the shrubbery, the grass, and her mosquito repellent. Glad I'm not a mosquito. My mind flies to the woods at Edgewater Beach, and one of my hands begins caressing her shoulders and back. Something's different now from just a few days ago—she doesn't resist. She softens and turns toward me. Then her hand is moving on my side. We are canoodling once more, and I feel myself getting warm.

"We better finish the job," she whispers, and she starts to get up. *Darn it all. She's right. Gotta do what we planned to. But it's not fair. It's* makeoutus interruptus. *I took Latin last year.*

We stand up, and I brush pretend-vegetation from all over her body. Then we walk down the road to the sign, hand in hand. There, I take out the paint and a bigger brush. She holds a flashlight on it, and I paint a broad line through "Swimming" and put "Polluting" underneath. It's not as neat as Lori's, but it's legible. It definitely talks back.

I finish and put away the paint and brush. Then I can't restrain myself. I grab Lori and pull her to me. I kiss her hard on the mouth as the waves lap on the beach and a cool lake breeze caresses us, and I feel her melt into my being.

THE END

Afterword

All characters and events in *Canoedling In Cleveland* are fictitious, and any resemblance to persons living or dead is accidental. The diner in the story is fictional, as are the bank building, real estate office, churches, and housing development.

The story takes place in a western suburb of Cleveland, Ohio, in 1960. Much has changed since then. At that time, the Cuyahoga River, from Akron to Cleveland, was dead, with no fish or fowl, and the beaches of Lake Erie near Cleveland were closed due to pollution. Today the portion of the river from Akron through Peninsula and Brecksville to Independence is part of the popular Cuyahoga Valley National Park. It has bike and jogging trails (the canal towpath), forests with hiking trails, waterfalls, caves, a scenic railway, and picnic areas. This portion of the river now has sixty-five species of fish. Egrets and herons stand by the shores, and eagles nest in the park.

The lower Cuyahoga River through the Flats is much cleaner today than in 1960, although urban runoff and combined sewer overflows continue to pollute the river during heavy rains. One steel mill remains, providing much-needed jobs for Clevelanders, and ore boats still ply the river's curves. Most of the oil refineries are gone. Freighters transport asphalt, gravel, petroleum, salt, and steel up and down the river. Once covered with oily brown scum, this part of the river now supports forty-four species of fish. I have even seen a mallard duck gliding on its surface. Since 1996, the Cleveland Rowing Foundation has hosted a major regatta on the river. The river was restored in compliance with the 1972 Federal Clean Water Act, which was passed partly in response to a fire on the river that occurred in 1969.

Today, beaches on Lake Erie are monitored daily and contamination advisories posted when bacteria counts are high and swimming is unsafe. According to the Ohio Department of Health (http://publicapps.odh.ohio.gov/BeachGuardPublic), Edgewater State Park Beach in downtown Cleveland was under advisory for high bacteria levels fifteen out of the ninety-two days (16 percent) between May 30 and August 29 in 2012. Yachting and sailing are more popular than ever on the lake. Environmentally, great progress has been made since 1960.

Rocky River Reservation, part of the Cleveland Metroparks Emerald Necklace of parks surrounding Cleveland, continues to be a popular recreational area with all-purpose trails, woods filled with wildlife, picnic areas, a nature museum, and three golf courses. In June 2007, *Field and Stream* magazine named Rocky River, which I call "Shale River," one of the "150 Best Places to Fish in America." In spring steelhead trout move in large numbers down the river to Lake Erie, and in fall move back up the river to spawn.

Good Samaritan Baptist church in the story is fictitious but was inspired by Shiloh Baptist church in Cleveland, which was originally built as a synagogue and which is on the National Register of Historic Places. Architecturally, I drew Good Samaritan in the New England style with a steeple over the main entrance, while Shiloh is a domed structure, modeled after the Panthéon in Paris, with six Roman columns supporting a portico over the entrance.

Regarding residential segregation, Cleveland remains one of the most racially segregated cities in the United States; the West Side suburbs are predominately white, and most African Americans live east of the Cuyahoga.

The canoe adventures in *Canoedling in Cleveland* have some basis in fact. I personally canoed Lake Erie and most of the rivers in my youth. The other autographical part of the novel is that in 1959 I asked my high school newspaper advisor why no Negroes lived in my town on the West Side and made a limited exploration to learn why. My surprise in finding that little had changed fifty years later led me to turn my brief high school quest into this young adult novel with fictitious characters and events. In the past few years, I have become aware that residential segregation is common in towns, suburbs, and neighborhoods across the nation (see *Sundown Towns* by James W. Loewen). Why I think it is significant enough to write about, especially in a young adult novel, is that I have found that one's attitudes toward people different from oneself are frequently modified by exposure to those "different" people; the polarization of the United States, in my opinion, is largely due to people not having significant contact with those who are different from us. Finally, if residential segregation is to change, it will be accomplished by brave and exuberant young people who have been exposed to people unlike themselves.

Special thanks goes to my wife Barbara, for her many readings of the book and countless comments; Stanford Pritchard, author of seven novels and books of short stories, and *The Elements of Style: Updated and Annotated For Present-Day Use* (with William Strunk, Jr.), for his editorial assistance; Katie Harrison for editorial assistance; Carolivia Herron, best-selling author of *Nappy Hair, Thereafter Johnnie, Always an Olivia: A Remarkable Family History,* and other books; David L. Levy, author of *Revolt of the Animals*; James Loewen, author of *Sundown Towns*; Antero Pietila, author of *Not in My Neighborhood: How Bigotry Shaped a Great American City*; John J. Grabowski, Associate Professor of Applied History, Case Western Reserve University, and Senior Vice President for Research and Publications at Western Reserve Historical Society, co-author of *The Encyclopedia of Cleveland History*; *Cleveland: Then and Now*; and *Identity, Conflict, and Cooperation: Central Europeans in Cleveland, 1850-1930*, and author of *Cleveland: A History in Motion,* for historical information on the migration of ethnic groups in Cleveland;

Virginia Grove; David Ramsey, canoe buddy; Alex Morris; Janis Rose; Svend Lauritsen; Bill and Stephanie Byers; Audrey Engdahl, for comments, interior graphics, and the cover painting, and Richard Engdahl for the cover layout; and many others.